COPYRIGHT

THIS BOOK IS AUTHORIZED FOR LEGAL DOWNLOAD/ SALE EXCLUSIVELY THROUGH AMAZON OR AMAZON KINDLE. ANY OTHER SITE OR ENTITY FOUND OFFERING THIS BOOK FOR DOWNLOAD/SALE IN ANY OTHER FORM IS GUILTY OF COPYRIGHT INFRINGEMENT AND INTELLECTUAL PROPERTY THEFT, A CRIME PUNISHABLE BY UP TO 3 YEARS IN PRISON AND A POSSIBLE £250,000 FINE.

If you downloaded/purchased this book from anywhere other than Amazon, it was stolen. By supporting pirate sites, you threaten authors' abilities to continue writing the stories you love.

Legal Ways to Obtain Free Books: Download Libby. It's a free library app that allows you to request and borrow free books from all over the world.
Amazon Kindle: Either through KU or pay as you go.

Request the book at your local library. Even if they don't have it in stock, they may participate in a library exchange program.

Sign up for ARC teams. Many authors distribute digital ARCs (and I do!)

Acknowledgements:

For my husband, kids, Tina, Nat, Aoife, Bek, Sam (my editor!) my sister, parents, in-laws and friends who I consider family, and other family members who genuinely know me & have helped me write another romance; thank you!

Copyright & Thanks
Acknowledgements:
~One~
Blythe
~Two~
Marcus
~Three~
Blythe
~Four~
Adrian
~Five~
Blythe
~Six~
Blythe
~Seven~
Marcus
~Eight~
Blythe
~Nine~
Adrian
~Ten~
Blythe
~Eleven~
Blythe
~Twelve~
Blythe
~Thirteen~
Adrian
~Fourteen~
Marcus
~Fifteen~

Blythe

~Sixteen~
Adrian

~Seventeen~
Blythe

~Eighteen~
Adrian

~Nineteen~
Blythe

~Twenty~
Adrian

~Twenty-One~
Blythe

~Twenty-Two~
Adrian

~Twenty-Three~
Marcus

~Twenty-Four~
Blythe

~Twenty-Five~
Marcus

~Twenty-Six~
Blythe

~Twenty-Seven~
Adrian

~Twenty-Eight~
Blythe

~Twenty-Nine~
Marcus

~Thirty~
Blythe

~Thirty-One~
Adrian

~Thirty-Two~

Blythe
~Thirty-Three~
Marcus
~Thirty-Four~
Blythe
~Thirty-Five~
Adrian
~Thirty-Six~
Marcus
~Thirty-Seven~
Blythe
~Thirty-Eight~
Marcus
~Thirty-Nine~
Blythe
~Forty~
Adrian
~Forty-One~
Marcus
~Forty-Two~
Blythe
~Forty-Three~
Marcus
~Forty-Four~
Adrian
~Forty-Five~
Marcus
~Forty-Six~
Blythe
~Forty-Seven~
Adrian
Epilogue - Blythe
Glossary

~One~
Blythe

"Grievson!" The distinctive holler of the Wing Commander's voice booms over my partner and me.

We stop and turn towards the sound of his voice. Annie throws me a nervous glance, and we wait for him to come closer.

"Sorry to holler at you like that," he apologises to me as he approaches. He turns and acknowledges Annie with a nod. "Holmes. I need a word with Grievson."

"Of course, sir." She nods at him, then looks at me. "See you in the mess hall when you're done," she tells me and walks off as best as her pregnant self can.

"It's going to be a blow, losing you two," the Wing Commander tells me as he indicates we're going to walk and talk.

"It is what it is, sir. We've more than done our time," I comment. Annie and I have been with the RAF for just over sixteen years. Our term was for twelve, and we extended it once. We've contributed handsomely to our military pension, but life is moving on. And we are moving on out. Annie's soon-to-be-husband doesn't want her to stay in the RAF, so she didn't renew her contract. I didn't want to stay without her, so I didn't renew mine.

"Yes, you both have. But, before you go…" He holds open his office door for me and guides me into his inner sanctum. Wing Commander George Davidson is in his mid-fifties, mostly white in the hair and beard department, but when he's in full dress, he displays a lot of fruit on that chest of his. He's taller than me, but most of the men on this base are, since it caters for strong, tall, vibrant helicopter pilots above all else. "We have a…guest," he spits out. My stomach sinks as I have a wild guess at what he's going to ask me to do.

"Aye, sir, I heard about last night's…situation." The wing commander's son was propositioned by a civilian contractor who didn't seem to take no for an answer. My Military Police colleagues had to lock up the contractor, and our "guest," as the Wing Commander has so eloquently put it, is now not welcome.

"Has everyone?" he asks in an exasperated tone.

"I heard your boy told him no; he didn't take the hint. I'd say he's lucky your son and his friends didn't go dump him in the North Sea, sir." I sit down as he indicates for me to do so.

Davidson looks like he's about to chew something and spit it out, his own tongue at a guess, but he schools his thoughts.

"I've spoken with my counterpart at Brize; they're expecting him back tonight at sixteen-hundred. I don't trust the little…" Davidson stops himself from saying what he'd like to, which I can only guess is going to be very unpleasant.

"To get there on his own, sir?" I gently venture a much safer answer to what he was likely going to say. Davidson smiles and nods at me.

"Exactly." Davidson might be in charge of RAF Lossiemouth, but his accent is anything but Scots. It's more English East Coast, very Inspector Morse like.

"And what would you like me to do to assist in that matter, sir?" I move in my seat to try and hide the excitement I can feel bubbling up inside of me at the mention of Brize.

"Escort him down to Brize. I hear your brother is deploying with the forty-seventh soon?" he asks, raising his eyebrows at me.

"Aye, I believe he is. I wasn't going to get to see him afore he went." As I speak, I sit bolt upright. I'll get to see Byron before he goes on another tour.

"Well, take our guest home and you can. I've instructed your pilot not to return until tomorrow evening. Twenty-four hours should be long enough, yes?" he enquires as he picks up his pen and a stack of papers.

I stand, understanding that I have my instructions. But what a set of final instructions six weeks before I walk out of here as a civilian.

"Aye, sir, plenty long enough," I reply then make my way to the door. "Did you want a spectacle made of him, sir?" I ask. There are two ways our guest can make his way to the helo. One of which is not very pleasant and reserved for actual criminals.

I see Davidson sit back and contemplate his answer. "Best not, unless he starts being a pillock," he says, nodding.

"Aye, sir, I understand." I turn the handle of the door. "Thank you, sir," I say. He looks up, gives me a smile through his thin white beard then turns his attention back to the paperwork, and I go to find our guest.

Outside the barrack room in question, two of my male colleagues stand guard. I nod to them, and they let me pass. The man inside jumps as I march in, unannounced, closing the door behind me.

"What's to be done? I know I screwed up," he wails at me. David Lloyd was here to upgrade some of the I.T. systems the RAF use. Unfortunately, he took a liking to the Wing Commander's son and didn't back away when he was told that Davidson Jnr wasn't interested.

"You're being returned to Brize, in about two hours. If you haven't packed, you have exactly one hour and ten minutes to do just that."

He slumps and sighs at me. His dark hair is slicked back, his rounded glasses are just sitting on his nose. He's slightly overweight and as tall as I am. Since most of the pilots here are at least six foot four and more, he falls into the short-arse category, like me.

"The upgrades aren't done," he tells me in a soft, Yorkshire accent, but I can only shrug.

"Not my call. You can either go nice and quietly back down to Brize, or go handcuffed to me and leave the base like a criminal. I'd rather you pick the first option and leave with some…decorum."

I can see the colour drain out of him, and for a white guy, that astonishes me as he's paler than the soles of my feet. My Italian heritage makes my skin look nicely tanned all year round, though getting out to Italy to see my ailing grandparents isn't easy. Something I plan to change very soon.

"What's it to be?" I ask. My hands are behind my back, my feet are set firmly and squarely at shoulder width. David stands and sighs.

"With decorum," he says and pulls out his case from under the bed he's been occupying.

"Great. I'll be back in an hour and five. We have a base helo down to Brize, so if you dinnae like flying, I strongly suggest ye dinnae eat until we land." I turn and begin to open the door. "Cause I'll no be clearing your mess up," I instruct him. He just nods at me, and I leave him to it, then I head towards the mess hall to find Annie.

I find her in a corner reading a book, her swollen ankles are resting up on the other plastic chair on her side. I smile, grab a coffee from the machine, and head over to her.

She looks up, smiles, and puts her book away. It's one thing we always love doing: reading a book together with a bar of chocolate, or other snacks we fancy, and just chilling in our room.

"What did the Fruit want?" she asks me quietly, her lips hardly moving.

"To take our guest back to Brize," I tell her. She gapes at me and then grins.

"Personally? Lucky bitch," she tells me. "Does By know you'll be down? How long are you going to be away for?"

"Twenty-four hours and no, I need to text him now." I pull out my phone and drop my brother a text with the good news.

"A free visit to Brize to see By afore he goes on a huge deployment? How'd you land that?" she asks, still not quite believing my good fortune.

I shrug. "Fruit was saying he's sad to see us going," I venture. "But I am not going to complain about it when he's doing me a solid. Byron will be gone for about four or five months. Ye ken I'll not hear from him until he's decamped when he gets back." Annie nods. After a tour, it's customary to spend some time just back on base, getting into the base routine again, de-stressing and talking with counsellors. It's de-camping as you're letting the pressure of the deployment go, before venturing back out into civvy-street.

"Aye. The de-camping will add a few weeks of radio silence. It'll be nice to hug the wee scroat once, afore he goes. Though, wee is relative." She chuckles and I join in. My "wee" brother is six foot three to my five foot eight, and he towers over both Annie and me. I sigh as I look at my best friend. We found ourselves sitting next to each other at our MP Training after boot camp, and we've been friends ever since. Now, Annie is pregnant, about to marry the baby's daddy out of some sheer sense of "doing things right," but I can't help but dislike Jim. He sets me on edge, and I'm one to trust my instincts.

"I'm gonna say this again: You dinnae have to marry him," I tell her, looking at the bump she's sporting. The light vanishes out of Annie's eyes, and I kick myself.

"I know, you've said. Dad has said it too. But, I have to give it a go, Bly. For the bairn's sake, if nothing else," she explains in a defeatist tone as she rubs her expanding stomach. I can only nod.

"If you ever want out of there, even after you've said, 'I do…'" I remind her. She nods and grabs my hand.

"You'll be there. Aye, I ken. Still, cannae believe that they didn't give me the message to get things updated," she laments. I snort into my coffee, trying to hide my anger about that set of RAF personnel communications. The thing she mentions was supposed to be a contraceptive implant update for us both, but the medics at one base screwed up and didn't cascade the information to the field base we were at, who then didn't enlighten our new base when we decamped. When we hit civvy street, Annie and Jim hooked up, and the rest is history in the making.

"Communication, aye? Serious lack of it." She grins, but it's an empty one. What's done is done. Six weeks from now, Annie will be married in an almost shot-gun wedding.

"You're still going to be there for me?" she asks. Her voice is quieter, shaky.

I nod. "I'll be there when the bairn is born too. Dinnae worry, I'm with ye," I tell her. Fuck knows if her to-be husband ever bloody will be.

We finish our coffee and head up to our room, the one we share. Women's quarters are in one building on base, men's are in another, marriage quarters are in clusters away from the singletons. I pack an overnight bag with some civilian clothes, change out of my fatigues, and put on the dress blues, including the snowflake cap.

"You know, I'll not regret leaving this behind," she tells me. I nod as I expected to be in the RAF until I retired, or I was stuck forever behind a desk. I'm nervous about what my future holds and what is waiting for Annie when she marries Jim.

"Aye, I hear you. I don't think I'll miss parts of this, but some bits I think I will," I tell her. I check my watch and sigh. "I'll see you when I get back."

She nods. "Aye, six more weeks for you, six days for me. Fuck, six days," she reminds herself, her eyes going wide. I giggle at her antics, knowing full well she's counting down the minutes and hours as well as the days. She's using her maternity leave to finish her contract early. Can't say I blame her.

"See you in twenty-four," I tell her. She nods and we hug, then I grab my small overnight bag and head to David Lloyd's room.

The same two MP's are still standing guard, and they grin at me. I walk in to find that he's packed and ready to go.

"Could you," he requests as he sweeps his hand over his bags. There's a posh suitcase on wheels.

"I am not your bloody bus-girl," I growl, but I grab the smaller bag, leaving him to drag the suitcase with the kitchen sink and whatever else he brought with him. Heading out to the helipad, I leave him to catch up to me. My two colleagues have the pleasure of following him, slowly.

I nod to the pilot and place the two bags I am carrying inside, then I turn and watch as he huffs and puffs his way across the tarmac. The pilot rolls his eyes at me, and I grin. We'd be in the air if it were just me, or even with Annie.

"Not taking Sherlock with ya?" asks the pilot in his strong Welsh accent as David finally gets close enough that I can start hauling his case on. I heave it on in one swoop and tuck it under a seat.

I look at him. "In her state?" I ask with my eyebrows raised.

His mouth forms an "O" and then he nods. "Sorry, forgot," he replies with a sheepish grin. I shake my head in disbelief.

"She'd soon remind ye," I warn him. He grins at me and nods.

"Yeah, she would! Can't believe you two are getting outta here," he says. "Thought they'd remove you both from the base when she gets decom'd," he teases. I doubt Lossiemouth is going to get decommissioned in my lifetime.

I ensure David's in and that his seatbelt and headphones are on. Helo's are noisy from the ground level; they're even worse in the air when you're confined in one for a few hours.

I put on my headphones as the pilot goes through his checks and speaks with traffic control. A few moments later, we're lifting off and heading south, over the border into England, down to Brize Norton.

There was hardly any chat on the way down. The wind made it so that the pilot needed to concentrate, and I couldn't blame him, I think I gave up trying to distract myself somewhere over Yorkshire. Finally, we enter Brize Norton's airspace, and we're cleared to land on the far side of the base. Our former guest looks a little green around the gills, and I make a note to inform the Commander of it. Even if I didn't remove him in cuffs, he didn't have a pleasant ride down and he's clearly not used to taking rides in flying machines. As soon as the rotors have slowed to almost nothing, the door is slid open and two other serious looking MP's from Brize take over, escorting David to their Wing Commander's office. Probably for a dressing down and, most likely, permanent removal.

I turn to Lossie's pilot, a tall, broad-shouldered man with typical military cut hair and tattoos. I notice the name Jones on the name badge. I chuckle a little at the relevance, and his accent now makes sense.

"I'll ride up front with ye on the way back, tomorrow, aye? What time is take-off?" I ask him as he runs through landing checks.

"Be back for fourteen-hundred. Just in case we need to leave early, the weather's not looking great for going back, and I might need to leave quickly to be in front of the storm."

I nod. "Sure thing, Jonesey! See ya tomorrow!" I yell as I head over to the bunkhouse. I sign in with base security and get told what bunk is mine for the night, then I get handed a pile of sheets and linen. It doesn't take me long to make the bed, shower, change into my civvies, and then I put on my ID badge and go to try and find my brother in the mess hall.

The mess hall is half full, which is a surprise. Brize Norton is home to the craziest of the pilots the RAF have ever trained. If you want a pilot to fly a LM C130 into a dangerous zone to retrieve a team, the pilots would be from the 47th. Men with steel balls, with egos to match; they are a tight group but crazy as all hell with demons on their asses.

I scan the hall, but I can't see my brother. I check my phone, he hasn't responded, and I make my way to the MP office to find out more.

Knocking on the office door, I confidently stride in as I would back at Lossie.

"Sorry to bother ye," I begin and three heads suddenly turn to look at me. They remind me of meerkats and I chuckle. "Sorry, didn't mean to startle ye. Sergeant Blythe Grievson from Lossie. I'm looking for my brother, FL Byron Grievson? I've twenty-four here and was hoping to catch him afore he deployed," I explain. The other MP furthest from me wears the rank of a Sergeant on his arm. He stands and comes over to greet me, shaking my hand as firmly as I do his.

"Grievson has a sister? He kept that quiet." He grins at me, and I smirk.

"Aye, he does. Is he on base or did I miss him already?"

"His squadron are on their last manoeuvres; they're not due back until oh-six tomorrow," another voice pipes up, a lady showing the Lance Corporal rank. She gets a glare from the Sergeant, but I speak up.

"Oh, bugger. Thanks! Saves me hanging about for his sorry arse to join me for a beer or two tonight. Where's good to go? I need a night off," I respond. The mention of beers and being off base suddenly has everyone offering where to go and what to do.

"We could join you for a few short ones," the Lance Corporal pipes up. The name on her lapel is too small to read from here, but she has a southern accent and her blonde hair is pulled back into a tight bun. A style I've worn for over fifteen years.

"That would be great; I don't know anyone here but By." And that gains a few more grins. Oh boy, my brother is going to kill me for using his family nickname.

"We'd love to," the other woman pipes up. A corporal rank shows on her left arm, and suddenly the Warrant Officer appears behind me, like a ghost.

"Can we help?" he asks firmly, his eyebrows raised. I get this is a military base, but I can sense additional tension here.

I go through my name, rank, and why I'm here. I smile, noting his name is Dobson. He grins, his shoulders releasing tension. "You brought the guest from Lossie down?" he questions me, but I suspect he's already aware of who I am and why I am here. I nod.

"Aye, sir, my Wing Commander was being generous and thought I might catch up with my brother before he gets deployed and I leave the service." That gets a few smiles and dreamy sighs, but they don't last long. "But, since he's not here and won't be, I thought a few beers might be in order, especially off base if there's anywhere decent and local." The WO nods.

"I'll leave you to make your plans, away from the office." His clipped voice leaves little to no room for negotiation.

"Of course, sir, apologies, I didn't mean to cause disruption," I offer and back out of the office.

"That's... Oh, bollocks, not what I mean. Sorry, bloody awful day," he tells me. I just smile softly at him.

"Understandable. I did bring an unwanted gift," I tease. He raises his eyebrows at me, then reads my ID badge.

"Ah, you did say where you were from. Yes, it makes a lot of sense now, you being here." He turns to the Sergeant and sighs. "Wrap up for me, would you, Bridge? I've had enough." He nods and heads past me, and the tension goes with him.

Half an hour later, I'm in the mess hall again, waiting for the two other female MP's to join me so we can head into town. Within fifteen minutes of them meeting me, we're in the centre of Carterton, at a bar with drinks and pool cues in hand.

The pub the girls have taken me to is not too busy. They nod to a few guys and they whisper their ranks to me, so I know who I am dealing with. Then they go all girly, giggly, and I turn to see why. There's a tall man, typically over six feet with non-military style hair and clean-shaven. His dark blue t-shirt pulls out over his muscles, highlighting every single pec and bicep he has. I can see some light tattoos on his arms, nothing heavy or tribal.

I turn my focus to the pool table and take my shot. As I come around for my next, I cast another glance at him, but I look away again to take aim, then sink another ball. The corporal looks at me in disgust.

"You've played before," she scolds. I shrug softly, offering her a hug.

"You didn't ask if I was any good, Steph; you knew I played, told you on the way over," I reply as I sink the black ball, winning the game. "But, the next round is on the winner, aye?" I offer. I don't need to be pissing people off when I'm only here for a short time. She grins and asks for vodka and Coke and the lance corporal, Denise Jackson, asks for the same. Two women after my own alcoholic heart. I head to the bar to order our drinks when the nice-looking guy the girls spotted earlier appears and leans in close. His proximity makes me hyper-aware as every nerve ending lights up in a way I've never felt before—with anyone.

"You're not usually here," he observes.

"No, just visiting overnight," I tell him, trying to keep my voice light and casual.

"Outta Brize?" he asks. His accent is kind of Oxford Uni with a hint of Scot, certainly seems more English.

"Aye. You?" I ask. With his hair, there's no way he's a serving pilot or anything else.

"I.T.," he tells me. So, he's a computer geek. Since when do computer geeks look like a blonde superman?

"With that hairstyle, had to be," I quipped, and I watched as his face fell. Shit! I need to add something to take away the slap I've accidentally given him. "Didn't have you pegged for a bus driver, or a snowflake." I wink. He perks up at that, understanding that I knew he wasn't serving in the military.

"Do you need to be on base tonight?" he asks in a low, sultry voice. My drinks finally get poured and brought to me. I breathe deeply a few times, trying to calm my nerves before I lift the tray of drinks.

"I'm supposed to be, why? Are you making a better offer?" I ask, licking my lips. Being this close to him has my insides doing something funny and weird, I'm not sure what. *Why is it so hot in here? Did that curl in his hair fall just for me to tuck it back up onto his head?* I keep my hands on the drinks tray so I don't try and tuck his hair back on his head. *Why do I want to touch him so intimately? I've only just met him.*

"I have plenty if you want to know about them." He leans in to whisper in my ear, "But, alone," and he pulls back with a wink, takes his drink, and re-joins his friends at another table.

I grin and take the tray of our drinks back to the girls.

"Don't tell me Marcus McGowan talked to you! He hardly says a word on base!" Steph whispers as I head back.

"Aye, he did. Why?" I glance across at where he's sat, and he nods to me very discreetly, but he doesn't do anything else. Steph and Denise are having a game, and Denise is losing already. I watch as she holds the cue and I can see why, so I step in and offer to correct her cue action. She gets a bit better afterwards, but then we're surrounded by guys. The table Marcus was at has joined us.

"How about a wager?" he asks, his voice developing a soft Scots burr. Steph and Denise shake their heads.

"He's a pool shark," whispers Denise as she passes me. I grunt a reply low in my throat. He's not the only one.

"Loser buys the rounds?" I suggest. Marcus shakes his head but looks at me with a quirky, half lopped smile, and his eyes dance. *Is he as attracted to me as I am to him?*

~Two~
Marcus

My brother being away for manoeuvres means I'm left to my own devices, and when I spot the gorgeous, dark-haired, Italian-looking woman come in, I can't pull my eyes off her. I see her pale blue eyes, a stark contrast to her black hair, and I have to remind myself to breathe. I peg her for being in the military straightaway, though being a pilot isn't one of the professions I think she's pursuing.

As she heads to the bar to fetch a round, I slip away from my friends and head over to her, hoping to hear a lovely, foreign accent. Instead, I get a strong Scottish one and my heart soars more. I miss Scotland, and I'll be glad when my brother's serving contract is up in a few more years. Until then, I'm honing my own skills on military I.T. systems and networking my arse off, making contacts so that the shared dream Adrian and I have had since we were little can become a reality.

"You're not usually here," I tell her, stating the obvious, and I kick myself for it. *How can she have me this flustered when she's not said a word?*

"No, just visiting overnight," she informs me, and my heart skips a beat. I know right now, if I don't get her details or even get her to my bed, it'll be a wasted opportunity. Something about her is drawing me in and I'm not sure what it is. She's not my usual busty type; she's far more dangerous, athletic, capable.

"Outta Brize?" I ask, wondering where she's based. She's not someone I've seen on base before, that much I know.

"Aye," she answers, and I realise I didn't ask the right question. I inwardly stifle a groan. "You?" she asks in return.

"I.T.," I tell her.

"With that hairstyle, had to be," she quips, glancing at the top of my head. I wonder if there's something wrong with my hair and run a hand through it. "Didn't have you pegged for a bus driver, or a snowflake." She winks. So, she knew I wasn't serving in the military but was linked to them somehow.

"Do you need to be on base tonight?" I ask as I notice that her drinks finally get poured and brought over. She takes the tray but holds it on the bar as we're talking.

"I'm supposed to be, why? Are you making a better offer?" she asks, licking those luscious lips, and my imagination begins to run riot.

"I have plenty if you want to know about them." I lean in to whisper in her ear and smell her scent. She's not used any perfume, but she smells of sea salt and petrol. "But, alone." I grin and head back to the table, watching her shapely arse as she goes back to the pool table.

Darren nudges me as I head back to my table.

"Putting another notch on the post?" he asks, and I roll my eyes.

"I am not a womaniser," I growl. "I happen to appreciate women and all their beauty." I watch as the woman who's enthralled me helps her colleague with their pool game, and I get an idea.

"Fancy a game of pool?" I ask him. Darren shakes his head.

"With you, yeah, against you?" He grins and his shoulders begin to shake as the laugh consumes him. "Not a chance against you!" he proclaims.

"Against them," I tell him, and he looks over at the three women still at the pool table. No one else has put their money down, so they're hoarding it. Still, it's generating money and they're not fast drinkers. I nod to her once as she glances over, a very slight, 'I see you' kind of nod, an acknowledgement.

"You're wanting a match against the military women?" he asks me, sipping the beer from his bottle.

"If they're up for it. Winner buys the drinks," I suggest.

"And if they win?" he questions. Because we've not seen the Italian-looking woman before, Darren has no idea how well she can play, if at all. I can tell she's competent if nothing else. I've not seen any trick shots, double backs, or knock-ons. She brings an unknown quantity to the table, and I'm tempted to let her win and offer to walk her back to the flat I share with my brother, knowing he won't be back until early in the morning.

"I'll still pay," I tell him. He ponders for a moment then nods, and we head over, the other two decide to watch, not wanting to play, and find a table closer to sit and observe.

"How about a wager?" I ask as I approach the three women. One whispers to the Italian Scot, and her eyes begin to dance. I can't help but wonder what she was told; the way she's looking me up and down as she is, it makes me react.

"Loser buys the rounds?" she suggests, her Scots accent so very different to the Oxford style I'm now used to hearing. The burrs and rolling 'r's has my heart soaring again for home and her.

"I was going to say, the winner buys, but either way works," I reply. She grins at me, her nostrils flare, and my heart begins to race.

"Toss for who goes first," she says. She turns to the darker haired woman who I know is Denise, who nods. Then she looks at Steph and nods. What are they planning?

"Doubles, alternate player, and we toss for the start," she states, her accent singing out in a strong and clear command. I try not to react to her, but I do. I look at Darren, and he nods.

"That's okay by me," he tells me. I nod in agreement and Denise pulls a coin from her pocket, a two pound one by the looks of it, and she tosses it, looking at me as it flips through the air. She catches it and covers it, so I can't see what side is face up.

"Heads," I say. Denise uncovers the coin to show both myself and the visitor.

"Ach, sorry, it's tails, my break," the visitor proclaims. Steph stands back and leans into her cue, trying to hide the smile that's dancing in her eyes. I look at our other friends, sitting close at a table, then I look at Darren. I've a sinking feeling developing.

Neither of us got to the table that first round. The visitor, whose name I still hadn't found out, and now almost didn't want to, had wiped the floor with us. She cleared the spots down in numerical order, even doubled the black off another of our balls, all from the break. She comes up to us now and grins.

"I suppose you're gonna want more than one match, aye?" Her eyes are twinkling. Steph and Denise behind her aren't even trying to hold their jubilation.

"You're a shark," I tell her, half teasing.

"Steph, am I a shark?" she asks as she chalks her cue. Her jeans are skin-tight, her blouse is pretty nondescript, it's a cream colour that billows out over her small boobs but pulls in at her waist. The boots add a few inches to her height, but she's pretty tall anyway.

"Not that I've worked out, Blythe, no." Blythe. That's her name and I commit it to memory.

"Okay, good, I thought maybe I'd sprouted a fin on my back." She grins again and winks at me, but sashays her arse to the end of the table where the balls come out and racks them up.

"Your turn, geek boy." She smirks at me and stands back to be near Steph and Denise. Darren looks at me and motions for me to break. I do, sinking a ball into one corner, but I'm unable to sink another of the same type. Steph takes a turn and sinks two of theirs, then snookers herself, and Darren knocks one down, but can't get at another. He groans as Blythe takes to the table; she gets the cue ball around one of ours, hitting hers and knocking another one she didn't aim to hit into the pocket. Darren and I can only watch as she clears the table.

I grin and then laugh, aware that she had me pegged from the start, thanks to Denise and Steph's inside knowledge.

"Loser pays, sure! What's it to be?" I ask. Blythe holds her hand out and shakes mine firmly in congratulations, lingering on my fingers a little too long. She's jubilant with Darren and sassy with us lads in general, but I catch her glancing at me regularly. They ask for three vodka and Cokes, and I head up to the bar to fetch them.

Then they do what women do; they head to the bathroom, together.

~Three~
Blythe

As soon as we're in the ladies, Steph and Denise laugh out loud, double over and are almost peeing their knickers because they're laughing so hard. I grin, but I don't quite get the reason behind their hysterics. Once we've used the facilities and we're all applying fresh lipstick, they tell me.

"Marcus is a mouse when he's on-site dealing with I.T. stuff. Here, he's a little more friendly, but he's a shark at the pool table. We tend not to play him as we know we'll never win. Where the hell did you learn to play?" they ask me. I shrug.

"Grandparents had a table. Byron and I used to play a lot when the weather was terrible. Italian rainstorms are something else," I explain. I don't share that they could last for days in Bologna or that Byron is much better than me.

"Grievson plays?" they chorus, which makes me wince.

"Don't tell him I told you," I urge. "I thought everyone would know," I share. He usually lords it over me when we play.

"He hardly ever comes out to this pub; he doesn't always get on with some of the other 47th." I sigh, hoping my brother hasn't made a dick of himself here, or that I've inadvertently made it worse.

"He has his close few; there are two sides of the 47th. The crazies and the real crazies. He's on the first side; Marcus' brother is more the second," Denise explains.

"Oh fuck," I curse. I was hoping to find a nice quiet corner with Marcus.

"Marcus, though, is a civvy and stands up to his fiery brother quite well. I've heard some of their arguments and, boy, both go as broad Scots as you when they're riled!" Steph admits, grinning. "Then they calm down, Aid apologises, and Marcus smooths things over. Then they do it again about four months later."

"I heard it's usually over a woman. Not one for gossip…" Denise pretends to zip her lip, but I get now, she can't and won't keep a juicy piece of gossip out of circulation. At least I've given nothing huge away for her to use against Byron. "But, I heard they like to share," she whispers, her eyes opening wide.

What she says does very strange things to my insides. *They like to share? One woman, two brothers*? My insides clench in response to that thought, and I begin to wonder if this is what I've been wanting or needing. I've never had one man satisfy me enough to quieten my sexual hunger for anything more than a night, sometimes not even that.

Steph nods. "I've heard the same, though it's never been substantiated," she informs us. "Just, either idle gossip or they've similar tastes in women. They're pretty close in age," she tells me. I finished applying some extra mascara, but what Denise said, if it's true, excites me more than I ever thought possible.

We emerge and then I check the time. It's nearly ten pm. Base doors shut at half past, and I inform Denise and Steph we need to get back. They nod and we head over to our drinks, thanking Marcus and his friend for the games.

As we're about to leave, Marcus manages to corner me as the girls go out to get a cab.

"How do I get you alone?" he whispers into my ear. He's not crowding me, but what he wants to say is for him and I.

"Invite me," I tell him, lifting my chin in a challenge. He licks his lips and looks into my blue eyes. I can see myself reflected in his amber ones.

"I'm heading back to mine for a nightcap. I'd like for you to join me," he tells me. There's an air of gentle authority around him as he offers.

I shiver in anticipation at his invitation, not many men can do that to me. He'll be the third. "I'd like that," I whisper back in reply. "Let me tell the girls to head back without me," I tell him. He nods, and I walk outside with him to find Denise and Steph are in the taxi, waiting to go back to base. I poke my head into the back of the cab.

"I'll check in tomorrow morning," I tell them, nodding towards Marcus. They nudge each other and then I shut the door and tap the roof, indicating to the driver that he can take off. I can see Denise and Steph turn and look out of the back window. I wave, hoping I've not made a huge mistake.

Marcus comes over to where I'm standing and offers me a hand. "I really want to know what you sound like when you come," he whispers to me in the darkness. "And what you taste like, here," he says, leaning in to kiss my neck which sends anticipating shivers down my spine. "Or here," he whispers, moving up to my jaw.

"Nightcap first, then if you can engage my brain, you'll find out," I tell him. He curls his lip in a smile, steps back, and offers me his arm.

"This way to the nightcap," he tells me and we walk through Carterton as the dusk begins to fall.

He leads the way to a modern block of flats and up to the top floor, motioning for me to go in first. I smile at his manners. He heads over to a small area and turns on a light, which reveals a drinks shelf with a little choice, a section for the glasses. The place has a feel of not being home, more of a place to rest your head.

"Not staying?" I ask as I look around. It's sparsely furnished, but more so than it would be if it were on a base.

"We know this isn't home; we have plans, my brother and I." He comes over to where I am and offers me the vodka and cola

I've been drinking all night. There's more vodka than cola in it, so I sip this one. He motions for us to go and sit on the sofa, and I smile at the invitation.

"What plans do you have?" I ask him as he takes up one end of the sofa. I remove my boots, then curl up on the opposite end. Marcus puts his drink down and helps me remove them with a smile on his lips and his eyes dancing.

"I can't do anything until Aid finishes his contract. He's got a few years left to serve and I have some more I.T. skills to learn." I look at him with my head cocked to the side. He sounds like he has a plan. "We've had a dream since we were old enough to work out that not everyone can stand up for themselves." I raise my eyebrows, questioningly. "To set up our own firm, protecting people. We figured the military would let us learn how, but I failed my basic training. Asthma, apparently. I went into I.T. as a civilian and I've loved it."

I grin at his story. He didn't let the avenue of one dream stop him from heading towards his final goal.

"I'll get out in six weeks," I tell him. "I've done sixteen years. My best friend is pregnant, about to get married and her hubby-to-be," I take a sip of the vodka so I can find the kindest way to describe her situation, "doesn't want her in the military."

"He's not willing to be a military husband?" Marcus asks.

I shake my head. "Hell no. He's got his own company, does well for himself." At least Jim has that going for him.

Marcus leans forward, turning to me. Our knees are almost touching. "You don't like him," he informs me, reading between the lines. I shrug my indifference.

"There are times, she comes to hang out with me and she's quieter, a shell of the woman I know she is. Whether that's because she's pregnant or not, I don't know. But every time I've met him, I've not liked the feelings he's left me with."

"And you? What do you want?" he asks me. I look at him, his mouth, his jaw and I can't tell him that right now, I just want him.

"I don't know. I want to see what's out there on civvy-street; I've not made any plans," I fib slightly. I've made plans to be there for Annie; I can sense what she has with Jim will be a load of trouble.

"But your friend..." he begins.

"Will need me when this goes south," I admit before I can stop myself.

"And what will you do for work? Head into the civilian police?" he questions. He takes a sip of his drink but doesn't nudge himself closer to me.

"What? No... Work private security, probably. Been police long enough. Edinburgh's a huge place, there's plenty of work to be had."

I pick up my drink and take a good mouthful. While Annie prefers spiced rum and cola, I much prefer vodka and this is decent stuff.

I turn to find Marcus has shifted to be closer to me and I reach out to touch his hair, then run my hand down his face, his jaw. I can feel his stubble and wonder what it'll feel like against my inner thighs. I can't wait to find out.

One of his hands scoops me behind my head and then he's pulling me in for a kiss. It's gentle, at first, then our lips part and his tongue begs for entrance into my mouth. I open up, letting him in and dart my tongue along his. Our tongues meet and dance and he pulls me onto his lap, leaning back onto the sofa, and I follow, straddling him, never breaking our kiss.

Long moments later, he pulls back. "I want to see you." And he's tugging gently at the bottom of my blouse. I grab it and pull it over my head, revealing the cream lace bra I put on to match the top.

"So perfect," he says, kissing my collarbone as he undoes the bra. It's off in moments and then his tongue is licking me, his teeth nip, and his hand plays with my other breast. I shiver at the coolness that's now hitting me and from his light touch.

"Take yours off," I command him, tugging at his t-shirt. He stops what he's doing and complies, revealing his pecs, abs, and everything else, along with a few phrase tattoos across his torso. I groan in delight as he does so and I wish now all geeks looked like Greek Gods. Maybe they should, the name is similar!

He pulls me in for a kiss, making me forget. Then I'm turned so I'm on the sofa, beneath him. His weight is perfect, solid and he's kissing a breast again whilst playing with the nipple of another. I groan and arch against him as he lights the fire within me and I push my hands into his hair as my breath hitches. He fills his mouth with as much breast as he can take, then he sucks and lets it pop out of his mouth. I've never had anyone treat me so deliciously before. He unfastens my jeans, removing them to reveal some matching knickers and I can hear him groan. I'm so glad I brought a matching set with me!

"Fuck, you're perfect," he tells me. I arch against him and can hear him chuckling. "Patience," he whispers and pulls my knickers down and off me so very slowly.

I can feel his stubble tickle my stomach as he kisses me, then lower as he makes his way down. Then he's kissing me and his mouth is on me, sucking and licking, sending shocks of delight and passion through me. He changes how he's lying to kneel and he turns me, right as his tongue delves deep inside me. I moan in ecstasy and arch back, fisting his hair and running my hands through it, enjoying the fire he's ignited within me. He pushes a leg back by grabbing my ankle, opening me up even more. I cry out as I shatter on his tongue and then he's over me, stroking my face.

"Bedroom," he hoarsely whispers, helping me up. He grabs our clothes and hangs my bra on the door. "In case my brother comes back early, just a way to tell him I'm busy," he informs me. I nod; it kind of makes sense.

In the bedroom, he turns on a small lamp and angles it away from the bed, diffusing the light, but it gives us enough to see by. He drops our clothes onto a chair and then he comes to me, pulling me close, kissing me deeply. My hands find their way down to his crotch, over his abs and his V.

"Undress me if you want," he tells me between kisses and I do. I unbutton him, and his sports trunks make me lick my lips. They're as fitted as his t-shirt was.

Slowly, I take all his garments off and he steps out of them. Dear God, he's beautiful, erect and dripping. I lick him, taking him into my willing mouth and he groans as I pull back and then swallow him deeper, fucking him with my mouth. I let the sounds escape, we're not in barracks, I don't have to be quiet or discreet. He pulls out of my mouth and grins at me as I look up at him.

He helps me up and guides me to the bed. From the top drawer of his bedside, he pulls out some condoms, rips one open and puts it on. Then he kisses me again, deeply, our tongues dancing and he bites my lip. The biting does something to me, releasing an animalistic tendency within me I didn't know I had and I bite his lower lip back.

"Make me come," I beg. God, I need to come. He nods before he holds my head more firmly, then he releases it and turns us so I am on top, in charge. It excites me that he wants to see and I sigh happily as I slide down onto him, enjoying the feeling of him as he fills me so fully. He groans, grabs my arse and I slowly begin to ride him. I'm either not fast enough or I'm doing it wrong, but he holds me still and then he's thrusting up into me, holding me as he accelerates his thrusting, slapping into me like a piston. He doesn't come, but after a few minutes, he slows and lets go of my arse to let me ride him again.

"Come 'ere," he tells me and I angle my head down to his, then his mouth is devouring mine as my hair cascades over his face, around us, closing us off to the rest of the room. He lets go of my arse and I change how my legs are positioned, so I'm more squatting and I continue to ride him. I can feel the pressure building, and I let out a moan or two. His hands grab my tits, fondling them, pinching the nipples, making me wild. He squeezes them tight, making me cry out as I climax on him for the first time.

He grins as I come down from the stars and pulls me in for a deep kiss.

"Not done yet," he whispers and with him still inside me, he turns us so I'm on my back and he kneels up. He pushes my knees up to my breasts and begins thrusting, slowly, deeply. I toss my arms above my head and moan in agreement as he hits the spot I find most men can't. His kisses are deep, nearly as deep as his cock is within me. Never have I had someone fill me so fully that I nearly orgasm just at the thought of it. The friction he creates builds within me, and I wrap my legs around him, holding him close as the pleasure we're creating mounts. I begin to moan and cry out, scratching his back, begging him to make me come again. He speeds up, pumping himself into me for all he's worth. The bed shakes, we shake, and then I forget, shattering around him once again as his cries join mine.

~Four~
Adrian

I sigh as I trudge up the stairs to the flat my brother and I share off base. It's five am, dawn is breaking and I'm dead on my feet. We ship out tomorrow at oh-two-hundred, something I need to tell Marcus about. My flight suit is all packed, but I need sleep. I enter the flat as quietly as I can and see the small side light is on. I look around and see a lace cream bra hanging from my brother's bedroom doorknob. Lucky git got himself laid tonight, so I know I need to be quiet. The bedroom door isn't shut tight, and I peek in. I can't see much, but I don't miss the shape of two figures in bed, entwined, fast asleep and she's dark-haired.

I grin, stepping away as quietly as I can, pulling the door back into place and making my way to my bed. It'll be months before I see any action of that kind, but by the time I'm undressed down to my boxers and my head has hit the pillow, I don't care.

When I wake up, the woman is gone. Marcus has left me a note to tell me he's on base, working and I check the time. It's nearly two pm. The coffee pot is ready to go and I turn it on as I grab a shower and decide what else I need to pack. I'm drinking my coffee, dressed in just bottom fatigues, when my brother returns.

"Good night?" I ask him, knowing fine well it was. He grins at me. We're eleven months apart in age, an academic year, but his civilian lifestyle lends itself to his looser, almost boho style of living than it does to mine. That said, he's a computer whiz and he's learning more than I ever thought would be possible or necessary.

"Fucking brilliant. She gave me a good workout. It's a pity we won't be seeing her again."

"We?" I ask him, raising an eyebrow. "Was she up for us both?" I enquire. Marcus and I shared a lot of things when we were kids; women are the one thing we share as adults but very carefully. Not everyone wants to be seduced by two brothers. I'm aware, as I know Marcus is, of our reputation on base from the one time we have—she wasn't terrifically discreet.

"I sense she might be. She switched from hard and fast, to soft and slow very quickly, it took a while to make her come with pure sex, but I wasn't giving up, especially as she begged me to make her come." He grins at me as he pours himself a coffee. He talks about her with some reverence and gentleness. I can tell he'd see her again if he was given even half a chance.

"She begged you?" I ask and he nods, a wry grin on his face as if he's remembering that particular moment. Then, he glances up at me.

"And she escorted that pillock of an I.T. guy from that other company down from Lossie. He tried to get it on with the base commander's son and didn't get the hint. The MP's had to separate him and the commander threw his arse back down here."

"So he's back on base?" I ask. The base jungle drums are rife with what happened and the snippets I heard at four am were enough to tell me who he's on about. He's tried to get friendly with Marcus and me, but we like our women.

"Nope! Our WC threw him out too, removed them from the contract. I've been picking his work up this morning, which is why I went in and escorted Blythe, my date, back to Brize." He sighs, happily. "She's a snowflake, but fuck…and she gets out in six weeks."

"She does, huh? Where's she going to be living?" I ask. I've never seen Marcus so enamoured by a woman before; his eyes dance either in memory or lust, I'm not sure which.

"Edinburgh. She's got a friend who is pregnant and she doesn't like the baby's daddy. She's going to be around for her friend as she can see it heading south already."

"Did you get anything more about her? Her last name?" I question.

Marcus stops and looks at me. "Grieves. I think she said her last name was Grieves."

I ponder. "We have got a Grievson on base," I tell him. "What does she look like?" He pulls his phone out and shows me a picture of her at a pool table. Long dark hair is pulled back into a light ponytail. Skin tight blue jeans and a cream top highlight her frame. The same black hair as the man I think is her brother. He's mentioned her a few times, but not often; he's quite private.

"She's an MP from Lossie?" I check with him. Marcus nods, his face contorting into a slight frown.

"Shit. That's Byron Grievson's sister," I tell him. Marcus drops his jaw; he knows Byron and I don't get on.

Marcus cackles as he sips his coffee. "You'd better not tell him I fucked his sister stupid whilst she was here then, had you?" he teases as he heads off to his bedroom to change out of the monkey suit he wears on base. No, I guess I'd better not.

~Five~
Blythe

"B_y!" I yell across the tarmac as I find my way to where I've been told my brother is currently located. I'm in base fatigues, my civilian clothes are back in my bag, which is packed and ready to go. He turns and doesn't acknowledge me for about three seconds, then recognition dawns and he's marching towards me, scooping me up and hugging me tightly.

"Bly, what the bloody hell…" he begins as he crushes me to him. *Bloody hell, it's good to see him!*

"Personnel escort. My flight back leaves in," I check my watch, "forty-five minutes. Can I snaffle you away for a coffee at least?" I ask him. He nods and we head over to his Flight Commander, who gives us a nod and tells us we have half an hour to catch up. It's better than bugger all.

"When did you get down?" he asks me as we march towards the mess hall.

I nudged him hard with my elbow. "Do you not check your phone?" I ask, exasperated. "What's the bloody point of having one if you don't use it?" I berate him as we head inside from the wind. I can see why Jonesey wants to take off at fourteen hundred; this wind behind us will be better than on us, or before us.

"Not had the damn chance," he tells me. "Ye ken we're off on tour for four or five months?" he questions me. I nod.

"When my WC saw that the guest had to be escorted back here, he offered me the chance. I had a few drinks out last night; I was hoping you'd be able to join me." I look up at him as he opens the mess hall door. "I'm glad I caught ye," I tell him. I'm not telling him I had the best sex I've ever had with someone competent enough to finally make me come during the act of sex itself and did so seemingly easily.

"Pity we can only grab a coffee, but ye ken what it's like," he reminds me.

"Aye, I'll not miss the deployments, but parts of this I will," I tell him as he hands me a black coffee. Then he goes to the fridge behind the counter and pours out the milk as we like it.

"I'll envy you that. I've another couple of years to go, then my dozen is up. I might carry on, not sure."

"Staying in the 47th?" I ask. Byron shakes his head, his short black hair not moving and his clean-shaven jaw is set. The same blue eyes I have stare back at me.

"No, something more…quiet. Maybe Lossie, or something more up North. There's the Red's out of Lincoln." He grins.

"Think you needed to have learnt how to fly something faster than a C130 to fly an Arrow," I torment him. He shrugs his shoulders, and we talk about family, our ailing grandparents. I check my watch, standing.

"I need to head out to the pad," I tell him. He stands and hugs me tight.

"See you in about six months," he tells me. I nod, poking him on his pectoral.

"You better do," I say. He grins at me and I sign out of the base as we head out to the helipad where Jonesey is waiting. Byron gives me one last hug and I climb into the helo, donning the co-pilot headphones as Jonesey starts her up. I can see By waiting to wave goodbye one last time and I wave until he's nothing but a speck in the distance.

~Six~
Blythe

Seven Years Later

I sigh as I hang my coat up on the hook. Another workday has ended and I decide I detest retail security more than on-site security. It's such a joke, the way kids think they can just take stuff without paying for it. It doesn't help that their parents pander to some of their antics and won't tell the child they're being ungrateful, spoiled wee shites. I feel my phone vibrate and I smile as I see a text from my brother, telling me he's landed safely at my parents' place in Italy. He extended his military contract and has another few years to serve, but he's taken a month's leave out of what he's owed and gone to see them.

I sent him a thumbs up; I'm glad he went to go and see them. They need cheering up after Papa lost both his parents so close together. I hear noises from the kitchen, and I smile as I hear my god-daughter and best friend going through spelling homework. Annie's not letting Elle get away with anything.

"Elinor Rose," Annie's voice cautions. My coming in has distracted Elle and I quietly slip off my boots and head into the kitchen. Elle is sitting on one side of the table, Annie at another and Annie's old, just working laptop is booted up.

"Ah, yer home," Annie cheerily greets me, but I know she heard me as well as Elle did. She turns to Elle. "One more time. Get it right and then you can say hi to Aunty Bee." Elle sits up and spells out the word 'occasionally' that Annie had told her to when I walked in.

I grin as Annie nods, and Elle jumps off the chair and bounces to me, wrapping tiny arms around my leg in greeting.

"Hello, sweetheart," I tell her, hugging her back.

"Mummy, can I watch some TV now?" she asks. Annie nods and Elle yips in delight and runs into the living room, and Annie smiles as she watches her daughter go. Then she looks at me.

"Had a shit day again?" she asks me, quietly. She doesn't need me to speak to know what kind of day I've had. I nod and sigh, then I put the kettle on. It's too early for vodka and Coke, so coffee will have to do.

"I found something," she tells me and she taps the newspaper. As the kettle boils, I notice she's taken a big black marker and circled a job advert for a local security firm that is after extra staff. It's coded and I can tell they're military-based or had the experience of it.

"Looks good, aye? Are you changing jobs?" I ask and she shakes her head. She wakes the laptop up and I see a CV with my details on it, a well-written cover letter, and she beams at me.

"I'm not, hell no; I'm wanting that promotion and I love what I do. But you should. It's all done, read through it, and we can change it if you don't like how I've re-written things." She points to a chair and heads over to make some instant coffee.

"How did ye notice it?" I ask, looking at the coded advert again. *Why was she even looking?*

"I've been looking for something for ye for a while. You need something better, more you. Retail security isn't it," she tells me. I nod in agreement.

"So you're not giving up being Lara?" I joke. Annie chuckles. Eighteen months ago, she answered an ad for a women's refuge charity shop. When she called and spoke with the woman, she was offered an interview, which was double-edged. Now Annie retrieves women from abuse situations, sometimes when and while the police are involved. It's not the first time I've known her to get the kids and the women out whilst the husband or boyfriend is distracted. I look at my best friend, the one who has my back. Her eyes are bright and animated. Her enthusiasm rubs off on me and I begin to grin.

I turn back to the advert she highlighted and check my CV over, along with the cover letter. I change a word or two here and there, but in the main, Annie has my style spot on.

"Right, ready to send it," I tell her and I log into my email on her laptop, then send both off and sigh, praying that this is better than where I am.

~Seven~
Marcus

Adrian sighs as he finally sits down. He's been on the go, I think now, for nearly ninety-six hours, and I know he's going to growl at me, but I have Tony's backing on this, so he's outnumbered and outvoted.

"Job is done," he growls. I push my chair back and turn to face him. After a moment, he lifts his head and looks at me. "What?" he asks me as he turns his chair.

"We need more staff," I tell him. We've only one other member who can help him out on security jobs and we're all overworked.

"Can't afford it," he begins, but I lift my hand.

"We can. The advert is out and I've received CV's already," I state, nodding to the printer.

Adrian pushes himself forward and growls. "How?!"

I look at my very overtired and workaholic brother. "Tony," I reply, simply. Adrian sighs and rubs his hands over his face.

"You went behind my back?" he asks. I lean over and hand him a pile of work we could do if we had more staff.

"Hiring people to do some of this alone, would pay Tony back, and more. We'd train them to do these jobs, which means they'll be trained for future jobs. We're turning clients away as we can't cope." I wait a moment, letting his brain catch up to where I am. "We either expand, taking on the work because it's coming our way due to our hard-fought reputation, or we fold."

Adrian's eyes go wide at that implication.

"I propose we expand," I state, heading to the printer to fetch off the CV's I've just sent to it. I've not read them yet and I sit down to do so. I can see Adrian chewing over my words from the corner of my eye. I don't need to push him, he'll come around to the logical way in a little while.

The first CV doesn't feel right; their lack of military background or general security training doesn't fit. The second makes me stop. I read the name again and I grin as my heart does weird things inside my chest that I'd forgotten it could do.

"Well, well, would you look here," I whisper, holding up the CV and the cover letter, stapling both together. I don't need to read the details; I *know* they're good.

"Found a decent one?" asks Adrian as he wheels his chair over to my desk. I grin and hand him the paperwork I've just put together.

He reads it and looks at me. "This her?" he questions, his voice quiet. I nod. I tried to reach Blythe at Lossiemouth when she left Brize that weekend. She never responded.

"Do you really want your fuck buddy in the office?" he asks me and I glare at him.

"One, she *isn't* my fuck buddy. We didn't have contact with each other again after that weekend. Two, she's got the training we need, probably more. Three, if she does become a fuck buddy and it screws us over, we let her go with a hefty severance and NDA."

Adrian looks at me, his face is like thunder and he's not too pleased by my words. I opt for a softer approach with him.

"Look, let's give her a trial. People with her experience don't just fall into our lap. We know she's got the credentials, we know who she is and we'd hardly have to train her to our standards." The RAF would have done that and then some.

I recall her mentioning a friend who was pregnant, the one she was going to be there to support if things went south as she expected them to. I wonder what happened there…

~Eight~
Blythe

My phone pings early the next morning as I hear Annie and Ellie getting ready for school. Annie's interviewing new candidates with the women's aid charity today, as a part of her new deputy manager's role that she was offered last night after Elle was in bed. Whilst it interrupted our movie night, a promotion for her is welcome.

I stretch and yawn, then rub my eyes and check my phone. I blink and rub my eyes again. Then I jump out of bed to go and find Annie.

"Hey, sweetheart." I smile at Elle as she munches on some toast, kissing her on the head as always. Annie has her usual bowl of porridge and she's got her dressing gown on over her suit. Well, what we have made into a suit. A skirt and jacket that goes with a neutral blouse and low heels. It's been a while since she was interviewed; doing interviews is a doddle and managing people is the next step up for her, at least in civilian life

"Could you read this for me? Are my eyes deceiving me?" I hand Annie my phone and she reads the email.

"You're invited to an interview," she begins.

"Aye, and who is it from?" I ask.

"Marcus and Adrian McGowan," Annie answers me, handing me back my phone. I bite my lip to stop myself from swearing in front of Elle.

"I'm sure as heck that he's Brize Norton Marcus," I tell Annie. "I can't recall his surname, but I'm certain it's them." It's almost comical to watch as the spoon stops between the bowl and her mouth, watching her eyes bug out and the words 'oh fuck' be mouthed in silence.

"I had no idea it was with them," she tells me in an apologetic tone. "I wouldn't have suggested it had I known. What do you want to do?" she asks me. "Your CV details point to here. They could easily come here to find ye if they wanted." She finally puts the spoonful of porridge in her mouth and watches me.

I sigh. "I don't know. Go, I think?" I question myself and my decision; I had never expected to run into Marcus again, though it's a night I've never forgotten.

Elle pipes up, as cheerful as ever a nearly seven-year-old can be. "You should go, Aunty Blythe. This will be good for you," she tells us. Annie and I look at each other and then at the bairn. Elle looks back at us with a mouthful of toast and the widest grin on her wee face.

I respond to the email as Annie takes Ellie to school on her way to work. Usually, Annie walks Ellie in, but not today. I drive them there as there's usually nowhere to park, so I drop them off, turn around on the estate the school is on, by which time Annie has escorted Elle in and is walking back. I find a place to pull up and wait for her, then I let her take over and she drives me home.

"What time are you wanting to arrange the interview for?" Annie asks me as she waits outside the place I've rested my head, and called home, for the last half-dozen years.

"Not sure, I'll let you know. They were quick to get back to me. I sent it to them yesterday afternoon at around sixteen-thirty, and that email reply was sent at oh-six hundred." Annie nods.

"Aye, let me know. Hopefully, you'll have good news this evening to match mine!" She's chirpy, buoyant and happy. It's been years since I've seen Annie like this on my behalf and I realise I've been in a funk, job-wise, for too long. *How has she coped with my miserable arse this long?*

"Later!" I call out as I climb out of her car and watch her drive to work.

Annie texts me that she's formally accepted the offer made to her last night; she's done with the interviews and wants to know if I've heard anything about times for mine. I check my emails, but still no time or date confirmation from Marcus or his brother about my interview. I replied to them, saying I was free later today or tomorrow due to transport and current working arrangements. As I'm tidying the kitchen around lunchtime, my phone pings and I nearly knock it off the counter to get to it.

I'm not sure if it's because I'll be hearing from Marcus, or if this is about a job I know I'll love that will finally challenge me and put all my skills to use. *Perhaps it's both?* The email is from them and I hold my breath as I open it and read it once.

"You are invited to an interview," it begins and I re-read it. Sixteen hundred today at a building I don't quite recognise. I check the address and notice from Google that the offices have been updated, renovated. They're near the City Centre and I recognise where when I see the images; it's in an affluent part of the city. I raise my eyebrows and text Annie.

B: The interview is at 16:00. Can I use the car if you're back in time?

A: I'll be back, gotta be for the school run! And yes, you can. I'll add some fuel.

I wince; fuel is expensive right now and we're both just treading water financially, even if Annie just got a promotion.

B: Ten should cover it. There's free parking on-site, so I have been told in the email.

A: That helps! Ten it is. Get a shower, ye smelly git!

I grin and look at the time. I'd better get my skates on.

Annie was back in plenty of time and as eager as I was to hear about her day and what happened with the formal chat and job offer, but she refrained, making me focus on my impending interview. She printed out a copy of my CV and what background information she could on McGowan Securities, including stuff from Companies House and legal suits against them. Thankfully, there were none.

"Pretty thorough," I comment at her, grinning. I've got a different blouse on, but I've borrowed her skirt, jacket, and shoes. Thank goodness we're similar in a lot of things. Civilian clothing for interviews isn't something either of us has splashed out on. Food on the table, paying the bills, decorating, and surviving have been our priorities. Things have been tight, but Annie does tell me what she's been offered as a salary. I hope things won't be as tight for her should she end up living by herself, especially if my job takes me away.

"Go! Slay them, and I hope they realise what a great asset you'd be to their company," she tells me. I smile, hug her, and then get on the road as she walks up to fetch Elle from school.

At ten to four, I'm outside their building, the butterflies cascading around my stomach. I've interviewed for civilian companies, but this is the first one with a military aspect to it; one that the owners know what the heck I'm talking about. There's some light scaffolding up on the front of the building as two men with drills and tool belts position a sign for the building name. Off to the side is a new sign, detailing the companies who are occupied within.

McGowan Securities is one of them and I see they're in Suite Four. Taking a huge breath, I venture inside and pray for a good outcome.

The receptionist is professional and there's another candidate there. He's tall and thin, slightly muscular, and the receptionist comes over with a coffee for him.

"There we are Mr McAulley." She hands him the coffee and he thanks her.

"Are you here for an interview?" I ask. He looks fit, but I don't have him pegged for being ex-military or being in any kind of security work. He grins at me with a lopsided grin and I immediately think Annie would melt at that smile. I'd like to introduce them, one day, if I can.

"No. I'm helping conduct them," he leans across and whispers, not too quietly. "I part own the company." He winks at me and I purse my lips together. "Tony McAulley." If the brothers are the brawns and intelligence behind it, then this man would be the money.

"Pleasure to meet you," I say and close my mouth. He nods to the receptionist, who brings me a coffee and something Annie once did strikes a chord here: Interviews are sometimes not conducted in the interview room, but outside in the more relaxed areas, like reception rooms, or mess halls. She found some key evidence on a case that had been bugging our WO for weeks, just by an informal chat like this over a coffee when the other RAF officer hadn't a clue who Annie was. Sheer genius but now I realise, bloody sneaky.

"How did you get to meet the guys?" I ask. I want to sound like I know them, despite only knowing Marcus on any level at all.

"Long term friends," he tells me and I nod. "What about you?" And he turns to me, coffee in hand. The interview has begun.

"I've only met Marcus, but I know of his brother by reputation." The fact that his reputation came as news from my brother isn't important. I know how pig-headed the older McGowan brother can be, but my brother can butt heads with the best of them over a fart.

"So what's your background?" he asks as he sips more coffee. Through two coffees and a glass of water, we talk. I give my background, experience and whilst I can explain what I've done, I don't go into details of past cases or too detailed on the incidents. I've not seen Marcus or even met Adrian since I arrived and it's not until the end that they appear.

As soon as you look at them side by side, you can tell they're brothers. Two peas out of the same pod. Marcus has kept his long hair and clean-shaven look; Adrian's hair is still quite military cut with more tattoos showing than Marcus, and he's sporting a short beard.

Adrian is also an inch or two taller and a good bit broader. Their eyes, though, are exactly the same shade, with the same shaped nose and kissable mouth. If I wasn't already aware that they sometimes shared their women, I'd be questioning what sanity I had by thinking that. All I can think about now though is very unprofessional and I focus on Tony to bring me back to the moment at hand.

He nods at the guys who give the slight nod most military personnel know. I wait, aware now that they were probably watching and listening in. Tony hands Marcus the Blue-tooth speaker that was on the table the entire time and I quickly understand that the device isn't quite what I thought it was. No one speaks, and I resign myself to the fact that this didn't go my way. I stand and look at all three men.

"Gentlemen, it was a pleasure. Thanks for the time and the opportunity." I smile, lift my bag and head out of the door, kicking myself for being a fool, thinking I had a chance.

~Nine~
Adrian

Marcus and I are listening to Blythe's interview with Tony. I didn't want to interview her with Marcus, so we asked Tony for suggestions on interviewing her without it prejudicing her chances, or having Marcus fuck her on the conference room table. He volunteered as the silent partner. I have to say, I'm impressed by her CV and how she's coping with this. One, she worked out pretty quickly that Tony was the one interviewing her, not Marcus or I, though I'm sure we were who she was expecting. Two, she went through cases and scenarios I'd expect of a military security person and of someone who has worked in the civilian sector, though she admitted it wasn't challenging for her. Three, she didn't give exact details, but the scenarios she speaks off, we're familiar with.

I nod to Marcus towards the end of the interview, just as Tony is beginning to wrap it up.

"She's clever, practical, sure, calm under pressure. You were right, she's the best of the candidates we've had come through," I admit. Fuck buddy to my brother or not, I agree that we have to have her with us. We stand and head out to the reception area. Bianca, our receptionist, has been busy taking calls, sending out emails and quotes for jobs the three candidates we're taking on will be tasked with, but she smiles at us as if this is normal practice.

Tony nods to us as we enter the reception area and I look at this woman for the first time with my own eyes. I can see exactly why Marcus is attracted to her, I'm tenting up and that's not just because I know he's slept with her. She is captivating, timeless. Elizabeth Taylor has nothing on this woman. Our silence is taken the wrong way, as she thanks us for our time, tells us it was a pleasure and heads out the door. I blink and look at Marcus and Tony, stunned.

"Don't you dare let her get away!" Tony points furiously as he instructs us to act. I march out the door to find her, expecting Marcus to be at my heels.

She's quick on her feet as I find her sitting in a small car in the underground car park minutes later. I've had to jog to catch up. Her shoulders are heaving and she's gasping in huge breaths of air whilst being hidden in the shadows of the car. Arse, she thinks she's screwed her chances over.

"Blythe?" I call out, questioningly, knocking on the window as gently as I can. She wipes her eyes and turns to me, winds the window down and she's swallowing hard before she speaks.

"I'll be okay," she tells me, but turns away from me and I see her heave in another huge breath of air.

"You will. You did great. Come and talk terms with us," I offer, holding out my hand. "I'm Adrian, but I think you worked that out."

She turns to me and she stops everything within me, breathing, moving, understanding. Her blue eyes hold my gaze and I don't know for how long. The space between us seems so vast, I don't want to move towards her, not yet. I shouldn't be thinking about how she'd feel between my brother and I, or even just under me.

"Terms?" I offer again. I need to get this back on track; now. That single word seems to galvanise her into action as she nods.

"I think I ought to freshen up a little," she tells me as she winds the window back up and climbs out. I nod and smile gently at her. This is where Marcus is so much better with women; my gruffness scares them away most of the time. *Where the hell is my brother?*

"We can do that," I tell her as softly as I can, holding out a hand for her again. This time, she moves towards me and takes it. Her grip is firm, but her skin is soft. She locks the car from her pocket.

"We'll explain why upstairs; I'm sorry you thought you weren't successful. You're the best we've seen by far, but Marcus knew you would be."

Her cheeks and neck go red from my compliment, but then she sets her shoulders and stands up straighter, her heels clicking on the hard floor as we walk.

Ten minutes later, we're all in the conference room. Blythe looks much more composed after a quick visit to the ladies. I had Bianca look after her, just so Blythe could ask questions if she wanted. I watch as she sends a text off to someone and sips her glass of water carefully.

"I had to borrow their car," she explains and I nod.

"Your pregnant friend?" Marcus asks, and I watch as Blythe gasps.

"You remember?" Her voice is soft and wondrous as if she can't believe someone would remember details from six or seven years ago. Marcus nods. His memory is longer than mine.

"I remember everything you told me that night we played pool," he tells us. I know he's slept with her, I doubt Tony does. I don't know if she understands I'd know, but she doesn't give anything away in that regard. With the look in her eyes and her set face, I decided never to try and play poker with her; she's got one hell of a poker face.

"And you did it, what you set out to do," she tells him as she looks around us. I look at my brother, and he just smiles.

"Yeah, we did. Anyway, because you and I have a history, Aid and I didn't think it was fair we got involved in interviewing you. But," he puts the listening device on the table, "we did hear every word you said."

He tosses her the device and begins to explain what he's designed it to do.

"It doesn't just listen if we need it. It looks like a regular Bluetooth speaker, something people have around them all day these days. But, this can also make it so your mobiles can't be used as a listening device." He flips a switch on it and calls my phone. I answer it and put it on speaker, but all we can hear from either mobile is static.

Blythe goes wide-eyed as my brother goes through some of the other tech he's developed that we use. Tony sits back and smiles. Ten minutes later, he's excusing himself, and Marcus sees him out; it leaves us alone for a moment.

"Are you feeling better?" I ask, watching her as she, again, slowly sips the water Bianca poured for us. The coffee pot in the corner gurgles as it finishes brewing the fresh pot, and I'll be glad when the kitchen area is complete later next week; the noise is distracting.

Blythe nods at me and fidgets.

"Something you want to ask?" I enquire, aware that my brother could come back at any moment, or that Bianca could waltz in with cups for the coffee. At that moment, Marcus appears, jovial and bouncy, the smile on his face reaching his eyes and causing him to almost dance on his feet. Blythe changes her look, her focus, and whatever it was that she was going to say; the moment is lost.

"Right, let's get down to terms, shall we?" he asks, and our negotiations begin.

~Ten~
Blythe

I didn't screw it up. I thank the heavens as I drive back, three and a half hours after my interview with Tony McAulley began. I pull into Annie's driveway, aware that Elle will just be going to bed and I heave out one last huge sigh of relief as I climb out of Annie's car, securing it for the night. I really thought I fucked it up somehow.

Annie meets me on the stairs as I enter; I've missed saying goodnight to Elle. I smile at my friend and nod, unable to stop the grin emerging on my face.

"Great news!" she cheers for me. "Go say goodnight to her; she wanted to be up for you coming home. I'll pour some wine," she offers and I head up to do as she suggests, taking the suit off which has brought us both luck today.

Half an hour later, we're comparing contract notes and salaries. Annie will be okay financially if I ever move out, something we briefly discussed before but do so again now in detail. I tell her what happened at my interview, but I keep Tony's name back from the information. Adrian and Marcus told me he was the silent partner, so silent he will stay, though I'll have to orchestrate a way for Annie and Tony to meet. He's just her type, tall but fit, thin, cheeky, funny and caring. It's amazing what you can pick up from people as you chat with them, and thanks to Marcus and Adrian, I know Tony's a multi-millionaire.

"I'm as glad as heck you sussed that out quickly, Bee! Congratulations," she tells me. I grin and she explains all about what she'll be doing. Not just working in the shelters here in Edinburgh, but in other cities, managing some of the teams that retrieve women from broken homes and situations, either with or without police assistance. Skills I know she has and still trains in.

"I'll still be on call every other weekend, which I can cope with. It gives me more money as the weekends are over and above my new basic salary. Ye ken the best bit? Using all that management training we endured for something good."

"Aye, that'll be good!" Tomorrow is Friday, and Elle will be going to her dad's for the weekend. The legal arrangement between them seems to be holding and has for six and a half years so far.

"Why don't we go out this weekend?" I ask her. Annie winces and shakes her head.

"I haven't got the spare cash, not yet. I've debts to clear first and the car to fix, afore I can think along those lines." I let my face fall; I want to celebrate.

"Let's think of something that's not going to break the bank though, aye? I want to celebrate too, I have a spare tenner," she tells me. I nod, but it's not what I wanted.

Friday night and Annie is training. She pays for her session by the block, so she's able to carry on training; she just needs the fuel to get across to the leisure centre and back. While she's out, I walk to the supermarket and get some fresh pizza, more wine, a chocolate gateau, and cheesy snacks. I walk back and hear my phone ping when I'm halfway there, but my hands are full and I can't do anything about it without stopping, something I don't want to do.

I carry on as quickly as I can and start the oven warming up as soon as I'm in. Annie will be back in about fifteen minutes, just enough time for me to get things organised. I plate up the cake and put things away where they should go, then I check my phone.

There are two notifications. One is from my bank and my heart sinks as I wonder just how overdrawn my account is now. The other is from a number I don't know but is quickly identified.

Unknown: Took the liberty of sending you some cash to clear yer feet. Yes, I went looking into your accounts, as we do with all new employees. Marcus.

I hold my breath as I check my bank account, seeing that five grand just got deposited. That doesn't just clear my feet, I can clear Annie's too, and get the car serviced, which it badly needs. It's been both of our lifelines for years, and she'd kindly added me to her insurance. Strangely, her premium was reduced by adding me, so that was a good bonus. It's also giving us funds to head out. I grin and reply.

B: You could have just asked me what financial state I was in.

M: I could. But I run these checks on all new employees. That's not an advance, that's from me.

B: Kind of you, but the first month's salary would have sorted it.

M: Now it doesn't need to.

I smile and immediately transfer Annie a grand; I'll explain why when she's home. After Jim screwed her over and controlled her financially from the start, I know she's going to baulk at what I've done. I'll just have to tell her a little white lie.

She comes in about ten minutes later from the garage. She'll have put her martial arts pads in the garage to air and the car away, or secured it. I grin at her as she strips off at the washing machine, dropping the lightweight gi she wore tonight straight into the machine.

"I got a salary advance," I tell her I lean against the doorframe as she undresses. She turns and looks at me.

"How much of an advance? And what did ye do that you had to tell me that?" she asks. I grin; we know each other too well.

"I shared some of it with you so you can get the car sorted and clear that credit card." I watch as she stops and looks at me.

"Bee, ye didnae need to," she tells me.

"Aye, I did. You've shared your home, car, and life with me, again, for the last six years. I've used that car as much as you, and ye ken it needs a damn good service and TLC. So, get it done. If you can't clear the credit card I know you've been secretly using, let me know."

She glares at me and I chuckle. "I noticed that the card was being used a wee bit more than usual. Clear it down for me, it'll make me stop worrying about it. And we can go out, say, tomorrow? Eastside?" I insist. *I really need to party in a dress!*

She sighs but nods. "Aye, okay! I'll get Hamish to look at the car next week. What are you going to do about going to work?" she asks.

"They're doing background checks, so it'll easily be about a week afore I get my start date." I don't share that they've likely done the checks already. "And I can use the bus to do the last week in retail," I suggest, but she shakes her head.

"Jack the retail job in, tell them you quit with immediate effect and you'll take their uniform in during the week. They've screwed you over with hours and conditions for too long. The shoe," she pats me on the shoulder as she walks past me stark naked, "is on the other foot. I'll be down in about fifteen," she informs me as she heads upstairs. I can hear the water running in the shower and I put the pizza in the oven. I sneak a quick text back to Marcus.

B: I fancy celebrating with my friend, care to join us at Eastside tomorrow?

M: We can't. We're heading down to Carlisle to quote on a job. But, I can spare you the Eastside cost. I'll get Bianca to drop the staff card in for you. Just you going?

I sigh, my sudden idea to get the McGowans, Tony, Annie, and me in the same place falls flat on its arse before it's even taken a step.

B: No, my friend is coming. She's had good fortune this week too, a new role on her part. Tell you about it one day.

M: Not a problem! I'll see you when we can get a start date sorted, which should be next week. You'll hopefully have a few new colleagues by then.

I raise my eyebrows and wonder just how quickly the brothers are going to expand their business.

~Eleven~
Blythe

Bianca drops off the card for Eastside as Marcus promised. It's the standard membership one, not one of the coveted black VIP status ones that I know exist. However, it will save us an entry fee, which means an extra drink. Elle went to her dad's as usual, nothing weird or awkward happened there this time, thankfully!

Annie opts for a trouser outfit with a silver top; I pick out a red dress I bought in Italy a few years back. I'm not surprised it still fits, I hardly change shape; even the RAF couldn't get me to do that.

We enter the club and it's quite busy. We grab a double round, drink the shot and head towards one of the dance areas. We cheer each other on and finish our drink before thinking about dancing. We somehow get caught up in a group of girls who seem to be on a hen do. They're quite merry, loud and brazen, but nothing unusual; they're how most drunken Scots lassies are when they're on the drink.

Half an hour or so later, the girls are making their way back to the dance floor as a large group, and we head off, leaving the girls to get on with it.

As we're dancing, the girls take it up a level and start hassling a group of lads, taunting and pushing into them, though I missed why. The bouncers notice, and the girls get asked to move on. A request they don't like and they make that fact known. Even in this noisy establishment, they're making heads turn for the wrong reasons.

Annie rolls her eyes at their antics. They'd be in the brig on a base by now if we were involved.

"I dinnae wanna get involved," she hisses, typically reading my thoughts in my ear.

"Me neither, but I wanna see how it pans out. I thought about bar security as an alternative," I admit to her. She raises her eyebrows and it makes me chuckle.

The bouncers and the girls are in a standoff, then one of them goads the bigger male bouncer and my anger at her disrespect mounts.

"Ach, fuck it," I declare and dance in front of the bouncer, up to the girl who seems to be in charge of the hen-night's activities, and I see Annie getting the attention of one of the bouncers, no doubt to tell him why I'm getting involved. I get up into the lassies' space, right in front of her and up to her ear.

"Listen, lass, there's undercover police in here and a big waggon oot the back. If ye want to be thrown into it and destroy yer pals' night like this, carry on. I cannae see ye being in the bride's good graces when ye both sober up in a jail cell, aye?"

She takes a step back and recognises who I am from earlier.

"Do yersel a favour, leave under yer own steam, rewrite it in the morning with yer pals, when yer safe at home with the hair of the dog for company, alright?"

"He told me I can't," she begins, and I nod.

"Aye, and he's got the power to remove ye, have ye cuffed and in that waggon afore ye can plonk yer arse down on the floor in protest. Dae ye want that, tonight of all nights?" She looks at me and as she tries to, I can tell she's three sheets to the wind.

"Pick another night for fightin', no the night," I instructed her as I nod towards the bride. I turn her around and help her and her friends gather their things together and help escort them to the door. They leave peacefully, even wanting to snog the bouncer, who gracefully declines.

I head back in with the big guy, who gives me a nudge and a gruff thanks.

"That was ace, cheers, hen!" he says, hugging me. I nod, slap his arm, tell him he's welcome, and head back to Annie, crisis averted.

"What do we call you?" he asks me as we leave a good hour and a few free drinks later.

"Dìonadair," Annie announces in Gaelic as one am fast approaches. "I looked it up earlier, it fits you," she tells me as the Uber comes around the bend.

"What kind of a name is that?" he calls to us as we reach the roadside.

"It means defender," Annie shouts back. We giggle and get into the Uber to head home. What a night!

~Twelve~
Blythe

Six Months Later

I drop my kit bag onto the office floor and flop onto the sofa in the reception area, allowing the exhaustion to catch me. The same sofa I sat on just over six months ago to be interviewed. We've been all over with this job, shadowing and protecting someone wealthy, a contact of Tony McAulley's overseas, training his staff while protecting him. Working in a sanctioned country was taxing, hard work, and dangerous. I'm looking forward to some serious decamp time, as well as some deep, undisturbed sleep. My boss, Adrian, and colleague, Duncan, look just as knackered as I feel.

"I've called you a cab. Fetch your car when you're safe to drive," he tells Duncan, who just about manages to nod in response. Five minutes later, Duncan's heading home to his flat, and Adrian and I are left in the office.

"Marcus will be here in about five. Where do you want us to drop you off?" he asks. I shrug.

"I might still have a room with my friend. I can call her to find out. I haven't had the chance until now." We left pretty early in one timezone and arrived here at almost the same time, though it was hours and a few thousand miles apart. Adrian shakes his head at me after checking his watch.

"We have a spare room in town, four bedrooms if you need one."

I've gotten used to his gruffness over the months we've been out on site. Adrian knows his stuff, he's fiercely protective, and he expects to be obeyed. He's scared a few of the businessmen's own men a few times; for as big as he is, he can be a shadow, slipping from here to there and not be seen or heard.

I check the time and it's five am. It won't be fair to Annie to wake her up or Elle; the poor bairn has school to go to and she'll need her sleep. Me traipsing through the door would disturb her. I text Annie though, telling her I'm back but have somewhere to sleep for a few days.

I nod. "Sounds like a good plan," I tell him. "Waking her and her lass at five am isnae something I wanna do." He grins at me, and I can see in his eyes, he's more tired than I am. Exhausted would be the right description. Right now, his demeanour reminds me of the time he and the client were sniped at. I wanted to comfort him then, being shot at isn't pleasant, but every time I tried to be friendly, he'd shut me down. Until now.

His phone pings and he nods, standing up. I do the same, grab my kit bag, and I follow him out as he locks up the offices.

A large, sleek BMW sits out front with Marcus behind the wheel. He nods to us both, but we don't say anything; we're both too tired to do so. However, I am glad to see him again; maybe he can explain his brother's extra gruffness to me. Adrian puts our bags into the boot as I climb into the back. He gets into the front passenger seat and Marcus drives us to their home. It feels like five minutes later that he's shaking me awake.

"Come on, sleepyhead, sleeping here won't be good for you," he tells me gently. I snap awake and climb out, offering him a tired smile. "You'll be in bed soon, come on." Adrian has walked off with our kit bags. I nod at Marcus and he guides me towards an elevator, putting us hot on Adrian's heels.

The elevator is old, a Victorian thing I think, given the age of the building we're in. "Tony has the top floor, we have the one right below on the fourth," he says. The elevator stops and Marcus helps me out; Adrian is still somehow carrying both bags. I don't think I've ever been this exhausted, even when Annie and I were on deployment. Marcus jumps from me to be in front of Adrian and unlocks the door, though I'm not sure how or why. Then I noticed a bio-scanner on the frame.

Adrian marches to a bedroom and drops my kit into it. He smiles at me and I try to smile back.

"There's a shower in there," he points to an en-suite that has all the amenities needed in a very masculine taste. "See you when you wake up," he tells me. He hesitates for a moment, his lips go thin, then he's gone and the door clicks softly behind him. I shake my head to remove the confusion it now holds as I quickly remove my wash bag and get the shower going. As it warms, I dig through for some sleepwear, then I shower the travel and muck off. I give my hair a quick towel dry and dress in fresh clothing. I sigh happily, then I climb into bed. There's a remote on the bedside table with two buttons on it.

I press the first and the blinds on the windows close. Then I try the other and the ones in the bathroom close. The room is now comfortably dark, so I put the remote back where it was. Within moments I'm asleep in a very comfortable bed.

I can hear raised voices and things being bumped into. I wake up with a jolt, confused for a moment by my surroundings. It takes me a few breaths to recall where I am and why. I want to check my phone, but I can't find it. I do find the remote and open the blinds. The light from the streetlights outside allows me to see where I'm going and I head for the door.

I find Adrian and Marcus in a tizzy, trying to find this or that.

"Hey, what's up?" I ask in a half sleepy voice. Both stop and stare at me, then Adrian swears like a scuffer.

"We've had the offices broken into; Alasdair got contacted by our automation system. The police are on their way." Adrian slides on a boot. Alasdair is the one colleague who didn't come out with us on the trip to Bosnia. He was doing other work back here; it makes sense he'd be called before Marcus or Adrian.

"Give me two, I'll come too," I tell them both and head back to the room they've given me. A few minutes later, I'm dressed, booted with a heavy jacket as I head back to the office, phone tucked away, wondering what the hell is going on.

The front door and the windows are in smithereens. Thousands of pieces of window glass are strewn over the floor as if they've been dropped from a height and left. Bianca is in tears and Alasdair looks sullen. I can see Adrian's jaw twitching and Marcus is heading off with another officer to check the offices further in. I head to Bianca and check she's okay. She is, it's just the shock of seeing the place so messed up. I see a shadow out of the corner of my eye and I instantly coil for action. However, I realise it's Tony talking with the police and Adrian. I breathe to calm myself, feeling foolish for a second; this isn't Bosnia. Marcus appears and chats with the police, who leave us with a nod, having already taken Alasdair's statement.

"What gives?" I ask as the three men head over to where Alasdair, Bianca and I have camped.

"Nothing is missing, but the paperwork has all been gone through. Chances are, we'll be missing files and not notice it for weeks."

Bianca scoffs. "I'd notice. I know how everything is filed off and it's all in the cloud, like you told me." She looks directly at Marcus. He nods and smiles at her.

"Good lass!" He turns to Tony. "Since we've got the chance, I propose we do that entrance upgrade now," he states. Tony nods in approval and looks around.

"How did they break *all* the windows and mirrors?" he asks. I look around, suddenly taking in what Tony's observed already. He's right, every window and mirror in the reception area has been blown outwards.

"They're all *out*," I whisper, understanding now what's in front of me. Adrian nods.

"Yeah, we know." He growls, but he's not seeing what Tony and I are.

"Out, as in, out*wards*. Do you see it?" I stand up and motion for Bianca and Alasdair to do the same. I pull the sofa cushions off but find nothing. Alasdair starts doing the same with the two chairs, but there's nothing weird. I look under the sofa and again, I find nothing. As I'm trying to get up from the floor in a tight space, I glance under the wooden coffee table. There.

"What the bleeding hell is that?" I ask, clicking my fingers to call attention to where I am. I point to it, and Adrian carefully lifts the table onto its end to find something attached to the underside, still blinking.

"I'll be damned... Bianca, who was here last week?" asks Marcus as he leans in to examine the device. He whistles and then licks his lips.

"No one of interest, I think..." she replies nervously.

"Careful," Adrian advises.

"It's a sonic bomb, harmless unless you're glass," Marcus informs us. He's focusing on the device and he grins. With a flourish of fingers, he deactivates it and drops it onto his hand. The coaster on the table that was metal falls to the floor, making us jump.

"Magnetic attachment, hence the coaster," he says. Adrian's mouth is tight and thin, his eyes slit. He's pissed off and the last time I saw that, we had just been fired upon by some militia group.

"Who the fuck would want to harm us?" I ask. Alasdair and Bianca shrug, but the glance I see Adrian throwing Marcus tells me they have an idea.

Marcus takes the device into a small electronics lab that we have on-site to start pulling it apart while the four of us get on with tidying up. There are buckets of glass around and we're all busy sweeping every last speck of it we can find. A buzz from the reception desk sounds out about an hour later and Bianca goes to answer it.

"The window company is downstairs," she tells Adrian. He nods and calls for Alasdair to accompany him.

"Stay with Bianca, please?" he asks me in a low, commanding voice. The look in his eyes suggests he's expecting trouble, a look I've seen from him before. I nod and stick close to Bianca as he and Alasdair head down to the loading bay. Ten minutes later, Adrian's back, looking somewhat more relieved, along with a few window fitters and they carry a few thick wooden boards between them. We leave them to measure up and do what they need to do. Adrian instructs Alasdair to hold down the fort and keep Bianca safe, then he motions for me to follow him.

"I'm glad it was actually them," he mutters as we head up to the mezzanine where Marcus has placed a small lab. Whatever Marcus designs, it's never done here in the offices. He can and does vanish for days or nearly weeks at a time, then he comes back looking like Tom Hanks from Castaway, though I'm sure Mr Hanks also smelled a heck of a lot better! I've only experienced him doing that once before we went to Bosnia for the last job, but Adrian has told me he's done it before.

"You've got an idea who is behind this, haven't you?" I ask in an accusing tone. He stops and looks at me, crowding me up against the wall.

"Listen, you smart mouth," he looks at my mouth as I lick my lips. I see his eyes dilate; this is as close to each other as we've physically been for nearly six months. "One of these days, Blythe." And I suddenly get it. I understand now his gruffness, the reason he's been cold, indifferent then the total opposite. I don't need to look down to know how I've just made him react. He's as attracted to me as his brother is, as I am to them both.

I grin as he backs off, and my treacherous mouth spits out, "Bring it," in a tone just loud enough for him to hear. He growls and I push myself off the wall, striding towards Marcus.

"So, what have you found and who the hell are you trying to protect by not telling us all what's kicking off?" I demand as I march into the lab. Marcus' jaw drops at my arrival and question, closely followed by the bear of his brother.

Adrian strides towards me, but I stand my ground. "I warned you," he starts, but Marcus steps between us.

"She's right," he states in an almost defeatist voice. "We're going to need more than just me and you to work this out." Adrian backs off with a growl.

"She's gonna get hurt," he starts and I shrug.

"Been there, done that, have done for years." I lean against a countertop, careful not to nudge anything. There are electronic devices, soldering irons, wires, clips, clamps, and goodness knows what else all dotted about at various workstations.

"So, give. Start at the beginning and don't leave a piece of information out."

The brothers look at each other and Adrian turns away from Marcus and I, the stress in Marcus' eyes is plain to see.

"Whilst we've been overseas, aye?" I begin. "What was the first time and why did Duncan and I not hear about it?" Marcus pulls out a stool from under a bench and motions for me to sit. I get the impression this is going to be a very long conversation.

Marcus heads to a wall and pushes it, revealing a filing cabinet in a hidden wall space. My eyes and mind boggle at the location of the cabinet as it clicks back into place. If he hadn't opened it, I might not have seen it.

"This is what they were after?" I enquire as Marcus hands me a file about two centimetres thick. Marcus nods.

"Most likely. It's backed up off-site in at least two clouds anyway, so even if they did…" He motions etc. with his hands.

I settle in on the stool and begin to read. The attacks began before I started with the company, but little things which seemed to be just computer glitches. They've escalated and recently, this being the most violent of any attacks.

"Do you know who is behind it?" I ask, looking at both of the brothers. They shake their heads in unison, and I carry on reading the details, which are more of a diary entry. I notice the dates, some of this happened a few weeks before I joined McGowans, but it wasn't understood at the time. Small virus attacks, mail being opened and diverted. Not large when you take each item on its own, but when you put them together...

"How much of this does Tony know?" I enquire. What they've put in place to counter it will have cost and most likely, him.

"We've told him enough, but he believes in us. We'd like to find this eejit and shut them down," Adrian growls as he paces up and down, his mind working as he paces. Then he stops and looks at his brother, who has gone very quiet.

Marcus looks at the device in his hands and then places it down very, very carefully.

"Military-grade components, fine work. I've not seen this level of work before, outside." Marcus is half talking to himself, and Adrian picks up some papers on a desk I hadn't paid attention to.

"You got a job offer?" Adrian asks in a quiet voice. It pulls Marcus out of his thoughts.

"I got what?" he asks. "Bianca opened them up and put them there the other day, but I've not had a chance to go through them. I forgot to do what she said." He blinks again, as if his brain is slowly switching to the conversation. "What did you say I had?"

Adrian hands Marcus a piece of paper on letterhead from another security company, one down in London.

"London?" I ask. I look at Marcus. "That's a big area; is there anything else on it, a name?" I ask, and I check the name at the bottom of the letterhead. Warren & Lloyd.

Marcus suddenly catches onto what I'm thinking. "I worked with Lloyd at Brize on the upgrades of the older systems; his removal was why we met." Marcus shakes his head, but he's looking at me. "I didn't know he was going into this business too," he mentions.

"Did you ever tell him this dream?" I ask gently. Marcus mentioned it to me, so he could have mentioned it to Lloyd or anyone else.

Marcus pauses, and I can see him thinking. His eyes are darting to the left, recalling things, his lips muttering, but nothing Adrian or I can work out. I glance at Adrian, then focus back on Marcus, who shakes his head. "Can't say that I ever did to anyone else but you. We hardly worked side by side. A few beers and some pool here and there."

He leans back against the countertop.

"I did the electronics, he did the coding…"

He picks up the device and checks it again, then he marches to a countertop on the far side and opens up a metal box. Then he drops what is left of the sonic bomb into it and closes it.

"If I'd designed that," he says, grimacing at his brother and me, "I'd have made it into a digital listening device too."

Adrian nods. "Who else did you work alongside down in Brize?" he asks as Marcus sets the metal box into the furthest corner possible. I just hope that box does what Marcus thinks it will do and stops any signals from getting out.

"A few people, some of whom applied here, but I discounted them."

I stop at the doorway as we prepare to leave and head down to the reception area. "Was Lloyd one of them?" I ask, looking at both the brothers. "Or anyone called Warren?"

Marcus shakes his head. "Nope, and to be honest, Lloyd was annoying, forever chatty and always needy, like a puppy. But this…" he motions to the reception area that's in a state of chaos and repair as we descend the stairs, "I'd say is beyond him."

~Thirteen~
Adrian

Blythe's smart mouth nearly had me kissing her in the office corridor. I've had to resist urges like that, and more, while on-site for months with her sassy observations. She's good, though, so I hold myself in check, again, which frustrates me to no end. We stay until the window company has secured the offices and I give Bianca and Alasdair the following day off. We change the locks as the window fitters fit the temporary boards in. The boards are at least fire retardant and thicker than the glass that was blown out.

"We'll be back after the weekend when we've made the bottom panels that you want. The glass will be about two weeks as that's triple reinforced and you want the front to have the frosted design," the main fitter tells me.

I nod. "That's great, thanks!" I shake his hand, and we let his guys go. Alasdair says he'll see Bianca home and as he sneaks a hand around her waist, I grin. I look around for my brother and he's lost in his thoughts. Blythe is in a similar situation, but she's chewing her bottom lip, eyes darting around. I've seen that look on her before, in Bosnia.

I can't help but admire the view as she walks towards the conference rooms and our offices. I lock the main door and follow her, which draws Marcus' focus back to the present. I find Blythe checking under every table and chair, in places that you'd not normally think to look.

"What are you—" I begin, but she holds her hand up and gives me the signal for silence. Then she tells me via hand signals she's looking around. I nod, understanding she's looking for something that's not normally here. Marcus picks up on it too and silently, we begin to search through the whole suite.

We search through every conference room, office, and finally, our office.

"Well, hello you, ya dirty wee bawbag," she utters as she looks under my desk. Marcus' eyes narrow as he takes the device in his hands that was hidden from normal view and in moments, he has it in pieces, pulling it apart from the inside out, his hands destroying it in anger.

"Not yours then?" asks Blythe, and Marcus shakes his head.

"No...It is the same design as the bomb though. Same workmanship and that," he motions to the device that was working three minutes ago, "was a mini EMP."

I look around at the computers here, and I swear.

"Thankfully, it hadn't gone off yet."

"I want their head on a pole," I growl. Neither Marcus nor Blythe offers any reply.

We visit Tony at his home in Newington, a huge place that's a far cry from where we all grew up and started life together. We bring him up to date and he sits there, pondering.

"Companies house, background information," he states, and Marcus nods.

"Already working that avenue," he replies, sipping the coffee Morag his housekeeper and friend has kindly brought through.

Blythe is sitting perfectly on the Chesterfield sofa Tony loves as if she's visiting royalty or in a commander's office. We might be more relaxed around him as we know him, but I can tell she's not, not yet anyway.

"There's something we're missing," Blythe mutters, and she shakes her head as if to clear it.

"What do you think we're missing?" I ask her, and she shrugs, but it's the kind of shrug I've come to learn that means she's thinking about things, churning them over in her mind. She usually can't sleep when she does this, and I need to give Marcus a heads up; he won't be used to her doing that, especially if she's staying with us for a few days. It was something I got used to very quickly in Bosnia.

"I'll let you know when I find it," she softly tells me and I can see the cogs in her head are working away. "Excuse me," she says politely and heads out of Tony's office.

I give her a few minutes and then go to find her. She's on the phone, rubbing her temple as she talks, pacing sometimes, stopping at others. I head out to the patio and listen in.

"Ye never met him?" she asks whoever it is she has on the other end. Blythe sighs. "Aye, I just wondered if he was capable of this, that's all." She perks up at whatever her caller has said. "Brilliant idea! Aye, I still have their contact. I'll call them now." She turns to look at me and she's animated, her nostrils are flaring and her usual cool blue eyes are a deeper blue than normal. "Catch up with ye soon, ta!"

She grins as she searches for a contact and motions for me to be quiet, winking at me as she does.

"Anderson?" she calls out as her call gets answered. "It's Grievance. I need some advice and I've been told you're still in the security sector. I've got two job offers on hand, not sure about either," she tells him. She listens for a moment. "Yeah, still with McGowans, at least for now."

She winks at me again, and a small sinking feeling hits my stomach.

"One is Warren and Lloyd down south, the other is McLeod over in Glasgow." She hasn't been back long enough to be offered anything, then her hand is placed gently on my chest and I hear someone walk across to us. Why she touched me like that now, after months of me avoiding her, both stuns and excites me. I reacted to her earlier and it took an age for me to calm down.

I turn to see Marcus approaching and she motions for him to be quiet. I glance at the house but I can't see Tony or Morag watching.

"Aye, just, if I'm gonna jump ship, which one is more sound, business-wise? I cannae use the systems at work to see who is doing what and how," she explains.

I grin, realising that she's being sneaky.

"Huh huh…is that so? Ach, that's nae good." She listens for a few moments more and I can hear a lighter voice at the other end. "Aye, but going south of the border wasn't that appealing," she laments. Marcus looks at me and I shrug. "Aye, would ye do me a favour and keep me in the loop? I've not got to answer back for a week or two." The voice at the other end cuts her off and Blythe chuckles. "Aye, I'll do that. Cheers, Anderson! See ya!" she says and hangs up.

She turns to me and holds my gaze as she says, "Interesting! Warren & Lloyd took over a few contracts from McLeod's, but guess who cannot deliver? He's desperate for staff, poaching people left, right, and centre. Not all of them have ethics."

I look towards my brother and grimace. Security personnel without ethics is a private army.

"It was an act." Her touch on my chest again makes me look at her. Her eyes search mine, and I want to believe her. "I'm not going to jump ship. Now, if it is Lloyd's doing, he'll probably hear that I enquired after him and his company, and he'll think he's won and come to offer me a job. If it's not, they'll also probably think that and might reveal themselves. I hope whoever it is does something really stupid."

"So, it was misinformation?" Marcus asks, taking a step closer to us. She nods and reaches for his hand, taking it.

"Aye, Sherlock was better at this than I was, but this was her idea: a misinformation trap. Now, to set up the other side and see which arm pings," she adds and picks up the phone again. This time, she calls McLeod's.

As Blythe speaks to Callum McLeod, Marcus pulls me to one side.

"We can add to this with a little misinformation of our own," he tells me. I frown, wondering what he's now also cooking up. "We can get the word out that the EMP went off, we've lost our computer systems, and we'll be back in about a week."

I shake my head. "That's suicide, business-wise," I tell him.

"It is," adds Blythe, coming across to talk with us. "And you won't need to do it that way. McLeod knows who Lloyd is, and he was quite clear what he thought of him. He's also backed by Tony," she says and nods to the house.

"Tony's backing McLeod's?" I ask.

Blythe nods. "Not as well as he's backing you two, I think, but he's invested in some of their technology." She turns to my brother, a soft smile on her lips. "Remember Denise from Brize?" she asks. Marcus nods, as do I.

"Snowflake," I mutter with a chuckle. Blythe turns to us.

"Yep, same as me. She's married to Callum now; they met when he was upgrading some of the I.T. systems back when you were too."

Marcus nods. "I recall him being there, but he was working on a different set of systems from me."

Blythe grins. "He's offered the use of his nearest but spare tech lab in Hamilton. If you can get the devices to his facility, he's happy to let you play, dismantle, or whatever it is you need to do."

"Why would he do that?" I ask. She nods at Tony who I can see in the window watching us. We head up to talk with him and he confirms he's called in a few favours for us, and I'm grateful.

We head off once we know McLeod's will keep what's happened to us to themselves, at least for now. We head back to the flat and it's getting on now; it's taken half the night to tidy up, call in favours, find out things. All our stomachs are rumbling, and my phone goes off, then I grin and read out Tony's text message.

Tony: Morag told me off for not feeding you three. There's a Chinese delivery on the way over to you, it'll be there in about twenty minutes. Don't miss the doorbell.

Blythe grins and leans back, sighing happily.

"Please tell me we have wine in the flat?" she asks. "Or beers? Fuck me, today has been bloody weird!"

I glance at Marcus at the use of her phrase then glance back at her, unable to hide my grin.

"What?" she questions, incredulously, clearly not realising what it is she's said. Marcus picks up on it though.

"Is that what you want?" he asks in a quiet tone that implies his hopefulness and his lust. Blythe leans forward from the backseat of the car.

"Are you offering? Honestly?" she enquires. Marcus glances at her from the rearview mirror, and I look between them both.

"We are if you're..."

"I am," she breathes in a rush, cutting me off. Her voice is low, lusty, and so incredibly sexy. "Have been since I was told that you two shared." Marcus glares at us.

"Who told you?" he asks, turning to look at her. Blythe slaps him and he turns back around.

"Eyes on the road," she scolds him. "And it doesn't matter." She pauses and her voice hitches. "Do you remember that night?"

"Haven't forgotten it," Marcus replies. "I've gone over it several hundred times in my head since."

"Do you remember how deeply we slept? I've never slept that deeply since. There's something…" She stops and sits back. She doesn't say another word until we're in the underground car park of the flat.

Marcus touches her face gently as he helps her out of the car.

"You were saying?" he asks in a low, husky tone.

"I hardly ever…" And Marcus gives her an incredible look of both disbelief and lust.

"You came for me," he tells her, finishing her statement. "Twice, if I remember correctly." He has her pinned to the car, but not enough that she'd be unable to get away. Like most military personnel, she's trained in several martial arts, and while Marcus might get floored by her, possibly harmed, I probably wouldn't, not greatly. I've also seen her fight and train others; she can be lethal.

"Never to be repeated," she laments at him. I'm on the same side as they are now and Marcus moves over to let me in.

"The deal is this," I tell her, stroking her arm, and I take a hold of her hand. "If you say stop, we stop. This is totally your call." I touch a small section of hair that's come loose from her ponytail and tuck it behind her ear. "But the idea is, we both give you what you need."

"And you both?" she asks softly as if we're going to be left unsatisfied.

"We'll get our fill, don't you worry." Then the timer on my phone goes off. "Our Chinese is nearly here. You two head up, get the wine poured, though make mine a beer, and I'll grab the food." I nod to my brother, who wraps an arm around Blythe, and I lean in to kiss her on her jaw. "Soon," I promise, "but we need to eat food first," I remind her as I look into her cool blue eyes. She nods and allows Marcus to take her up to the flat as I head to the front door to collect the food.

~Fourteen~
Marcus

An hour after the food arrives, every food box is empty. Tony had ordered us a huge selection, but like the ravenous ex-military beasts some of us are, we ate the lot. We hardly exchanged a word as we did so, and I could only watch as Blythe and Adrian devoured a huge chunk of it. I wonder when was the last time they ate. I feel fulfilled and much calmer, but still nervous. There's still an air of sexual tension between the three of us. She leans across for her glass of Malbec and grins at us.

"You were going to say something in the car," I prompt her as I top up her glass. She swallows and nods.

She looks like she's going to say something, then stops, then tries again. I move closer to her and stroke an arm. Adrian is on the other side of her, waiting. The soft stuff, he usually leaves to me. He's not great at displaying his emotions, but I understand him, which helps.

"You'll think I'm crazy," she whispers. I shake my head and lean in, kissing her gently on the lips.

"Not crazy," I tell her. "Uncertain, perhaps. There's nothing here between us that you need to worry about." I kiss her gently again and notice she closes her eyes.

"I have a...darkness within," she stammers, and some tears threaten to fall.

"A need?" Adrian ventures. He's shuffled closer so that our little triangle is made up of Blythe and me on the sofa with Adrian on the footstool on her other side. He's stroking her right arm, and she sighs after a moment or two. She nods and looks at him. Then she turns to me.

"You managed it that night, to be all that I needed. But I think I wore you out," she chuckles slightly and I grin.

"Maybe, I don't recall." I recall perfectly, but I'm not going to tell her that. I was bloody-minded that night to make her come on me, and I'm glad now I did. "How do you want it tonight, Bee? Can we call you that?" I ask, touching her upper thigh and running my hands down into her inner thigh. "Tell us how you want it, darling," I request. She reaches across and touches my face with one hand, Adrian's with the other, and I see his hand is on her other leg, stroking up and down, squeezing her flesh.

"You can call me that," she answers, her voice breaking in a husky tone. "Both ways, any way." She leans in to kiss me first. I wrap a hand around her neck and draw her in, opening her mouth to let our tongues dance.

"Taste her," I huskily tell my brother, and his hand strokes the side of her jaw. She leans in as a kitten would, and he draws her in for what I think is their first kiss. I've already fucked her, made her come, and this time, I decide it's his turn.

Both his hands come to cup her face, and they kiss, deeply, sensually. Watching them makes me harder, knowing I'll be with her again makes my heart soar. Their breathing gets more ragged, and I reach up under her top to undo her bra. I remember these small breasts of hers, perfectly sized, responsive, sensual things that drive her mad when they're tweaked, sucked, or nipped the right way.

Adrian pulls back, and I lift her top from the waist, taking her bra with it, revealing those perfect, shapely breasts to him. He groans and leans in to suck and play with a breast. One of her hands is in his hair, and she turns her face to me. I capture her mouth and kiss her deeply, leaning her back so that Adrian can play.

He moves from one breast to the other, appreciating the taste of her skin. She's watching me, and I caress the side of her face, feeling its softness, tasting the food we've all shared on her tongue, the wine she and I drank.

Blythe moans as Adrian stops doing what he's doing and removes his work shirt. I follow suit, appreciating the groan Blythe makes. The lust in her eyes spurs me on.

"You like what you see?" I ask, and I receive a slight nod in return; Blythe's eyes follow every movement we make. I sit on the sofa and pull her onto my lap, her back to me, allowing me to fondle her breasts as Adrian pulls her skin-tight jeans down. The ones I have been admiring her perfect arse and legs in all night. He pulls Blythe down so that I can see over her shoulder, and he kisses his way down her body, sending shivers through her. Her breath hitches as he finds sensitive spots on her ribs, across her stomach. She has on some pair of tight black fabric sporting knickers and as Adrian removes them, she moans, making me harder and almost desperate to be inside her. I move her so that she can turn and I can kiss her again, both of us occupying both of her lips.

As Adrian licks, sucks, teases, bites, and pulls, I do the same with her mouth. She comes in a shudder of waves and convulses as Adrian feasts on her, but I absorb her screams and cries. He doesn't stop, making her convulse and come again. I can see her legs clamp around his head, trapping him to her.

"Bed," I say, wanting her on a flat, softer surface than the sofa.

Blythe relaxes when I say that, and Adrian extricates himself from between her gorgeous thighs.

"Please," she begs, not wanting it to stop.

"Bed," I repeat, and she nods, understanding the word she somehow missed earlier. Adrian scoops her up and takes her to his bed, the largest in the flat.

~Fifteen~
Blythe

Adrian's mouth on my clit, whilst Marcus kissed me was as hot as hell. I've come twice already just from their magical mouths, and I miss why Adrian suddenly stops. It's when Marcus says "bed" that I understand.

Adrian scoops me up and takes me to a room I've not yet seen with a bed big enough for three. He lays me down on one side after Marcus has pulled the sheets back.

"You're both not quite naked enough," I tease, noticing that they're both tenting their jeans. They look at each other and shrug their indifference, then they strip. Almost in synchronicity, they remove their jeans and sports boxers. I mean, come on. I know Marcus is older than I am, but not by much. Adrian is slightly older than him, again, a year or so.

How can they look so damn fine, defined and together?

"Jeezus fuck," I whisper.

"I don't know about Jeezus fucking you," Adrian growls as he tosses his brother a silver packet, then he strides towards me with a condom in hand prowling onto the bed. "But I know I will."

He leans in and kisses me, pinning me to the bed. I can feel another weight, Marcus, as he comes towards my head and begins kissing me. He pins my hands above my head as I lie diagonally across the bed. It takes a few moments before I feel Adrian inside me, and Marcus backs off.

"Fuck, yes!" I cry out, and Adrian does just that. He's fast, furious, and intense, pushing himself within me so deeply, making me forget everything but his cock, I think I'm going to rip apart. I shatter on him, arching up, unable to see, and then Marcus is back, kissing me, tweaking a nipple, sucking on the other. Somehow he moves so he's between my legs and then he's inside me, loving me, slowly while Adrian kisses my mouth and tweaks my breasts. Marcus is thrusting deeply, kissing me when Adrian backs away. It's a different style of loving from his brother, but so intense are the feelings and physical touches they're both giving me, I orgasm on Marcus too.

~Sixteen~
Adrian

I've wanted this woman for so long, at least since we interviewed her. Being close to her for half a year, thinking she was just my brother's old fuck buddy, messed with my head. I wish I'd asked her about all this months ago. But, I didn't. I'm making up for the lost time.

Having her come on my cock almost sent me over the edge, but I somehow held back. I need to come in her mouth, or inside her. Marcus fucks her slowly, sensually, making her writhe and arch up as she comes. As she calms down from her climax, we switch places, and I bury myself straight back inside of her. Wrapping my arms around her, I roll us over so I am on my back and she's above me.

"Both of us?" I ask her, wanting to be sure she can take this or is even agreeable. We might need to work up to it, but she nods.

"Yes!" she exclaims. Marcus nods and grabs the lube from the top drawer, and she squeals.

"It's cold!" she laughs, trying to turn to look at Marcus. I kiss her, deeply, and I can feel her pulsing around my cock which is harder than steel.

"Relax," I tell her, feeling her tense up slightly, even though we've both just made her come. "Let us," I whisper as I kiss her again and pin her to me. I love how she moans and claws at me as I nip and tweak her perfect breasts. We're kissing deeply, and I feel Marcus between my legs, shuffling forward inch by inch; I feel her tense up slightly.

"Breathe, it's okay. You're in charge," I remind her before I kiss her again to distract her. She lifts herself slightly, and I tweak both her nipples as Marcus pushes her down onto me, and I can hear him swear.

"So fucking tight…" he groans, and so does she, then she clamps down on me as my brother's penetration makes her climax again.

"So perfect," I tell her, scooping some of the black hair away to look at her blue eyes. I pull her down to me to kiss me, and I can feel Marcus withdraw then slowly slide back into her. I match his slow rhythm, both of us withdrawing and pushing forward at the same time. I can feel him inside her, nothing but thin, expressive, sensual walls separating us from each other.

"Fuck!" cries Blythe as we withdraw slowly and drive forward together as one. We slowly pull back, and Blythe lifts her head, her eyes unfathomable with lust, desire, and ecstasy. She cries out with every thrust we make into her, her mouth drops open, and her hands grab anything soft that they can. We've made her experience this.

"Come for us," I command her as Marcus and I thrust into her. She shatters on us both, screaming in pleasure, her eyes are unable to focus, her eyelids droop as she shakes between us both. She's stopped kissing me, and I'm holding her to me so she doesn't fall. We thrust into her a few more times, slowly, then Marcus withdraws, discards the condom, and I can tell he's jerking off onto her arse. I hold her to me by her waist and I can hear him grunting and swear as he shoots his load over her arse and up to the small of her back.

She kisses me as he wipes her down and backs off. I grab her arse and hold her, thrusting into her from beneath. Her head is in the crook of my shoulder and my mouth is near her ear.

"So fucking good, Bee, you're ours." I hold her arse open and Marcus inserts a finger into her as I thrust up. Her reaction to that triggers yet another climax for her and, finally, my own as she clamps down on me like a vice.

    I'm not sure how long I'm holding Bee in my arms, but Marcus finally moves and eventually gets in on the other side of the bed, and I turn, depositing Blythe between us both so we can cuddle, caress, and care for her. I quickly throw the condom into the bin as he pulls the quilt up onto all three of us, and we lay together, stroking Bee until we realise she's asleep. We kiss her goodnight and snuggle into her, not daring to let her go.

~Seventeen~
Blythe

I awake in the middle of two men, the brothers who I was told years ago shared their women. The need within me to come multiple times, the darkness I tried to describe to them, isn't there; I've found my Nirvana. To experience what I did with these two men has let me be at peace, at least for now. *I never want to be shared by anyone else. I also don't want them to share themselves with anyone else,* but I don't understand why. *Am I jealous?* Perhaps. *Overzealous?* I haven't been before, so why now? I lie between their heat, eyes closed, but my mind is running at a hundred miles an hour, asking questions I can't find the answers to.

This...was...is magical.

I move, slightly, which causes a moan from the man in front of me, and the man behind me pulls me in close.

"Yer deep in yer head, woman. Penny for them?" he asks in a low tone. I sigh, wishing my mind would shut the hell up for once.

"Come on, talk with us," pipes up a sleepy Marcus from behind me. Now I've woken them both, and they've propped themselves on an arm, stroking parts of my arms or moving my hair out of my face, looking down at me.

"I don't want this to end," I admit, closing my eyes as I say it. I'm waiting for the boot to fall, the need for me to crawl back to Annie's, though I know I'd be welcomed with open arms, a coffee, and she'd be around here making a scene.

"Does it have to?" asks Marcus and I look at him.

"You mean it won't?" I breathe out in the shakiest voice I've ever heard emerge from my lips—so unlike me, but it matches the huge knot in my stomach.

"Not unless you say it does," Adrian comments, his voice is more growly this morning than usual. "We need to communicate exceedingly well if we're going to fuck and work together. And I mean better than we ever did when we served," he says, stroking my arm. Adrian is usually the big, gruff, boss man, especially if he's at work, on duty, or pissed off. He's showing that he's also tactile, gentle. This is a side of him I never thought he possessed.

"What is it you're scared of, beautiful?" Marcus asks as he leans in to kiss my right shoulder.

I look between the two of them and swallow, commanding the fear that's rising up to back the hell off. Fear can make you do really stupid things, but it can also give you strength. Gigi always told me, if you're going to lose something and you're afraid about losing it, you're meant to fight for it.

"I don't know… Are we together, the three of us? I started thinking about you two being with someone else," Marcus tsks, but Adrian's eyes narrow, "and I didn't want that. Do I have a right to be possessive, this soon? Or am I just jealous and what was said last night," I look at Adrian, aware he told me I was theirs, "was only said in the heat of the moment?"

Marcus scoots closer to me, draping himself over one of my legs.

"Are we together?" He touches the side of my face with his right hand, cupping my jaw, turning me to face him. "I bloody hope so. I so want to do that again with you, or watch you and my brother, have him watch you and I." Marcus' eyes are tender and soft. "So you'd better move in, permanently." I blink and go slightly wide-eyed. *So soon?!*

He looks at Adrian, expecting him to make a statement. He acknowledges his brother's silent instruction with a quick nod and then looks at me, his free left hand is caressing my side, my ribs, sending ripples of desire through me.

"I don't say things I don't mean. You know that. If I'd known last night was even possible, I'd have had Marcus shipped out to our location in Bosnia, and we could have been doing this months ago. As for someone else? No. You've played on my mind so much over the last six months, but I didn't pursue you, thinking you had a thing for just Marcus."

He leans in and kisses a breast, and Marcus' hands reach down to my thigh, where he tugs and massages it.

"Now I know it's not, that it's both of us and I'm just late to the party." He grins and then he turns his attention to the other breast. "I'm happy." After a few moments, they stop and come to cuddle into me.

"The one with the say here, Bee, is you. This isn't going to work if you have doubts," Marcus informs me, his voice gentle, loving, and soft. "Do you want to move in and stay here?"

"I've never dated two men before, or been with two until last night." Marcus leans in and kisses me softly. "I never want to be with two others again. Or even anyone else but the pair of you."

I hear a groan of satisfaction from Adrian, and the sigh from Marcus touches my shoulder.

"That was a deep sigh," I tell him, reaching up to run my fingers through Marcus' long hair.

"I thought you'd tell us that was the only time," he breathes.

"You were scared I was going to run off?" I rub my thumb across his stubble. Where Adrian usually keeps his beard short, and I found it soft, Marcus is clean-shaven, but his five o'clock shadow is showing and I kinda like that.

"It was a possibility," Adrian admits, and I turn to him. "You can end this in a heartbeat and there'd be nothing we can do about it. We have morals." He leans in to kiss me and does, softly. "We'll never force you." His eyes stare into mine, and I reach up to him, pulling him down for a kiss.

"And if I need some female time? When I'm on or just cranky?" I ask and Marcus chuckles.

"You get it. This is more than just sex, Bee," Adrian huskily tells me. "This is about us, you, me, Marcus. We want to know all about you, your life, your friends, your hates, likes, dislikes. The whole nine yards."

"A relationship?" I breathe, not quite sure I'm hearing what I am. *Surely I'm going to wake up in a moment and find that this is just a dream?*

"Aye, that's what it's called!" Marcus quips; his voice gets lighter, teasing, and even has a laugh in it. I nudge him and he laughs, but not at me. He's laughing because of me, something only my brother has ever done in my lifetime.

"A ménage or polyamorous," Adrian confirms. "Just us, no one else. We won't entertain the idea of another woman with us."

"And we don't expect you to be with anyone but either of us," Marcus finishes.

"And if someone else comes along? Or you meet someone else?" I ask, glancing from one to the other. They both shake their heads.

"There won't be," Adrian tells me emphatically, to which Marcus nods slightly.

I wiggle a little, and the guys back off slightly.

"You've thought about this," I state as I sit up a little more in bed. "Before I came along?" My eyes go wide, and I'm not sure what reply I'm expecting.

"We talked about it after we were together down in Brize, but not since or because of anyone." Marcus holds my gaze. "We decided when the 47th came back after that tour what we were looking for, wanted, and needed." Marcus swallows hard and looks at his brother.

"But the chance of anything happening was lost, until your CV landed on his desk." Adrian nods to Marcus. "That's why we had Tony interview you. If he thought you were a good fit, being the silent partner, you were in and not because the boss had a thing for you, or you had a thing for one of the bosses."

I grin, but Adrian's face is dour. "What else?" I ask, my voice shaky and hesitant as I try to catch Adrian's line of sight. Haven't we just worked all this out?

"Your brother," he breathes and I frown at those words.

"What about him?" I ask, wondering what the hell he has got to do with this.

"We don't get along very well," Adrian admits in a low voice, and he looks at me as if he's about to break.

I nod, understanding him now. Adrian's pre-empting an issue so expects the worst. "That'll be a bridge we need to cross when we get to it. But, at the end of the day, this is my life. My wee brother doesn't make the decisions for me."

"What do you want to tell friends? Family?" Marcus asks me, and I pause for a moment.

"The truth," I gently confirm. "My parents, brother, Annie— they get the truth." I sigh, releasing the nerves as we work through these small hurdles. "No one else needs to know," I tell them. "Unless you want the crew at the office to know?"

Marcus chuckles. "They'll work it out, but you're happy for them to be told we're all together?" he asks as he strokes the side of my face.

"Yeah, I am, if you both are?" I check with them. They nod. "We're together, that's it. They don't need to know the specifics." I grin. "But, let's keep it professional in the office or friendly when we're with others, aye?"

My stomach rumbles, and the guys chuckle but agree with me as they kiss me with mumbles of reassurances and agreements.

Then they each kiss me deeply, leaving me breathless, before Marcus leaves the bed.

"I'll put the coffee on. Try not to break her while I'm gone," he teases. Adrian flips him the middle finger, then he holds it up and grins.

"Oh, look what I found!" he proclaims and places it gently at my throat, then slides the finger down the middle of my body, between the valley of my breasts and down to my core. I shiver in anticipation with every nerve ending he touches. He slides it up and down my opening, gently teasing as he leans in for a deep kiss. As we kiss, his fingers strum me slowly, and he touches me where I am now sore, making me wince.

"Sorry, sweetheart." He stops with the finger action and withdraws his hand. I whimper in frustration as he licks his finger clean. "We'll have to be more gentle with you when you have us both," he admits. I smile into his shoulder as he hugs me, then Marcus comes in with the coffee.

"You broke her!" he teases as he sets two mugs down on Adrian's side.

"Nope, I think we both did; someone's a little tender." Adrian smiles at me as he shifts up the bed to sit up, then he motions for me to do the same. When I do, he passes me a cup of coffee, and we all spend some time in bed, sipping coffee and just being.

Adrian checks the time, and we decide we'd better head into the office to retrieve the bombs that went off yesterday. With the doors secured, the alarms were back and working, or we hoped they still were!

We wash and dress, though I take my shower in my own room, feeling decidedly fragile but fulfilled this morning. Thirty minutes after we left our collective bed, we're at our office block. It looks normal, exactly as we left it.

We head in, cautiously, Adrian taking point and me bringing up the six, Marcus between us. The alarm beeps, demanding our attention to disarm it before it calls the police. Marcus gets to it in time, and we fire up the lights. Nothing has been moved since yesterday, but we're still apprehensive about being in our own offices after yesterday's attack.

"I'll wait and secure here," I tell them, locking the main office door. Adrian nods and he motions for Marcus to follow, setting a quick pace to the lab where the EMP and sonic bombs were deposited.

Ten minutes later, they come back with the metal box in hand and Marcus has a determination and attitude about him now that wasn't there before we left the flat.

"Let's get this investigated," he states. His attitude now reminds me of Adrian on a job that hadn't headed south. At least, not yet.

"Where are we headed?" I ask him. He shakes his head and motions to the box he's carrying with a nod. As we enter the car park, he heads out towards a Defender 90. I had no idea those cars belonged to the Agency! I loved driving those when I was in the RAF and my heart soars at the thought of getting behind the wheel of one again.

"We aren't," he says, his jaw as set in determination as Adrian's is when he's made up his mind. "Aid is going to follow until I get to Hamilton," he holds his hands up as I begin to protest, "then he's coming back. This might take me a few days to dismantle and learn about." He points to the metal box he's tucked under a rear bench. "But I hope I'm quicker than that."

"So what leads do we have, besides Lloyd?" I ask, wanting to get stuck in to find the reason behind this nonsense. If Marcus doesn't want the distraction of me, or anyone being there, I can still make myself useful.

"Alasdair is on his way over to help search through things with you and be an extra body on site. I'll come back and relieve you both in a few hours." Adrian looks at me affectionately, and I nod in reply.

"Those papers on the lab desk? I haven't been through them for weeks, and they might hold an answer," Marcus suggests. I nod, then I kiss him deeply.

"When did you pack?" I ask, and they grin. Adrian points to the other bench seat in the back; hidden underneath is an RAF kit bag. I smirk, I hadn't seen it. It makes me wonder what else I've missed with these boys that is hidden in plain sight.

~Eighteen~
Adrian

I can tell Marcus isn't happy as soon as he puts the two devices together. Usually, it's me that's the grouchy bear, not him.

"She'll be fine," I tell him, guessing at what's caused his foul mood. He looks up at me and nods. Then he stacks the papers up that I disturbed yesterday and makes them neat, adding more to the pile. The file we've been building is there too.

"Talk with me, brother," I demand. I know he can go sulky, but it's usually because the tech isn't behaving, not a woman.

"I'll be away too long," he tells me. I shrug at his pang of jealousy; there's no need for him to be so.

"It is what it is." I look at him and can tell he doesn't want to leave, but this is too important. "Marc, I've only worked with the woman for half a year, avoiding social situations with her like a damn plague. Until last night." He smiles at me. "Which was fucking magical, let me tell you. But the quicker you can find something out or discover something about those devices, the quicker you can get back to us."

"And in the meantime," he adds as he secures the box with a carabiner, "you get to fuck her."

I pull my shoulders back. "Only if she wants it. And she might not. She was quite tender this morning, and I've still got all day to piss her off." Marcus knows my ability to piss people off is legendary, and it makes me think of her brother. We spoke once and from that first and only conversation, Byron and I had avoided each other, thinking the other was an arse.

That reminder makes him chuckle. "Honestly," I promise to him, "I'll do my damnedest to ensure she isn't pissed off at you."

Blythe's figure disappears into the distance as I follow Marcus in one of the long-wheelbase vehicles we have. Blythe's eyes nearly popped out when she realised these were ours and not someone else's. Marcus and I are on Bluetooth, and I tell my phone to call him.

"We can't have forgotten something already; we're not even out of Edinburgh," he teases as he answers.

"I've realised, Blythe doesn't know the same level of stuff we do," I begin. "The cars, the resources…" I could go on, but I know I won't have to. "She knew the set-up for Bosnia in a matter of days, but not here. We never got the chance." I follow Marcus as he takes the road out of Edinburgh to the motorway and Hamilton.

"I'm okay with you bringing her up to speed. She knows we have an Eastside club card," he tells me. "I lent it to her just as we hired her."

"Oh, ye did huh?" I tease. Marcus and I have very different tastes in clubs. I don't mind them, the noise within is like a C130 ride, it's just background noise. I'm glad Blythe has a thing for clubbing at Eastside, as I do too.

"Yeah, they were both celebrating new jobs and, well…" He hesitates, and I wonder why.

"What did you do?" I ask with a groan. I get a chuckle in return, and we both synchronise our driving.

"I sent her five grand," he tells me.

"Was she that much on the breadline?" I ask in disbelief. I make a note to check in on her finances when we're alone.

"She was. I also figured she'd share it with her friend and she did. She sent her two grand, and the credit score at that property went up."

I swear slightly at his comments.

"She knew I sent it, I told her, but she's been fine since. She's been building up her savings and has hardly any outgoings."

We change lanes out to overtake a caravan and car, then pull back in, keeping each other in range.

"You've checked?" I ask, knowing he can quite easily.

"Yep!" he answers back enthusiastically as if it was normal to be worrying about a new lover's financial need.

"Did you ever ask her why she didn't get back to you?" I ask him, realising we had the chance this morning over coffee.

"Fuck! No…" he growls.

"Focus on the road. I can ask her when I'm back at the flat with her," I tell him. I can hear him muttering in the background. Then, he speaks.

"I'll ask when I get back. I'm going to be incommunicado while I work on these. And we need a backup site," he tells me.

Oh hell yes, we do.

Three hours later, I'm pulling the one-ten back into its usual parking spot at the office. I have to admit, McLeod's got a fantastic backup facility, and I can't help but wonder what plans Marcus is going to hit Tony with when he's back.

I dart up to our floor and let myself in. The place is quiet, then I hear Blythe's voice call out from the mezzanine.

"There you are! We've been watching you on the cameras," she tells me. "We're in two," she says as she vanishes from the balcony view. I grin and climb the stairs to see what they've come up with.

Across the largest conference table we have is all the paperwork.

"Do not touch or move a single piece," Blythe growls as I enter. Bianca, Alasdair and Blythe are all on different sides. There are sections and piles and...I notice coloured wool between various piles. I blink.

"You found something?"

Blythe's eyes are animated, shiny. Alasdair has one of the tablets out, watching the cameras on the doors and car park bay.

"I think so...I'm just not quite sure what it is yet," she says. Bianca calls her over, and they go through a pile together, then another piece of wool is used to link it to another pile. Alasdair shrugs and looks through more papers, then he too makes a wool connection of a different colour. This goes on for another half an hour before all the paperwork from the original file and what was on Marcus' workbench has been gone through.

Blythe sighs and stands up, arching her back against the curve. Bianca does the same and then they look at me.

"From what we can gather, there's a hint of an attack depending on some correspondence that's sent to Marcus. Not usually you, though we think you got the last one. And it's always sent when you're heading home." Her lips are thin and her eyes have taken on an icy blue hue. I'm not sure what is going through her mind, but if ever there was a hint that a woman is pissed off, Blythe just demonstrated it. I only saw it once in Bosnia, right after we'd been shot at. It was when I discovered she was a crack sniper when she needed to be.

The buzzer goes and Alasdair checks the cameras. "Duncan's here," he says. I nod as he gets out of his chair to let in our other employee.

"What kind of hint?" I ask. She comes around to the side I'm on and she and Bianca carefully pull out three distinct piles of papers. As they explain what each coded message seems to be, Duncan and Alasdair walk back in.

"Whoa!" exclaims Duncan after seeing things for the first time in a few days. "What the actual hell..." And Alasdair begins to take him through what they've pieced together and why.

While the guys are talking, Blythe takes me through the coding she and Bianca have broken down.

"This was a warning," she says and shows me a code in some spam email Marcus printed off. It looks like a phishing email, but it must have triggered something in Marcus' psyche for him to print it off and keep it. Bianca has highlighted some words, and it's clear when she does that it was a warning, but it looks incomplete. "When it was ignored, as you would do given how it was delivered, your systems were hacked. Marcus got the virus out, but when you were back four months later, another one came in." She walks me through all the times I was away on jobs, sometimes with Alasdair, usually without, when Marcus was holding the fort with Bianca.

"It goes on and on, in different forms of email. From what looks like phishing," she holds up another, and Bianca works her magic on it, "to this." She holds out what looks like a standard enquiry form from our website, but with Bianca's magic, the message is clear. Close McGowans or suffer the consequences. It was dated a week before Blythe and I returned, and I notice I'm copied in. Marcus wouldn't have known I'd not seen it.

I frown and sit down for a moment, trying to work out why I hadn't seen it.

"Al, where are the tablets we used in Bosnia?" I ask. We were on our client's network over there, and something Marcus told me ages ago about I.T. systems now surfaces in my head.

"Let me fetch them," he tells me. He comes back five minutes later, and I find the exact tablet I had. I fire it up, and everyone gathers around. We watch as the emails update, then the one we're looking at on paper appears in the middle of others I've read and replied to. Unread.

"Firewall," breathes Blythe. I look at her.

"I was thinking that, but I have no idea what the heck that means," I tell her.

"I do. It means that the Bosnians have better I.T. security than we do." She leans back and folds her arms. "It could also mean that the earlier attacks were either a test or the back door is still in our I.T. systems."

I narrow my eyes at her intimation that we have a Trojan in our computer systems.

"What if that EMP was meant to wipe the computers out, eradicating the trace of it?" asks Bianca in a questioning tone. Everyone turns to her as understanding dawns.

~Nineteen~
Blythe

Bianca's innocent but pertinent question sets us into a dour mood, but the one person who can maybe secure it, or do something with that knowledge, isn't here. Marcus.

We add in an extra secure lock to the conference room door, something Duncan got quite good at in Bosnia, then we re-secure the offices and head out. Alasdair is wrapping an arm around Bianca as they head to the car park and Duncan bounces off towards Princes Street. It leaves Adrian and me alone for a few moments.

"He needs backup," I say out loud, airing my thoughts. Adrian gives me that weird look of anticipation, frustration and curiosity. How he conveys all three emotions at the same time is beyond me.

"Who?" he asks as he watches me sling my coat over my arms from the back of the chair in a flurry of leather.

"Marcus. If anything happened to him, who the hell would we rely on I.T. wise?"

Adrian is walking with me, but he stops dead as we reach the building foyer. "We do need to plug that hole," he admits. "No more chat about it until we're back at the flat though, aye?" he asks me with his face set. I nod, and we head out of the building and turn towards Princes Street, following Duncan's path.

Princes Street is a colourful, mile-long pedestrian street of cafés, shops, and bars. Our residential building is on the other side of it, and this morning we walked in, enjoying each other's company. The smell of coffee, cake, and pastries hits my nose, and my stomach growls. So does Adrian's, and we chuckle—we forgot to eat. Then a voice cries out my military nickname.

"Grievance?!" I turn to find Annie quickly marching towards me, brown paper bags from a high street store in her hands.

"Sherlock!" I cry out, pleased as heck to see her. "Where's Elle?" I ask, realising that my god-daughter is not with her.

"With Jim, as usual on a Sunday morning!" she replies, chuckling, and I go red, realising I should have remembered.

"Annie, this is Adrian McGowan, one of my bosses," I say, introducing them both. They shake hands and again, our stomachs growl in unison, Annie's joining in because it can.

"Fancy a Flo's?" she asks us, and we nod.

"So you would be…" Adrian asks as we walk down the hill to our favourite cafe.

"Blythe's old partner and bestie, Annie Holmes," she tells him with a grin.

"You wouldn't have happened to be pregnant six or seven years ago?" he questions, and Annie throws him an inquisitive look.

"Aye, I was. It's why Bee ended up down Brize, and I was stuck back at Lossie," she smiles at him as he opens up the bright orange door, "Why do you ask?"

We find a table in the corner and sit down, Annie putting her bags into the corner of the booth seat.

"She mentioned a friend who was pregnant; we haven't had the details yet." Adrian guides me to a booth seat. "This is on me, what are you having?"

I order a small Scottish All Day breakfast, Annie asks for some cake and a latte and I watch as Adrian goes to the counter to order and pay.

"So," Annie asks me, her lips hardly moving. "What gives? Have you switched brothers?"

I shake my head. "No…" I reply, also hardly moving my lips. It was a skill we learned whilst an MP, ventriloquism. "Both," I reply, keeping my voice low.

Annie leans back and gives me a look that borders on pure elation. "And it's what you want?" she asks. I nod, joining her mirth-like grin.

"Yes," I whisper. My heart soars to privately admit how they've made me feel in such a short space of time, especially to my best friend.

"Explains the light that's in your eyes now. Good!" She grabs my hands, squeezing them, then winks at me and motions to the counter area. I don't need to turn to know Adrian is coming back.

We eat, talk, and drink, then talk some more. Coming across Annie, even though I can't talk to her about work, given where we are, is a welcome breath of air. It's normal, historic, and familiar. Adrian is still on alert, something Annie picks upon.

"There aren't any AK47's pointed at you," she tells him in a low voice so only we can hear.

"Work issues, I'm just on edge," he explains. Annie nods.

"Aye, I hear you," she nods back at him; she understands where we're coming from, even if she doesn't know exactly why. She looks at me and smiles. "I'm gonna get back, tidy up a wee bit afore the wee tornado comes home, and hide these," she grins, holding up the bags as she slides along the booth seat. "Adrian, it's been nice to meet you, thanks for the refuel." She extends her hand again and leans in, muttering something to him. He nods, replies, and then Annie blows me a kiss to vanish out into the throngs of Sunday shoppers.

"What the heck did she say?" I ask as I watch as his smile gets broader, his shoulders shake, and his eyes close, then he hits his hand against his knee a few times and breathes in deeply, calming himself.

"That we're to treat you right, let you sleep in a few times a week, and that the nearest sex shop is only two streets away," he replies with mirth.

I scowl, calling her names under my breath, then I laugh. Bloody Annie!

We tidy the flat and chill out for the rest of the day. Annie texts me and asks me if I need or want the rest of my stuff if I'm going to be staying here, to which I say yes. Adrian just nods and gives me a hug, reminding me I have my own space if I want it. Unless I screw this up, I'm going to be living here from now on. Adrian lends me a Defender 110 that is in the car park and I make the run to Annie's as Jim is dropping Elle back. I give the munchkin a good cuddle, hardly believing that she's a good few inches taller than when I last saw her. Jim doesn't hang around, a fact Annie thanks me for when we're briefly alone.

"Is there anything else ye wanna take?" she asks as we load up the last of the boxes. Like a good friend, she kept all my stuff in storage whilst I was gone. It was all sealed and packed, waiting for me to find somewhere.

"No, I've got it all," I tell her.

"Aye, ye do." She grins at me, and I recall now her parting comment to Adrian. Checking Elle's not around, I firmly slap my friend on the upper arm.

"Your bloody comment," I tell her as my grin gets wider.

Annie tosses her head back in laughter, which does bring the munchkin to come and see what all the noise is about. I'm leaning against the Defender, trying to stay upright. Elle just shakes her head and goes back to doing her own thing.

"Did ye go down there?" she asks as I slam the rear door shut. I shake my head in answer.

"Not yet, there's time," I reply, winking at her.

Annie sighs deeply and looks at me. "Ye deserve this, Bee, be happy for us, aye?" She hugs me. One day, I hope she'll be happier than she is now. She needs a good man, one who has her back and can make her laugh, be there for her. Like me, until now, we'd never found it. We're in our forties; this is something I didn't think I would find.

"It's been a damn long time coming," I tell her, and she nods.

"Aye, it has," she responds, her words choking on emotions. "Go on, get outta here and have fun; the banana boat needs sailing away into the sunset," she tells me. I grin and climb in, then beep the horn at her. I bloody love my best friend!

Back at the flat, Adrian is waiting for me in the car park, and he has a dolly-trolly. A fairly largish trolley with wheels, sides, and a pull handle. He looks pleased as I jump out to greet him, suddenly aware of everything around us.

"What's wrong?" I ask, the tension building inside of me.

"Nothing new!" he explains, a smile on his lips.

"Then why are you here?" I ask, confused as to why he's here and waiting. He points to the car.

"GPS," he tells me, and I relax, then smile at him, chuffing out a chuckle, or was it a snort?

"Well, that'll be very useful." I motion to the trolley and open the rear door. We both start taking boxes and stacking them carefully, fitting six in. I've fourteen boxes so I pick a lighter one and carry it up as Adrian kindly pulls the dolly. Another trip later, we've secured the car, the boxes are in my room, and I sigh. Some I know I can unpack now as they're full of clothes. As I'm putting a load into the machine, I become high on smelling the freshly brewed coffee, Adrian taps me on the shoulder and motions for me to follow.

I set the machine to go on a setting that I think will do that load in an hour, then I follow Aid to the living room. On the tablet, via secure video call, is Marcus.

"Hey you, having fun?" I ask as I sit down next to Adrian. He hands me a coffee, and I thank him, then we sit back and get on with our observations of the data that's on the conference room table. As we explain what we've found and the ciphers, Marcus begins to pull faces, almost chewing his tongue. A thing his brother does too. At least Marcus doesn't rant and rave like Gordon Ramsey doing it! I can only guess that us telling him about whoever is still in our I.T. systems is making his brain ache.

"If we're being warned, do we want to increase our firewall and email filters to as high as the Bosnian's systems?" he asks.

"I'm not qualified to answer that. In one way, I'm glad we found the coded messages. In another, I am not. If we had someone else technical, we could have a better discussion," I observe. Marcus goes wide-eyed.

"What does that mean?" he asks.

"It means if you get killed or hurt, there's no company. At the moment, you're the weakest link, and I am not happy about that," Adrian tells him in that stiff, 'obey me' tone he used in Bosnia with the client's own security staff we were training.

Marcus sits back in his chair, and I can tell he's thinking. He's got a pen in his hands, which he twiddles in an annoying fashion.

"Okay, you're right. And I could do with someone technical, server-side, to chat with. I've so many ideas, and I need someone else to understand them. By the way, I have accessed the firewall and I've had to close up some of the ports that…" He stops and laughs. "Yeah, okay, I've lost you." He grins and Adrian looks as confused as I do.

"Assume for a moment, you haven't," I pipe up, pretending that I know what the hell is going to come out of my mouth next, or that I actually listened to the Unix guys years ago when they tried to explain what they were doing. "What ports did you have to close up, and can you explain in stupid terms to us, why?"

We watch as Marcus laughs and we listen, understanding as best we can. Marcus explains what the firewall does in simple terms, that he has closed some of the high-level ports and the lower ones that should be closed over anyway, but weren't, and that he kept the internet ones open. Beyond that, it goes over my head. I can see from Adrian's confused expression, he probably understands as much as I do.

"So, how is ours configured now? Will those messages still get in? And how can we check it?"

Marcus holds a hand up and grins. "One question at a time, Bee darlin', honestly!" He chuckles, but I can only grin.

"Our configuration is tighter, and the messages could still come through via web traffic…" Marcus' face contorts and he swears as much as Adrian or I would.

"What is it?" Adrian asks.

"I need to do another system sweep. I'll be back tonight, maybe tomorrow; these bombs are military-grade, but the guy that makes them is down in Essex and sells them on, not tracking what device goes to who, though he has sales records. He won't share who he sold them to, client privileged information. I don't want to hack him to double-check. That puts us back at square one." He grins at something above the camera view for some unknown reason, like a child caught with their hand in the cookie jar. "And I won't be coming back alone," he tells us. I frown at him, curious as to what or who he's bringing back with him from Hamilton.

He grins at us.

"I.T. backup," he tells us. Then he swiftly bids us bye for now, and the call ends. Adrian looks at me with his eyes wide.

"Guess we'll see who tomorrow then," I comment as I clear away the mugs.

"Aye, guess we will," Adrian sighs as he leans back on the sofa. I smirk and leave him to his thoughts, rinsing the mugs and stacking them in the dishwasher. I get on with tidying the kitchen area, but I jump when strong arms wrap around me.

"Bloody ghost," I chastise him. I didn't hear him move. "What are you thinking?" I ask him, not turning to him. I can feel him pressing up against me, and he's getting harder every second.

"That we should go out for dinner." He steps back and opens the fridge. I gasp and put my hands on my hips.

"I'm gonna move back in with Annie! Seriously, you guys wanna fuck me stupid and not feed me enough to keep my strength up?!" I hold my cross look for a few more seconds as fear appears on his face, then he looks into the fridge, and I laugh when he realises the lack of food. And the awful smell.

"And oh my God, what the hell died in there! Do you guys never clear it out?!" I proclaim. "Come on, let's get this cleaned." He chuckles, grabs me, and tickles me until I'm screaming,

"You sassy tease," he admonishes. When he stops, he brings the bin over and we get the fridge cleared, cleaned, and closed again. I glare at Adrian as I open the freezer to find it's a frost-free version, and I'm glad, even though it is quite empty.

"We can look after ourselves, ye know," he growls as I close the freezer door.

"Aye, it sure looks like it!" I go to empty the bin and Adrian grabs my wrist.

"We can, clearly Marcus hasn't been great at it. Go and shower; I'll empty this and then grab one myself. Half an hour," he tells me in that instructive voice of his.

"Bossy," I snip at him. He grabs me and pins me up against the fridge, and even though I'm wearing trousers, he runs his hand up the inside of my leg and palms my crotch which sends fire through me. My insides quake in anticipation of what he'll do next, or later.

"Yep, and?" he growls as he nuzzles me. "I'm hungry for food, you…" He pulls back and looks at me, then he kisses me intensely, roughly, and completely. "Will be dessert," he tells me when he breaks the kiss. "Go be a good girl and get a shower, but wear a skirt, no knickers."

I can feel my eyes going wide at his command.

He leans in and whispers into my ear, "We can't fuck in the car, away from the cameras, with barriers in our way." He waits for me to react, and my slight nod is all he needs. "And heels…wear heels for me." He kisses me again, gently, then he lets me go, takes the bin liner out of the bin, and vanishes. I grin and look where he's gone before I go and grab a shower, taking care of the important bits. I've never been told what to do like that and in most cases, I would tell them to fuck off. *So why are his commands making me wet and shudder in anticipation?*

~Twenty~
Adrian

Knowing I can answer Blythe's sass, that I can act on the emotions she invokes in me, is as intoxicating as it is powerful. Her face as I told her not to wear any knickers, but to wear a skirt and heels, was a mixture of 'what the fuck' and 'fuck yes.' She didn't quite know what to respond with, but she pushed into me when we kissed after I told her. I don't know if she realised it, but I did.

I drop the bin bag down the rubbish chute, listen to it slide down to the bins, and head back, checking on her as I enter the flat. I can hear her shower running, so I march to my room, stripping as I go. Today's been a bit mixed mentally and emotionally. First, the thought is that someone wants to shut us down. I don't understand why. Learning that Marcus confirms and thinks they're maybe still in our I.T. systems bugs the fuck out of me. I can't wait to find out who they are; I'm going to rip them a new one.

As I shower, I recall meeting Blythe's friend, Annie. I can see why they had a reputation in the RAF. Annie missed nothing in the forms of cues, hints, body language. Even six or seven years out of the military, she's as aware that something is going on as we are, though not why. Marcus said she got a new job role when Blythe joined us, so that was about seven months ago.

She would be a great asset to the team, and I decide to sound out to Blythe about Annie maybe joining us. Then I remember, Annie's got a bairn, a wee one, and is single. I can ask, but I resign myself to the fact the answer is likely to be no and I'll not push it if that's the answer.

As I dress, I hear Blythe moving around the laundry area. I can hear the tumble dryer startup and doors close, and I surmise she must be about ready.

I find a jacket to go over my shirt and put on some boots, heading out to the living room as I put the jacket on. I stop dead when I see what she's wearing. A denim skirt that's angled with frayed bits covers her lower half down to her knees, partnered with a V-neck low cut tunic top in a darkish red and looks phenomenal. I'm semi-hard just looking at her as she slides on some red heels. It makes me wonder if she did as I asked.

She twirls around for me and I groan in frustration.

"I did as instructed, sir," she teases me. Fuck, at this rate, we're not going to get where I plan to take us.

"Come on," I growl as I motion to the door. She grabs her leather jacket and a small red bag, then we're heading down to the car park.

I pick a Ninety that we've had configured with a proper back seat, not the usual Defender benches. Marcus fell in love with these things when he was in Brize, though I've never really had a love for them. Blythe, though, has to put her eyes back into her head. I grin, then I remember I need to tell her about all the resources we have access to.

"You drive out, I'll drive back," she tells me. The sassy woman is giving me instructions again and I growl at her. "What? You know where we're going," she protests as I open the door for her.

"Don't tell me what to do." I stare at her. She grins.

"Yeah, not nice, is it, big guy?" She pats me on the chest and climbs in, still giving me that sassy grin as her eyes dance in the low light. I huff at her, shutting the door hard, and ponder her observation as I get into the car. I set the SatNav and drive out of the car park, onto a back road, out of Edinburgh, heading north.

"Do I really talk to you like that?" I ask, glancing at her.

"You do it when you want something. On a job, I accept it as normal. When we're being us, our trio or a couple, it's…I don't know. If I didn't know I was going to sleep with you again, or even before last night, I'd have told you to fuck off until you can find some damn manners." She sighs. "I don't know…it's like when we're at work, I expect it. The bedroom, that just makes me react," I glance at her as I drive, "but when we're not, it doesn't seem to sit well with me, the example being now."

I take the junction to the northern part of Edinburgh's borough, heading for a small coastal village in Leith I know with great views and food.

"I get your point, I think," I tell her. "You telling me that you'd drive back, how you told me, I think I get it."

She nods. "We just need to change the tone when we're away from work, but I'll do you a deal. I'll try to phrase my ideas as questions if you can do the same when we're alone or it's just us three."

I nod. "That I can do, I think. Bite me if I get it wrong though, aye?" I put the car into the highest gear to cruise along the dual carriageway.

"Oh, biting… What else do you like?" she asks with her voice all sultry and sexy. I growl again in frustration, and she tosses her head back in laughter. "Yes, sexually…we might as well get all the kinks known about, aye?" she asks.

"Aye, we might as well. But, I need to talk about some work stuff first," I tell her, glancing across. I can see her tilt her head at me and a small frown forms on her brow.

"Oh?"

"Aye, in Bosnia, you knew what cars we could use, resources, different buildings, safehouses, etc. Here, we've not told you, simply because the timing has been shit, and we've gotten into a situation as soon as we got back." I can see her shoulders relax a little and a small sigh escapes her lips. "And why are you so on edge all the time?" I take the turn as the SatNav suggests and we're on quieter, slower, residential roads.

"Like you, I expect the worst, aye? Anything else is a bonus," she says. I chuckle at her observation of me.

"Aye, but we need someone else who knows what we do, worst case. And it's a sergeant thing, aye? Third in command," I tell her. Her face is a picture, frozen in a moment of understanding and realisation.

"Because of…?" she enquires in a hesitant voice. Just because we're together, isn't the whole reason.

"We need someone else who can take charge if Marcus or I end up hurt, or worse. We've spoken about it; we want that person to be you." I turn off the engine outside the restaurant and shift to her in my seat. "You were the highest rank out of all of us, and you're by far the more experienced of anyone else beyond the three directors. Tony marked you as a leader right after your interview and, well, now is as good a time as any to make the company more solid."

She smiles, but it doesn't get to her eyes.

"We'll talk more inside, aye? Something's bothering ye." I sigh. "I told Marcus it wouldn't take me long to piss ye off." I climb out and head around to her side. A few hours to do exactly that is a record, even for me.

"You haven't," she breathes at me when I open her door; her eyes are smaller, contracted, a sign of fear. We're not in danger right now, so why? "I just expect the boot to fall all the time. Working through it," she tells me with a soft smile. When she climbs down, I pin her against the side of the car and lean into her ear.

"We're never going to tell you we don't want ye anymore. If anything, it's going to be you telling us to fuck off." I pull back and the fear slowly disappears from her eyes and her face softens.

"Breathe, lass, yer fine," I tell her. Then I softly kiss her. Before it develops into anything more, I pull back and take her hand. "Come on, let's go eat," I say, taking her into the coastal Italian Restaurant that Marcus and I have loved for decades.

The owner greets us enthusiastically, bringing over wine. Blythe waves the car keys at him and she declines. We place our drinks order once we are seated at a sea-view table. Blythe looks through the menu quickly, then closes it. Her nostrils are flared and she has that tell-tale smirk of trouble on her face. Then it fades and she's calmer again.

"What's gotten into you?" I ask. She is hard to figure out, changing tact and body language at the drop of a hat.

"Nothing a good dinner won't sort! I'd like to do the ordering for us both if that's okay?" I grin at her request, something we both said we'd do. I nod, wondering what she's up to. I tell her what I'd like and when the owner comes back, she greets him in fluid Italian. There's no hint of an English or even a Scottish accent on her lips; it's like a switch.

She speaks rapidly and doesn't even look at the menu. Giovani Rossi chuckles and responds to her with a loud booming voice, some hand gestures, a squeeze on her shoulder and a wink at me.

I sit back, stunned.

"You speak Italian? Fluently?" I enquire. That conversation was more than school taught Italian. Blythe laughs and her eyes dance. At least she's back on happier emotional ground.

"My grandparents were Italian on my father's side, remember? He came over here for a holiday with a friend, met my mother, and never went home. Hence the long, black Italian hair." She swishes it around a little. The ponytail goes this way and that.

"And the blue eyes?" I ask. Black hair and blue eyes are a striking combination.

"All Mamma. Dad's eyes are a weird colour, Mamma's blue was clearly the most dominant, but By and I have this shade." I nod with a smile.

"Do you visit your grandparents in Italy much?" I ask as the drinks are brought over by Giovani in a flourish of Italian, to which Blythe responds, again with no Scottish accent. She smiles at me when we're left alone again.

"Used to, every summer from when I could fly at a year old to when I enlisted. Some of the storms in Bologna are brutal, and my grandparents invested in a pool table when Byron was about four…I'd have been about six. Every summer since, we played when it was raining. We got good at it, as you'd expect. Ask Marcus how that went down the first time he played me."

I chuckle at the memory. "Yeah, he told me about that first game. I came back early that morning but saw he was engaged, and after I checked you two were okay, I headed to bed. You'd gone by the time I woke up. Then, I was shipped out for nearly five months at oh-two-hundred the following morning. We'd been getting used to the time change we'd need beforehand, which is just as well." I shudder at the memory. "We were as busy as all hell when we got there, and it didn't stop for nearly four weeks. Then, things calmed down, but being on stand-by for that length of time…" I shrug. Blythe nods.

"Prague was my last foreign deployment before we got shipped to Lossie. That's why…" She pauses. "Ach, she won't mind."

I give her a curious look.

"Marcus kinda knows, so do you. It's how Annie ended up pregnant." She sighs, sits back and begins the tale.

"We were heading back from Prague, decamping at Manston before being redeployed up to Lossie. We're heading to Lossie, heads kinda on straight but in need of a session, aye?" I nod and she continues. "So, Annie and I stop for a night in Edinburgh. She hooks up with this guy for the night, then we head up to our new base. Only, six weeks later, she's having to go back down to Edinburgh to find him to tell him she's pregnant. Prague was supposed to tell us to get our contraceptive implants sorted. They didn't get the message until we'd left, but they didn't send it onto Manston; they forwarded the message to Lossie. We weren't *at* Lossie, so Lossie filed it and didn't tell us until six weeks after we'd landed there. Before you get that stuff sorted, you're tested. Annie's result was positive, mine wasn't."

Blythe shrugs. "Jim seemed all right, but we never intended to see those lads again. And then Annie…" Blythe shivers. "Had a difficult, hard delivery. She needed a blood donation afterwards. Thankfully, I was on hand. Bitch is, I got to hold her daughter before she did."

"Yer the same blood group?" I ask. That is useful to know.

"Aye, but it means Annie can never give blood to me or anyone else, in case she passes on CJD or something that leads to it. She's a fighter, always has been. It took her five whole days to recover enough to hold her daughter. Then she got a bunch of other complications because she hadn't fed her daughter naturally." Blythe shrugs and I notice her eyes are an icy blue.

"Hey," I reach out and touch her hand, squeezing it firmly. "It's in the past, ye cannae change it. Annie's here, alive, and thanks to your help, her daughter has her mum," I remind her. Blythe nods.

"They got married weeks afore, and Jim agreed for me to be godmother after Elinor Rose was born, because I stopped him from becoming a single da. Still dinnae like the guy, he's a banana boat driver," she scoffs. I chuckle at the old RAF reference for an aircraft carrier seaman.

"And after? They're divorced, aren't they?" I ask. Blythe nods.

"Aye, it lasted six months or so. Jim's…" She bites her lip. "If ye cannae say anything nice," she quips. I get it. She hates him but tolerates him for the bairn's sake. Time to shift this conversation along.

"Do you think she'd move jobs to work alongside ye again?" I ask her. I watch as she grins, then shakes her head.

"No, because of Elle, naw. She needs to do the school runs; though Jim has the bairn on the weekends, she'll not sign up to do just a few days. What she does now is just brilliant." Blythe sits back with her chest puffed out, clearly enamoured with her friend.

"So what does she do?" I ask as the starter gets delivered. Blythe waits until we're alone. Then she leans forward and lowers her voice.

"Ye ken about domestic violence victims?" she asks me. I nod, we had a few incidents on base at Brize the dozen years I was there. "Well, she goes in and gets the women and kids out. She's been in a few scrapes, but she usually gets her woman out. Sometimes it's a pickup from the police, sometimes she goes in when the police have the husband or partner distracted."

I gape at her. "People actually do that?" I ask. Blythe nods.

"Aye, and Annie does. She…" Blythe chuckles. "She dresses up, tight black gear, you would think Lara Croft or some comic book hero. Croft on speed, maybe, or something else. Annie takes it up a whole level, but she'll go looking for runaway victims too, so they don't end up on the streets. That's taken her to some really rare parts of our country."

I blink as I eat. "Why dress up?" I ask.

"Disguise, I guess. You try finding someone who is dressed like a ninja in day to day clothes. Would you have pegged her to be doing that when you met her?"

I ponder. Of all the jobs I thought Annie did, that sure as heck wasn't one of them.

"No, have to admit, I wouldn't."

"Annie treats it like a uniform. On duty, off duty, dangerous, not so dangerous."

I nod. "Makes sense, allows the mind switch to happen," I say, and Blythe nods.

"Exactly that. We went through the setup when she started, and every change since when she's gotten hurt," she says.

"Makes sense, you were living there." I recall the address in Edinburgh. "Decent schools in that part," I comment, and Blythe agrees.

"She needed that, even if it wasn't the house she originally wanted, she got the area." I grin, and our mains are brought out and not quite what or how I expected it to. Blythe has ordered more than I thought we'd need, but as we tuck in, I realise she's ordered several sharing platters, food I'd not normally try.

"You have to try this," Blythe says, pointing to something on the platter before us. The main dinner turns into some sort of buffet and at the end of it, I am stuffed. Blythe, though, looks incredibly happy.

"So that's what you were doing?" I say as I wave my hand over the numerous empty plates. There's not a scrap left on any of them, and I'm stunned. She grins and nods.

"Annie learned quite quickly to let me order in Italian. I guess it's like the Chinese or Greeks; if they go into a restaurant of their home country, they get better food and better service. Speak the language of home and the doors shall open." She gesticulates with her arms and I laugh.

"But, back in Bologna, that's what dinner would be. Not set meals as we have here on civvy street, more like we did in the mess-halls. On Italian night, they'd rope Annie and me into making dinner. We got two weeks out at my grandparent's place after MP Training and before Officer's the first time. Then a few times again afore they passed away. My grandparents fell in love with her and taught her to make some traditional family dishes. She can make lasagne and bolognese better than me, but I love the shrimp ravioli." She smiles as she wipes her mouth, and Giovani comes over to ask how it went.

Blythe grins and replies to his questions in English. I chime in with some praise of my own, and we settle the bill, though Blythe has another discussion with Giovani in heated Italian. As we head to the car and I open the door for her to get into the driver's seat, I ask her what happened.

"He didn't want to let us pay," she tells me. I narrow my eyes and look back at the restaurant. We're coming here again, for sure!

"How did you persuade him?" I ask.

"I told him his momma would smack him up the side of his thick head with a pasta roller and ask him where his brains had gone." She chuckles and I do recall him wincing a little and rubbing his head.

"He told me his wife would do the same thing, so I told him to never let me find out who she is because I'd tell her!" I laugh at Blythe's antics and am sure she would do that too.

We climb in, and she starts up the car, happy as Larry to be driving one of these.

"Oh, I've always wanted one of these!" She stomps on the headlight button near the clutch to turn the lights on.

"Take us home, McDuff," I tease her. She glares at me, then her lip curls and a huge smile appears with a glint in her eyes.

"Aye aye, Captain!" She winks and begins to follow the mobile SatNav, taking us home.

~Twenty-One~
Blythe

I get to drive one of my all-time favourite cars home. There was one particular Defender 90 on base I just loved, but this is a damn close second to that. I follow the SatNav, taking unfamiliar roads and Adrian pauses it at a junction, asking that I head out to a bluff point. I do and as I pull up, we can see the North Sea, the far side of the Forth, the jagged edges of the cliffs, and a bird of prey swooping around. It's still light; sunset will be a few hours yet.

"White-Tailed Eagle, one of three mating pairs this side of The Highlands," he tells me. "It's why we picked it for our logo. Marcus and I grew up on this side of Edinburgh, Tony too."

I nod, aware now that the company logo has a meaning. It's a link back to home, to this raw, small corner of Scotland. The North Sea can be rough, and you have to have balls of a certain size to survive. The White-Tailed Eagle has it in its talons. We watch as it soars, then dives and returns with a fish in its claws. I gasp, feeling sorry for the fish, but we've just eaten seafood and ours wasn't as fresh as what the raptor just caught.

"She's magnificent," I breathe, watching the bird closely.

"That's a male. Darker plumage, bigger wingspan, whiter head. But yes, either way, magnificent." I look at him and wonder where his knowledge came from. "What?" he asks as he sits back. "We used to climb up to a buff further down and watch them when the weather was decent. It gave us something to do in the summer, other than avoiding the damn midges." I chuckle. The Scottish midges are wee horrors in their own right and are quite feared worldwide! Give them tasty blood like mine or Annie's, and we became an all-day buffet. Thankfully, the military has better midge repellant than what is available on the high street.

We watch until the bird has eaten his fish. He flies off and catches another, then he heads away from us and I groan.

"Aww, he's gone. I hope he's happy!" I muse.

"Why would ye care about whether he's happy?" Adrian enquires as I start the car up again and turn us around.

"Everyone and everything needs to be happy; we all need it in our lives. That bird is just as sentient as you and I." I glance across at him as we talk and I make my way back to the main road and head towards Edinburgh. "You have had people to take care of. The crew out in Bosnia, for example, when we were there. The women, another example. They're not just pretty little things anymore," I remind him.

He laughs, shaking his head. "No, they're not! You did a heck of a job with them! Femme fatals for sure!"

I chuckle and check the mirrors as I drive. As I take the turns the SatNav suggests, the car behind follows me exactly. Adrian looks at me as I check the mirrors again, ignoring SatNav.

"What we got, Bee?"

"Someone is following us…"

"Give me your phone," he instructs. His phone is doing the SatNav as the phone holder is a magnetic one and I don't have that type of case.

"Code?" he asks, and I put my finger on the screen to unlock it. Within moments, he's got the car's dash-cam on my phone. "Need their licence plate," he tells me and I nod. Instead of driving straight onto the dual carriageway, I take a side road. It's a longer route, but I should be able to get him close enough for the cameras to help us out.

I don't like what the guy behind us is doing, and I shift in my seat, preparing to do something crazy and probably downright stupid, but hopefully, it'll stop him from following us. "Aid, pull yourself in," I bark at him as we come to some farmland out of the housing estate. He does as I tell him, without a word of objection, and I swing the car into a tight one-eighty so I am facing the oncoming car, which looks like one of those new Ford things.

I hit the accelerator and drive straight at the person who has been following us for too long. At the last second, we both swerve. They manage to keep their car on the track, but it's made me aim for a bank, and I stamp on the brakes, hoping she'll slow down quickly. It doesn't happen and there's a loud bang, I see the sky, then we're pitched sideways, the car tilts, metal groans, my weight is shifted into the door, then we stop dead.

"Fuck!" I swear and try to move and as soon as I try, I yell in pain. "Oh shit…" My mind begins to understand what I've done to myself. Again. "No!" I yell and Adrian reaches across to grab my free arm.

"Why'd we topple?" he asks. I'd shrug, but I can only guess that the bank was steeper than I thought.

"Least of our problems," I whine, the pain excruciating.

"What's broken?" Adrian demands, his voice a growl.

"Shoulder, dislocated, again," I snap at him. "Can you get out?" I ask, trying both not to cry and scream in pain.

"Yeah." He manages to get out and I can hear his boots crunching on the ground. Trust this time to be the one time I'm in nice heels, no knickers and now any chance of sex is out the bloody window.

"Bee, stay there. There's a farmhouse about half a mile down the way, I'm going to go and see if they can…"

"We have a winch!" I yell. I love winches.

"Yeah, on the front and the car is on its side. The winch is of no use."

I sigh in frustration, the pain is now getting intolerable. "Be quick!" I yell. Fuck, I really need to not be dealing with this shit shoulder again. It was why Annie and I returned to Lossie. An op in Prague got me a dislocated shoulder. There's one person who can set it right the first time, and she's not here.

"Blythe!" I can hear Adrian calling my name and I come to. Shit, I must've blacked out. "Blythe!" he yells again, this time there's more urgency and apprehension in his voice.

"Here!" I holler back. "Can't go anywhere bloody else," I seethe under my breath.

"We're going to push the car onto its wheels. Let the brakes off," he commands and I check. The Ninety has a transmission handbrake and is really only a parking brake, which is disengaged. I would swear blind that I'd engaged it as I was trying to slow down. I can't tell anymore.

"You're good!" I yell, knowing in about thirty seconds or so, I'm going to be biting my tongue and tasting blood so that I don't yell out. He probably doesn't know how badly this hurts or that I've done this too many times already. Nothing about me can be fixed if this car isn't moved. I can hear another vehicle, and I concentrate on the revs of its engine, which will tell me when this car is about to be pulled. I can hear the car get closer, slowly, then something metal is being tied around the top frame. I hear a winch being used and I sigh, understanding how they're going to pull the car upright. I just hope whatever tree they're using can take the weight.

I double-check the brakes are all off again as I hear the car door shut. Grabbing the steering wheel with my left, I try to brace my body for the jolt of movement. It comes when the car is over the tilt angle she needs; the car groans as she bounces onto all four tyres again. I bite my tongue, tasting the blood I knew I would in an effort to stop myself from crying out as the jolt sends searing pain through me. I don't think I succeeded. The fresh air tells me Adrian has gotten the door open and I'm crying in relief, pain, and ready to faint.

~Twenty-Two~
Adrian

Seeing the car on its side and the bank it tried to climb at speed was astounding. I did take a photo, Blythe will never believe she got a Ninety to tilt over. Help was already coming by the time I'd gotten halfway to the farmhouse, and they gave me a lift back.

I knew Blythe had an old shoulder injury, but I had no idea what. When I returned, she didn't answer my first few calls, which worried me. Eventually, she does and I can't get this car back onto its tyres quickly enough, though I know we have to be careful.

The farmer nods after he's set the pulling winch and he gets his Toyota to pull slowly. Painstakingly, the Ninety is winched back onto her tyres and I am sure I heard Blythe cry out as the car bounced back onto its shocks. The side of the car is scratched and dented, but it's fixable, I just hope we can get it going again.

I pull the driver's door open; Blythe is still in the seat, looking totally horrid, pale, her lips are dry, despite the tears she's crying, likely from the pain. I get her out as carefully as I can, but I accidentally touch her shoulder, which makes her vomit. Thankfully, I wasn't in front of her. I manage to guide her to the Toyota's flatbed so she can sit, as she looks like she's about to collapse through sheer pain or exhaustion.

A jolly lady huffs up to us, carrying a huge first aid kit. The kind I've seen paramedics carry.

"What do we have here?" she enquires in one of the most professional voices I've ever heard.

Blythe's eyes open and she immediately tries to push herself off the Toyota, holding her injured arm with one shoulder clearly out of alignment with the other. As she tries, she collapses onto the road and I can't get to her in time from where I am. Her eyes are wide, and she's clearly avoiding what appears to be a qualified paramedic.

"I won't hurt you," the jolly woman says. I have no idea what her name is, but my priority switches to Blythe.

"That's what they all say," Blythe snips. I begin to tell her off, but the medical lady just lifts her hand, indicating I should shut up. I do.

"Had a shoulder injury before then?" The medical lady smiles softly at Blythe, gets down to her level. Blythe nods in reply, but she's still scowling. Both women are on the dry road track, but neither seems to give a damn. "Tell me about it," the nurse lady commands.

Blythe's head shoots up. "Dislocated it one time, a medic on site was too new, didn't take the time to set it properly. I had to have it dislocated and put back in a second time. Hurts like hell when it does, but it has to be put in at a certain angle on the rotation. Only two people ever do it right. Been out five times, no, six now." Blythe goes even paler than she was, telling me this isn't just physical. Her anticipation and expectation are adding to it, and I know that's not good.

"Okay, I'd suggest you are taken to—"

Blythe cuts her off. "No, please! They'll insist on surgery, and I'm not consenting to that." Blythe stops spitting her replies out. "Maybe, next time, I'll consider it..." She softens her gaze to the paramedic lady, "But right now, no. I just need it rotating back in and strapped to me. But, properly, please?"

The lady nods, her round glasses make her eyes seem bigger than they probably are. "Where does it need rotating to?" she gently asks.

Blythe indicates somewhere just above her temple and I blink, knowing that's too high to rotate it up to, normally. The farmer taps me on the shoulder and motions to the Defender, and I can see the damage to the doors and rear panel. A few seconds later the birds fly out of the trees as Blythe's scream cuts the air in two, and I let out an involuntary growl.

Over half an hour later, I aide Blythe into the passenger seat, her colour no better, her arm strapped to her, making it immobile. The whiteness of the sling is a stark contrast to the dark red top she's wearing, though I've managed to get her jacket over her so she's warmer. The paramedic nurse told me what to do when I got her home, and I nodded in agreement, though I'll be having Eric, our company medic, look at her and double-check it when we get back. That will be the first call I make.

I strap her in and the sassiness she'd give me about helping her like this has gone. I don't blame her, the scream from her as her shoulder was reset was blood-curdling for the wrong reasons. The nurse dried her tears and strapped Blythe up, with instructions not to use it for at least four weeks. She also told Blythe to seriously consider an operation to tighten the muscles again, so that this type of injury is reduced.

I check we have both phones, and we do. I'm grateful perhaps that I only had one beer at dinner, but even if I hadn't, the following incident would have sobered up the most drunken bum. I restart the Defender and then thank the farmer and his wonderful wife once again. She nods to Blythe, who I think mouths the words "thank you" at her, then I take us home.

The call to Eric gets placed as soon as we're on the dual carriageway and twenty minutes from the flat. He agrees he'll meet me there and check Blythe over.

"Are you asleep?" I ask her gently over the roar of the engine. Defender engines aren't the quietest of things.

"No, hurt too fucking much," she replies in a gruff growl.

"I should have driven," I comment and I'm kicking myself that I let her persuade me to let her drive back, though she was as excited as heck when she saw this car.

"It didn't happen that way. Stop beating yourself up over it," she states. Her tone is flat, clipped and I can only imagine the pain she's in.

"Do you want some painkillers? There's a pharmacy on the way home that's open late," I suggest, knowing that there's none in the car's kit. She nods.

"Yes, please. The highest dose you can get over the counter, and a bottle of water if you would. Though, some gas and air would be the better option."

"Absolutely," I reply. "Tell me about that shoulder." I heard what she told the paramedic, but I have no idea what caused it.

"Prague, RTI with a drunken local half a mile from the base. The field medic was new, got flustered, and somehow put it back in wrong. It took a more experienced medic to sort it, which involved forcing my shoulder back out to go back in correctly, the following morning. I was in agony for months. It took a fair amount of deep physio in England and Italy to un-pinch vital nerves, rather than dislocate my shoulder again."

So far, she's talking, distracted, and I ask more questions.

"The third time it popped out, Annie reset it for me. She was the first one to get it back in right with the least amount of pain. Until tonight." I cringe. If this is the least amount of pain, what the hell kind of pain is she in usually when it happens?

"Pharmacy," I tell her, pulling into the parking bays. "I'll leave the engine running so you stay warm. Back in a few." Blythe nods. Five minutes later, she swallows a double dose of the meds, and there's some colour to her face now, but she's still as white as a ghost.

Twenty minutes later, Eric is checking her medically, and she's putting up with it, but she positively growls when he prods a little and asks if this hurts. She's trying not to snap at him and I doubt she has much patience left. I'd have chewed him out by now.

"Well, I concur with your paramedic's suggestion; keep that strapped up for the next four weeks unless you need to shower or dress." Blythe gives him a look that could kill. "Have you had any painkillers?" he asks, but he looks at me. Blythe huffs and leaves the living room, heading to her own room, slamming the door behind her.

"Oops," Eric breathes. "Maybe I should have looked at her when I asked," he says, packing up his medical bag. "Listen, that's going to hurt like hell for a while. Given her history of it, maybe beyond the four weeks and, yes, I agree with getting it surgically looked at. I'll check in tomorrow and start loosening it up with her when she thinks she's ready, but she'll need something soft behind that shoulder so she doesn't roll onto it tonight. That will hurt more and there's not much you can do about it."

I nod, angry now at myself that this situation was caused just by me not being the one driving.

"And for what it's worth, it probably would have happened had you been driving; that was a heck of a knock from the back." It's like Eric's read my mind.

I frown, not understanding. "The back?"

Eric nods. "Yeah, it was pushed out from the back. I think she turned in the driver's seat, yanking on the wheel as it flipped. Happens regularly in racing, not so much in four-by-fours. Must've been a hell of an angle to tip a Ninety over." Eric nods to me, then he leaves, meeting Marcus on the way in.

"Why was Eric here? Are you both okay?" he asks, rushing in to check on us. Only, the door to the room that has the answers is closed.

~Twenty-Three~
Marcus

I agreed with Callum McLeod that we would borrow his firewall and software engineer for a few weeks. Keith apparently writes weird custom software when he's not tinkering with firewalls and protecting I.T. systems—two skills both Callum and I personally lack—but we know you can't do it all, and Keith isn't his only firewall guy. Keith, for his part, has family in Edinburgh and wants to see them, so I drop him off at theirs on the way back to the flat earlier than planned, agreeing to pick him up early tomorrow morning.

I'm as eager as heck to see both Adrian and Blythe, but seeing our usual medic, first aider, and qualified A&E doctor leaving our flat, I get into a panic. Adrian is standing tall, though he looks visibly shaken.

"Why was Eric here? Are you both okay?" I drop my bag and look around. Blythe isn't around; the door to her room is closed. It's not often, if at all, I see Adrian flustered, but this is the second time and again, it involves Blythe.

"We got followed," Adrian tells me, then he proceeds to tell me how Blythe got injured. I don't give a shit about the car, though I'll pull all its details off later.

"Fuck, do not leave her alone." I point to her door. "Go, check on her." I can see him hesitating. "You were with her, go to her. That's what I'd be telling you if it were just she and you together. Now, go! I have a text message to send."

I pull out one of Callum's mobiles and text Keith. Until we secure our systems, I can't trust sending any communication via our systems or directly from our mobiles. Keith texts me back, telling me to make it a seven am start. He's got a beer, and he'll have the program ready to load tomorrow.

I look up to see Adrian walking out with Blythe, and I make room for them both on the sofa. Fuck, she looks so tired and, I guess, she's in a fair bit of pain. I reply to Keith then focus on the two people before me.

"Hey, how are you doing? Have the pain meds kicked in yet?"

Blythe gives me a non-committal answer and gently eases herself back into the seat.

"I hurt. I need to sleep, but I need this strapped back onto me." She holds up a triangular piece of cloth and lets it drop onto her lap. "I can't be arsed, not tonight. I don't want to move, think, breathe, feel…"

I nod to Adrian and the bandage, and he picks it up.

"Let's get you strapped back up, then we'll help you get to bed. Do you want to sleep in with either of us? Or on your own?" I nod, pleased that he's giving her the choice and not demanding it of her.

"On my own, I think. I really don't need this being knocked out during the night, and I can't blame either of you if you're not there." I notice she's holding back tears. "Who the fuck was that in the other car? It was a male, right?" She checks with Adrian.

He nods once, confidently. "Yeah, it was. Didn't get a good look at him, and I'm hoping the dash cam did before we tipped over."

"That was bad driving on my part." Her voice is low, her eyes are closed. My stomach sinks as I listen to her. "So bloody stupid, and I know better… I think I hit the accelerator and turned it away from the bank, not into it." She grimaces as she talks. "And this," she motions to her shoulder, "I can do without."

Adrian leans forward and touches her knee, causing her to look up.

"It's o'er and done with, time to move on, aye?"

Blythe shakes her head. "Next step is to find the bastard." She wiggles forward then pushes herself up from the sofa. "I need to sleep. And I'm sorry I've not been better company for ye this evening." She looks at Adrian, then blinks away tears and takes a step to her room. Adrian grabs her by the left hand and holds her fast.

"I understand why. I can't imagine having your shoulder dislocated for the sixth time is any fun."

I blink. Six times… Oh, bleeding Nora!

"But we're here." He doesn't look at me; he doesn't need to. I look up at her; her right arm is pinned to her body now, thanks to the sling. "You let us know if you need anything," he tells her.

Then he takes the hand he's holding and kisses it, and we watch as the tears start to fall.

"Come on, lass, yer beyond tired. Let's get you tucked in," Adrian states, taking charge.

Twenty minutes later, we have a beer in hand, and Adrian tells me off for the state of the fridge. I nod, guilty of it.

"She's not going to be able to go out on jobs for a few months," Adrian confirms, thinking out loud. I nod.

"Did you speak to her about being the third in charge? The resources?" I ask. My brother nods and takes a swig of his beer.

"Yeah, we spoke on the way up. She thinks that it's because she's dating us." He sighs.

"Not why at all! I hope ye told her that?" I enquire, and he nods. "She looked good in that skirt and if she had heels…" I add, which makes him laugh.

"She wore them." He points to where they're discarded in the hall. Usually, he's a neat freak; Blythe must be too. Those are discarded and I get why. "Told her not to wear knickers; she didn't."

I gape. "She did that?" I ask, amazed.

He nods. "Yep. We never got to do anything though, that eejit followed us, and she picked up on it quickly enough."

I nod.

"I'll pull the camera info off tomorrow." Adrian looks at me.

"I already did it, saved it to the cloud, in case it gets wiped," I tell him. He smiles at me and he un-tenses as he absorbs what I've said.

"So, what did you find at McLeod's?" he asks me, finishing off his beer. I've hardly touched mine, but then, I haven't been in a car incident.

I go through what I found. That the bombs, while clever, were single function, but they've given me ideas for lots of new toys. Exclusive toys for us to use.

"The firewall, we're sure is compromised or they've gotten past it. Keith is pretty sure they're still in there; his small suite of programmes tomorrow will tell us. He's finishing one up tonight." And I grin, knowing what Keith is making it do. "And we're going to reboot the whole lot tomorrow after Keith's done what he needs to, so that the second part can be implemented."

My brother gives me the usual frown of uncertainty, and I chuckle.

"Additional firewall software that the box will run. But, he needs it to be the only machine up. Each machine will need to be swiped and configured for this software before it goes onto the network."

Adrian nods. "Anything we can do?" he asks. "To help," he adds as he fetches us a measure of whisky. He must be feeling pissed off; it's the only time he drinks Scotland's best export.

"Yeah, we use a smaller room to do each machine swipe once the firewall is as Keith wants it. So bringing the machines in that aren't servers, putting them back. Tablets too. It'll take most of the day, so help in ferrying the kit back and forth." I stop talking as Adrian nods with a grin on his face.

"This is what got you enthused about what we did. I think you've forgotten about your role here." He leans back into the sofa, and I sigh.

"I also think we need more staff when this nonsense is over. A few other technical people, a HR person, certainly more on the cameras, people we can train." Adrian nods at my suggestion.

"I've had the same thoughts, but I want to deal with this bloody idiot first." He finishes his drink and smiles at me.

"I'm going to check on Blythe, then get to bed. Are you doing an all-nighter?" he asks me as he gets up. I shake my head.

"Maybe tomorrow, when we're clearing the systems down, but not until," I say.

He nods and heads to Blythe's room. Then he's out a few moments later, closing the door softly behind him.

"She's out like a light. See you in the morning," he tells me, and I nod, silently thanking the Gods they're alive.

~Twenty-Four~
Blythe

I woke up a few times through the night, mostly for my shoulder hurting like an absolute bitch. By four am, I am swallowing yet more painkillers and I want to ask Eric for some stronger ones when he comes to check on me later. I do what I have to do in the bathroom and doing it one-handed makes life interesting and bloody difficult. Last time, Annie and I were roommates, so it was much easier to ask your best friend to pull your knickers down, put your bra on or your top. I think this time, I'll just stick with the crop bra and sports knickers. At least I can work those with one hand!

As I'm sitting on the bed, there's a knock, and Adrian pops his head around the door.

"Hey, how are you feeling?" he asks, coming to sit next to me on the bed on my 'good' side, my left.

"Had an okay night…but getting dressed…" I sigh. I'm still in my pyjamas, which Adrian helped me into last night. That was embarrassing, being so damn helpless.

He grins at me and strokes my leg. "I can help ye with that," he quips, standing up. "What do you want to put on?" he asks, looking around. Well, since he's good at undressing me, he might as well get good at dressing me. I pull out the soft-crop bra, something that won't dig into my shoulder. Adrian helps me get dressed as carefully as he can. We deal with the top half first as that's the hardest; moving my arm is bloody painful.

Also, with one hand, I need to pick something that's going to make it easier to go to the bathroom. One-handed is hard enough as it is without complicated clips and things on jeans. I dig around for some black jeggings that I know are in the boxes around me. Finding them, I sit back down, and Adrian carefully straps my arm back into place once I've done some basic movements with it.

"Should you be doing those?" he questions as he straps my arm into place.

"Maybe, not exactly sure. It's one exercise I was told to do after the third time, to help. The muscles are what's causing the pain now as they've been rudely shoved out of place twice and they're tightening up." I wiggle my fingers to keep the circulation going and sigh as Adrian pulls my jeggings up for me. I know that trusting him like this is important and reaching for a kiss seems wrong. I sigh in frustration as he stands and smiles at me.

Once dressed, I just need some socks and something light on my feet, so I dig out a pair of lightweight pull-ons. They're purple and black in colour, but I couldn't care less. I can get them on with the one hand I can still use.

Adrian nods to me and guides me to the dining table, where he's set out coffee and orange juice. He looks pleased, perhaps nervous.

"Careful, you'll let your gruff side down if people find out you're a gentleman too," I tease. He tries to hide the grin, the light in his eyes, but he can't. "Thank you," I say to him softly. "And I'm sorry I was a grouch afterwards," I add, reaching across for a mug and managing to pour myself a coffee without spilling it. I'm surprised my left hand is doing what I tell it to.

He smiles as he pops some breakfast muffins into the toaster. "Ye were in pain," he acknowledges. "I get that." He leans against the counter as the muffins toast.

"Still, there's no need for me to be a bitch. I'm sorry." I hold his gaze, watching his amber eyes dance and react.

He nods, accepting my apology. I look around, Marcus' door is open slightly, indicating he's not here.

"Where's Marcus?" I ask, sipping some coffee. It feels weird to be using my left hand for everything right now; I'm so right-handed, it's unreal. Still, the refresher it'll be going through will ensure I'm ambidextrous again in no time flat.

"He went to fetch Keith at around half six this morning. He's at the office. Told me not to come in until around ten. He said they need to get the servers and firewall cleared first. And we didn't want to wake you." He smiles.

"You've been awake since oh-six-hundred?" I ask. He shakes his head.

"I went back to bed for a few extra hours; I've been up for about half an hour, and I put the coffee on when I heard your toilet flush." He grins, and the toaster makes him jump as the muffins pop up.

He butters mine up and brings it over on a small plate, then butters his own. I wait for him to join me before I begin, even though I could have wolfed it down as he prepared his own; my stomach still hasn't stopped complaining.

"So what's the plan? Do we head in?" I ask. He leans back in his chair.

"I was going to ask what you feel up to doing," he says and checks his watch for the time. "We're still about an hour from any contact from Marcus. Until then, we're on our own time. Eric should be here in a few moments though, to check you over."

I nod. "Good. I could do with something stronger than what you managed to get. I'm taking too many to combat the pain levels, and I dislike taking drugs at the best of times." I sip my coffee.

He nods. "Same here. Harder drugs but fewer of them, I am totally with you on that one," he agrees as he folds a muffin into his mouth and eats half of it. I chuckle at the spectacle he makes; he can be funny. Something I didn't see from him in Bosnia.

"Do we have a gym on-site?" I ask, finishing up my muffin. I've only been living here for a few days and now I'm injured; I can't even use one if I wanted to.

Adrian shakes his head. "No, we don't. We have staff memberships for a gym a few streets away from the offices, but that's kinda outta your limits right now."

I grin at him. "Walking isn't. If and when the weather turns, because let's face it, we're in Scotland where we can get all four seasons in a day. I'd like to be able to walk on a treadmill."

"See what Eric says first, but I get what you're saying." He stands and clears the plates into the dishwasher. I finish up the coffee and pour myself another, then I stand up, taking it to the living room, and I find a corner seat, keeping my bad side away from everyone else.

I close my eyes for a moment, absorbing the pain and letting it go.

"Hurting again?" he asks. I nod.

"If I move, it hurts. When I shift positions, it'll hurt. It's going to be this way for a few weeks, at least until the muscles stop bitching."

"Is there anything we can give you?" he enquires as the door to the flat is knocked. I shake my head.

"Nope! Not unless you can give me a new shoulder, or you can rewind time so the five times before and last night didn't happen?" He chuckles and shakes his head whilst he checks on his phone who is at the door. He smiles at me and motions to the door.

He opens it to reveal Eric, and I smile gently at him. Here's to more pain.

Eric firmly straps my arm back across to my opposite shoulder after checking out the joint; he only gently poked me.

That's the most comfortable position for me and even he winced when I went through how it was dislocated for me the first time and the five times again since.

"That small exercise you're doing, keep on doing it. As for the rest of your body, do what you can. I'd avoid crunches or stomach work as it'll pull the shoulder along with it, but some light leg work…" He gives me a look with the word 'light.' He really does mean light! "Will be okay. Walking is good."

I nod in reply and ask him about the pain meds.

"I can give you something better, but here's something I have in mind for you to take in small doses. Every few days only if you're really bad, or it gets knocked somehow, okay? But I'll add in some stronger painkillers for you to take as normal." I nod, understanding, and he writes out a prescription. "These big ones are likely to knock you stupid, so please be very sparing with it, and tell Adrian or Marcus if you take it. You're only getting five doses. It usually has to be ordered in, but if you go to this pharmacy," he writes down the address of a small independent pharmacy just off the high street, "and present it, they'll more likely have it in."

"Thanks!" I say, taking the paper from him. "Five doses only, huh?" I ask, grinning.

He chuckles. "Yep, five, so be selective with them. I'll check back in a few days." Eric gives me an evil grin. "Oh, one, sorry, two more things. No alcohol at all with that drug, and no driving at all with that arm."

I gape at him. "None at all?" I ask.

His grin becomes wider as if he's enjoying telling me that I can't drink alcohol with these drugs. He leans down and whispers, "Don't even sniff the stuff." He winks to imply he's maybe teasing me, then gets up and leaves, patting Adrian on the arm as he goes. I look at the drugs he's given me and gape. I've never heard of it before.

At the pharmacy in question, half an hour later, the pharmacist tells me exactly the same about one drug: No alcohol is to be taken with this, it's to be taken in extreme pain conditions only, and I'm to have my boyfriend be aware I'm taking it. I grin, glancing at Adrian. I know he wouldn't stop me from taking it, but if he's aware, then maybe I might not do crazy stuff. The pharmacist hands me over a small box of the drug and the stronger, but regular painkillers. As soon as I see the horse tablets, I get why. These things are 800mg of drugs. I can see others on the shelf at the back, the same name, but at 400mg. These things are double the dose and they're a good three centimetres long. I nod as I take both boxes, pay, then I tuck the drugs into my clamped arm, and Adrian escorts me out, holding the door for me.

"Interesting looking drugs," he tells me as we head towards the offices, past Flo's. I make agreeing noises, and I find I can't walk as fast as he can. I can't use my arms to get the pace up. Adrian slows to match my pace I can just about manage.

We stop off at Flo's, and Adrian puts in a huge order for brunch, to be delivered in about half an hour for eight of us. Flo grins and thanks him for the business, and we head to the offices to see what catastrophe Marcus has gotten himself and us into.

~Twenty-Five~
Marcus

"Got ya, ya little shit," Keith exclaims as he bangs on the table as the firewall is swept with another of his programmes. That's the fourth Trojan he's found and the second piece of self-developed software he's run on our boxes. He lives and breathes firewalls, and I can only watch as his screen flashes red, then black, then green.

"Okay, that's his nose out of the firewall. Next server," he says. And slowly, we bring the network back up online. The coffee is flowing well, and I watch as Keith loads some software onto our firewall.

"Another beauty of mine," he grins at me. "The firewall software is hackable, it's standard code. My programme," he points to the USB drive, "should make it respond to a DoS attack quicker than usual. If it can't, it'll shut the firewall down, closing all the ports to protect the systems behind it."

"Firewalls do that anyway," I tell him, and he nods.

"Yeah, but by the time they do, the nosy gits are in your network, and you're sitting with a firewall that's rebooted, an error log you have to fish for, and the ports shut down. We don't want them back in," he tells me as he slurps the coffee with a grin that reaches his eyes. He stands up and his rather rotund frame threatens to knock his coffee over. Somehow, he manages to avoid doing that.

"I can write code, but these boxes," I say, pointing to the servers we have, "are a little beyond me."

Keith nods. "Usually, out of the box configurations are okay. I will tell you this, whoever got through, knows what the hell they're doing." I nod in reply, the uneasy feeling I have had since I awoke now intensifies. Given the attack on Adrian and Blythe, this isn't random. It probably never was.

Keith tinkers with the firewall a little more and tells me off for not having a logging server configured. I shrug, but he grins and tells me he'll sort it. The code and electronics I learned, taught myself, didn't include this.

Keith and I talk as we sweep the file server. He feels he's not challenged at McLeod's anymore, and he's too far from most of his immediate family. He hints that he's after a change, and I nod, telling him I'll see what my brother and I can do, enquiring if he's interested in joining us. He is, providing he gets time to develop his little software packages and test them out. I grin; it sounds like a fair trade.

The software he's running on the file server goes mad, beeping and flashing red, as does the programme on the firewall. Keith almost cackles in delight as his software chases down the rogue programmes and kills them off. The firewall isn't letting the traffic out, never mind in. Our I.T. systems are as offline as they can be, almost 1980 solo.

"Having fun?" I ask as I watch the screens flash various colours. He turns the beeping off, telling me it'll be making noises for hours as we slowly sweep the systems here.

"But yeah, it's wonderful to see something you've created, the code, work and do what you meant it to do." I grin; there is a satisfaction in that too. "Cal said you were working on some micro tech?" he enquires as he turns away from the two server screens, but I hesitate. "Oh, we can leave that. The file server is going to take a while, the program will need time to scan everything on it." He grins, and I motion for him to follow, taking him to the lab as his stuff does what it needs to do.

By ten am, the file server is done, after being cleaned, scanned, and goodness knows what else by Keith. We slowly fetch each laptop, tablet, and device that connects through our systems. I check with Bianca what tech is off-site and she tells me nothing should be. I frown; if that's the case, we're missing a device.

I go through the entire cabinet we keep the tech in. It's not shielded yet, but it will be when the new one arrives, hopefully later this morning. I hear voices and go to investigate, finding my brother and Blythe walking in together. I feel a little better, seeing her on her feet, even if her arm is pinned to her. They smile at me, and I grin back from the mezzanine and motion for them to come on up.

Bianca and Alasdair arrive a few moments later, followed by Duncan, and the whole crew is here.

"Let me introduce you to Keith Williamson," I begin, and everyone greets him. He goes to shake everyone's hand and it's comical how he realises he can't shake Blythe's hand. I get jealous for a moment when he takes her offered left hand and kisses the knuckles. I'm not sure who growled louder, Adrian or me.

"Oh, the lady's taken." He grins at my brother, then winks at me. We're not usually possessive, but after the last four days, I guess even our nerves are showing. "The missus will be pleased," he teases, and Blythe grins.

"Okay, here's what we've got," Keith begins, and he takes us through what he's found in simple terms. Bianca asks a few questions, and she nods in understanding as he replies. Even Adrian seems to be following what's being said.

"So no one took a tablet device home? Or has it in their bag, desk, or anywhere else?" I ask. Everyone shakes their head. I look at my brother and Keith. "Then we're missing one," I tell them. Adrian scowls.

"Do you have a list of the devices and known IP addresses?" Keith asks me as he pulls a can of cola from his bag.

"Yeah, we keep it on the cloud," I tell him. He nods.

"When we're done, we'll pull that down. We can give it a little welcome home party when it reconnects to the Wi-Fi. Which, by the way, I want you to change the password on. It needs to be sixteen long, alphanumeric, and strong," he tells me. I nod. The buzzer goes, and Adrian asks for Duncan and Alasdair's help. Five minutes later, they're back with three boxes, and the smell of the food permeates the air. As the software does what it needs to, we refuel.

I grab Adrian's attention, and we head out to our office, quietly talking.

"You've swept the place?" he asks, and I nod. It was the first thing Keith and I did when we entered. "Good," he growls. I can deal with finding electronics, and given the presents that led me to meet Keith, I've swept the place.

"Two things," I begin, looking at my older brother. "I want to offer Keith a job here; I've spoken with Cal, he's okay with it." Adrian nods.

"The second?" he asks, and I grin.

"Blythe..." He nods again. At least we're in agreement about her role in the company as well as our lives.

We discuss the terms we'd like to offer to Keith. Fifteen minutes later, we're making a verbal offer, which he counters and pushes us up a little on the salary. I get a quick nod from Adrian, and I agree with Keith's terms.

"As soon as we're back up, I'll get the contracts drafted," I tell him.

He grins at me. "There are a few support holes I can see you've got," he adds and suggests others he's worked with, those who are good at surveillance, camera work, and surprisingly, a hacker come cryptographer. "One with ethics, she's good."

"A hacker might land us in seriously hot water," Adrian reminds Keith. Keith grins.

"Internet research isn't easy. She won't go into something like the Pentagon or GCHQ, but your mobile phone bill? She can do that. Do you want to know where a call was placed from, or who agreed to meet who where and when because it was discussed on Facebook? Give her a little to go on and watch her work. She's scarily good, but just hacking for hacking sake? Naw…"

"On retainer, perhaps?" I suggested to my brother. "We do have a need for those skills, just not all the time." Keith laughs at my observations.

"That's why she always takes a junior position in the companies. No one ever suspects the Internet Research Assistant or Junior Firewall Engineer to be a hacker or cryptographer, especially when you look at her." Adrian raises his eyebrows at me; Keith knows a heck of a lot about her.

"Who is she to you?" I ask. He winks and leans in.

"The missus," he tells me. I chuckle, but Adrian nods.

"We'd like to meet her, see what she can do," Adrian offers, and Keith agrees.

"Part of what I wrote, other software, is to keep the trackers that go after hackers off of her. I've managed it, but she doesn't do crazy stuff. Other stuff we have access to as normal, she's just good at finding out things you'd never think were relevant." Keith takes a mobile out of his pocket and sends a message to someone. He gets a reply back pretty quickly and grins.

"She's driving up from Galashiels," he tells us. "She'll be here in about an hour. Is that too soon?" he asks. I shake my head, and I have the perfect idea of who can interview her.

Keith heads back to the server room and carries on running his software across all the devices. None of the tablets are running rogue software Trojans and neither are the other laptops.

"They didn't need to," he tells us.

"Because they were getting it from the file server?" asks Blythe as she leans against the doorframe of the small office we're using to sweep the devices. Keith nods.

"Yep. As for your missing device," he says, using one tablet to track the others. Now that our systems are clean again, we can start tracking things. "It was seen here two days ago." And he brings it up. Adrian goes wide-eyed.

"That's the one I was using in Bosnia," he says and gets up, heading to Conference Room Two as I follow hot on his heels. Bianca and Alasdair are there, going through more of the paperwork and there are more woollen threads joining this pile to that pile.

"Bianca, do you remember what happened when we were reading that email update the other day?" Bianca blinks and looks at him.

"Sorry, boss, no." Blythe hmms and I look at her.

"Bianca, recreate it with me," Blythe instructs and I watch as they recreate what happened the other day. Blythe gently pats down on piles of papers and grins when her hand hits a particular pile.

"Could you carefully remove that, please? One hand," she quips, and Bianca nods, then slowly removes the tablet from the half ream of paper it was buried in. "Thanks!"

I sigh, grateful that we're not missing any tech.

The rest of the day, I spend adding to our security as Keith brings us back online. Blythe and Bianca are going through the paperwork; even one-handed, she gets stuck in, and it makes me smile. I'm testing the new cameras when I see a lady pausing outside the boarded-up offices. Then she makes a call, and I hear Keith huffing as he quickly aims for the front door, then he realises it's locked.

"The wife," he puffs as he sees me behind the reception desk. I grin and get the keys to let her in. As I open the door to allow her entry, the elevator pings and the new sonic/EMP bomb-proof storage cabinet is wheeled out on a trolley. I call out for Adrian to come and help once I've signed for it, and we're busy setting it up and securing the tech for the rest of the day.

By eight pm, we're all tired. Blythe interviewed Keith's wife, who frankly, you could pass in the street and not notice. Rebekah, Bianca, and Blythe chatted on the sofa, then they got Bekah in linking and finding digital connections to all the printed paperwork. She did that and then went digging on her own. Just as we're clearing up for the day, she tells us what she's found. Adrian quipped they were the "Three Bees," and the nickname seems to have stuck.

She's an older lady with grey, straight hair. Totally not what you expect a hacker to look like.

"The messages you've received have come from one of three devices. I've gotten Keith to flag these up on the firewall if they come through, but also on your tablets, like this." She shows us one screen where it's in a royal blue. "It'll be more noticeable that way, and they seem to switch the devices each time. Never the same device in a row and never the same location in a row."

"The emails tell you that?" Blythe enquiries. She's looking tired; her shoulder must be giving her grief, but she's not being snippy.

"No, but what I can find on them does." Bekah winks, and Blythe grins. My phone pings, and it's from the window company. I read it out.

"We have the replacement panels for the bottom of your windows ready to go. We can be on-site at eight am, if you can be there at that time. Please confirm." I look at Adrian and he nods.

"We can be here at eight am," he confirms and I send that information back.

"One other thing…" I say and everyone stops. I have the anti-listening device already on and nod to Adrian who closes the office door, ensuring that we're secure. Everyone looks at us as Adrian comes to stand near my chair.

Adrian carries on our train of thought. "Things are crazy right now. What's happening isn't random. We're," Adrian looks at me and Blythe, "being targeted. If anyone doesn't want to work here anymore, let us know now." He looks around at everyone but no one moves a muscle. Everyone is looking at him, the big, tall, ex-pilot. "Thank you. Secondly, if anything were to happen to either Marcus or I, or you can't get something approved by either of us, Blythe is the next in line." I watch her as she blinks and gapes. We didn't tell her we'd be making it formal this soon.

"Guys," she begins, but Bianca cheers.

"Good for you!" Bianca offers her a gentle hug, not nudging Blythe's bad side. I look at Alasdair and Duncan, who both look relieved and congratulate her. Bekah grins and snuggles into Keith. For now, our little work family has something to celebrate.

~Twenty-Six~
Blythe

Adrian's announcement at the end of yet another hard, weird day, leaves me feeling discombobulated; they made no indication they'd be telling the team today. They had me interview Bekah, pretty much in the style I was interviewed, which was easy. She's got skills we can use and having her dig into the digital versions of the communications we had on paper was the best task I thought to start her on. She found some good answers and another clue. I just wish I could see how the damn pieces fit together already. Sherlock would live up to her name at this point I'm sure.

My neck hurts, my shoulder aches, but not as much as yesterday. I swallow two of the stronger painkillers, but save the heavy-duty ones for another day and time. Ten minutes later and I'm happier, the pain is reduced, and I can focus on what we're needing to do. Keith and his wife sort out the tech, stacking it into the draining racks we're using to hold the tablets that we'll keep in the new anti-EMP cabinet.

Keith was travelling to Hamilton one day, staying for four, then coming home. His wife is as pleased as punch that she has got a new steady job and that he's going to be home more often. From not seeing each other often to being under each other's feet almost, it's a huge change, but they seem happy as they've been teasing each other about it.

Efficiently, Keith and Bekah get the cabinet set up, everything has its place, and everything is in its place. Adrian calls it a night soon after and we depart.

"Dashcam!" I exclaim, just as we're locking up. Keith nods.

"I secured that system right after the file server, so you can review the footage when you want now. Good night!" he calls out, taking Bekah home. Although Adrian and I walked to the offices again today, I'm too beat, tired, and sore to walk home.

"Take-out," Marcus states. I laugh.

"Try doing some food shopping so we don't get fat," I tease. He grins at me and guides me to the BMW. Then, he takes us home. An hour after we've left the office, Marcus is gently shaking me awake. It takes me a few moments to register Adrian is carrying large shopping bags past the car window.

"What?" I ask, confused and bewildered. As Marcus helps me out of the car, he cuddles up to me on my good side.

"You fell asleep. I'm guessing the painkillers are to blame?"

"Not sure…I took two standards," I inform him. Higher-strength co-codamol is excellent when it's not the weaker over the counter strength.

"Well, we did some food shopping, as you suggested," he tells me and motions to the boot where there are two other huge bags. Marcus hands me the keys and takes the bags out. Once he's clear, I close and lock the car, then we follow Adrian up to the flat.

The guys unpack and put things away, and I quickly scan through what they've brought. As they stack the fridge, freezer, and cupboards, I pull things out to make a bolognese sauce.

"We brought some," Marcus tells me, holding up two pre-made jars. I begin to tell him off, in Italian. He gapes at me and turns to his brother, who holds his hands up and laughs.

"Told ya not to get that stuff," Adrian quips, chuckling as my Italian expletives fill the air.

"Why would you buy that crap?!" I exclaim and forget for a moment that the sling is strapping my arm to me as I try to gesticulate. I wince but carry on with my small tirade anyway. "Honestly, so much salt and water…" I shake my head and begin to pull out other ingredients and tools.

"Do you have a blender?" I ask, switching back to English and Marcus finds it. It can't have been used for ages; it's covered in dust and crap. I look at it and him, and he frowns, then pulls it apart and starts washing it. I find the fresh ingredients from the bags and make up some fresh sauce once the blender is clean.

"Time to learn how to do it from scratch," I tell them. I walk them through what my grandparents taught Annie to make, showing them tricks like how microwaving the garlic cloves for twenty seconds loosens the skin, or that you can add fresh herbs to the tin of plum tomato, a little salt, tomato puree to thicken it, and since they bought it, one of those jars. As the sauce is mixing in the blender, I get Marcus to dice an onion and start frying it while the kettle boils.

I walk the boys through it step by step. It's not fresh beef tomatoes off the vine at Grandma's, but it would be close enough to get a pass from her. I ask Marcus to start browning the mince as I add some cornflour to the sauce to thicken it again as the jar stuff is too watery. Once the beef mince is browned off, I toss the sauce over it and get Marcus to stir it all in with the chopped mushrooms, slowly.

"We can let that simmer for ten minutes, while someone starts the pasta. What type did you get?" Adrian points me to the cupboard with almost every design of dried durum wheat pasta I've seen. I grin. "Did you get any garlic bread, mozzarella, or parmesan?" I ask, hopefully. He points to a double packet of baguette garlic bread that's fresh, and I ask Marcus to turn the oven on high. I pick out pasta I can stab with one hand; spaghetti is too much work for a single-handed woman.

Half an hour after we started boiling the pasta, we've cleared our bowls. The boys at least have decent pasta serving dishes, and while it wasn't the restaurant standard of a platter with this and that, it was good, filling, home. Adding cheese to the insides of the garlic bread as it cooked helped fill us; I was ravenous. Two baguettes that dripped in garlic butter and cheese, between the three of us, was enough. Then Adrian holds up a supermarket version of tiramisu and I grin, nodding. At least I won't get drunk on that version.

Hours later, we're chilling, and Marcus asks me a question that comes out of the blue.

"Did you ever get a message from me, after you returned to Lossie?" he asks as he holds his beer. I've stuck to squash because of the drugs, and I see Adrian has too. Marcus has hardly touched his drink; I can see the bottle is half full and there aren't any droplets on it anymore.

"No...I never did. I didn't think to try and stay in touch with you. I wish I had," I lament. "You tried to reach me?" I ask, catching up with what he's saying, and he nods.

"I just assumed you didn't want to," he replies with a sullen voice.

"Far from it." I reach across and touch his face with my working arm. He leans into my forehead, and we sigh together. "Do you remember who you spoke with?" I ask, wondering if he got through to just the gatehouse or my actual office. He shakes his head.

"Nope, sorry, can't say that I do, not after all this time," he explains.

"What matters more," says Adrian as he comes to sit behind me, gently on my bad side, "is that we're together now." I can feel Adrian's hands around my waist, his hands radiating warmth through to me, even through my clothing. I want to lean back into him, but my shoulder pain is too great.

"Easy, Bee, I just want to cuddle into you, okay?"

I nod, aware of Marcus' words, but I can feel the heat from Adrian. I wiggle back, gently leaning against the larger of them, then Marcus is on my left, and I'm warm. It's intimate, just cuddling on the sofa. I see Marcus reach over and press a button for the blinds, which turn to close. It's the last thing I remember.

~Twenty-Seven~
Adrian

Marcus chuckles a few moments after Blythe cuddles into us both. I frown at him, wondering what on earth he finds funny.

"She's spark out," he tells me and I grin in response. She pushed herself today and I wonder just how many painkillers she's had. Marcus helps get her standing, and we tell her to walk with us to bed. She does, but it's slow going.

Getting her into bed and out of those jean things was interesting. We left the top half of her clothes on; I know she picked stuff that was comfortable to wear all day. Picking up the drugs from her bedside table, I can see she's only taken four of the standard ones through the whole day. Marcus is still sitting on the bed, watching her.

"Is her breathing normal?" I ask. We watch her for a few moments and her breathing is conducive with sleep. I sigh, pleased that she just seems to be tired or exhausted from the continuous pain.

Marcus gets up, and we leave her to rest, cancelling the movie we were going to put on. We put on the sports channel and chill out.

The following morning, I'm up and out of the flat to be at the office at eight am for the window fitters' arrival. They're on time, efficient, and they begin with the doors. At least it gives an indication of us being open for business. It's another weekday, and the fitters and I engage in idle chatter as Alasdair and Bianca arrive. Motioning for Alasdair to follow me, I head to the office area with him following, leaving Bianca to do what she does best.

"Can you pull the Defender's dashcam from the other night out of the company cloud? Take a look at it, see if you can see who the other driver was, will you?"

Alasdair nods, giving me a firm slap on my arm, and I go to grab a laptop as I head back to the reception area.

As the last new window is being secured in the door, frosted glass the right way around, Alasdair grabs my attention from the mezzanine balcony. I nod, check Bianca is okay and head up to see what he's found.

"You're gonna love this," he tells me as we head into one of the smaller conference rooms. The largest is still set up with all the paperwork threads and we've left that alone. Alasdair turns the lights off and I watch the dashcam footage be projected onto the white wall, keeping my nerves, anger and frustration at bay.

"Took me a few times to see this," he says as he pauses it. I watch as Blythe turns the car around and faces the Ford pickup, both cars heading right for each other. "Here," he says, pointing at the driver's face.

"Obscured," I say, knowing that the image wouldn't be movie quality.

"Huh uh... Watch," he growls as he unpauses it. A few seconds later, the man, for it clearly is, can be seen behind the wheel of the car. It's not David Lloyd.

"That's not who we thought it would be," I share with him. Alasdair grumbles.

"We need Bekah to go find him, but I'll tell you now, with those clothes, he's in our industry." I nod in reply and absorb his words. Now I really want to find whoever is behind this. I want to know why.

Bekah and Keith arrive as the fitters are leaving. The fitters told me that they'll be back next week with the other windows, which we have to wait for as they're being made up. I nod, thank them, and send them on their way. As soon as I can, I ask Bekah to check in with Alasdair, telling her what room he's in.

"You know, we could do with an incident room," Bianca chimes up as she hands me a coffee.

"Where would we put such a room?" I ask. She smiles at me and motions for me to follow but stays on this floor. The servers, working offices, and two of the conference rooms are on the mezzanine, but the others are down here.

"Knock these walls out and make this whole section open plan. We can see who is coming and going anyway," she tells me. I contemplate her idea and I like it; the rooms are too pokey, something I don't like. I knock on the wall and Bianca laughs. "Stud walls, boss. Easy to knock down and tidy away. It'll mean new carpet or laminate, but that's okay. We can do most of this work."

I smile at her and nod. "We can," I confirm, it's something we have to do when we're putting cameras into client houses or premises. Bianca walks back to the reception desk and I follow.

"And we've had some speculative CV's come through that would suit camera operators and some of the other roles that were discussed yesterday, I've picked out the best ones," she hands me a small pile of papers, "I thought you'd want to look through them first."

I grin and thank her. She heads to her desk and busies herself on her computer, her fingernails tapping the keyboard at a decent rate, and I walk to my office with that sound reverberating in my ears.

I pop my head into the work area; Bekah and Alasdair are there with the radio on low. Keith isn't with them.

"Server room, adding in a logging server," Bekah tells me without looking up.

"I won't ask how you knew I was looking for him," I state clearly. I was going to ask where he was. Bekah hits the keys on her keyboard and looks across at me.

"Too many years of Keith and his work colleagues, I'm well practised," she tells me with a broad smile. "I'll let you know when I get a hit on that driver," she adds and goes back to her dual display. Now that I think about it, we should have this floor more open-plan too, though, at times, I like having a private word with my brother.

~Twenty-Eight~
Blythe

I stretch and wince, but breathe out deeply as I slowly awaken. I glance at the clock and it's gone nine am. What the ever-living hell?! I jump out of bed, and my shoulder twinges, then I slump back onto the bed. Okay, that's not a wise move.

There's a knock at the door and Marcus steps in.

"Morning! Coffee is on, need some help?" he asks and I nod.

"Yeah, please! What happened last night?" I enquire in a questioning tone.

"I shut the blinds, you went to sleep. I think the painkillers, food, and being snuggled between us got to you, finally." Marcus grins as he helps pull my knickers off and I use the toilet. It's just as well that they've seen me naked.

"Could you help me shower?" I ask, nervously, though I have no idea why. In the military, you showered at least every day, mostly because you needed it. Here, right now, not so much because of my injury and a lack of actual exercise. I am now starting to hate being in my own skin.

Marcus chuckles and nods. "Sure, I'll just grab my stuff," he tells me, and I gape at him. "Can't help you fully clothed, babe," he says with a wink, cupping my jaw and kissing me. He still has that silly grin on his face as he goes to his own room and a few moments later, he's back with a towel, clean clothes and his shower gel.

Fifteen minutes later, I'm wrapped up in a towel, being gently dried by Marcus who is making it very hard to concentrate or for me to not jump him. The towel around his middle only adds to my distraction as his entire upper body is just an eye fest. From biceps that bulge just by using them, to pecs that almost dance on cue, down to his V with tattooed words scattered across his very toned and not too pale body. The guy shaved my legs, my armpits (after I gently moved my bad shoulder), washed and conditioned my hair, and did everything that I would do and how I wanted it. Every touch sent zings through me, lighting me up, and my shoulder hurts from the tension of trying not to react to him.

As he helps me into fresh clothes, I can't help but be thankful that he's here.

"Thank you," I tell him in a voice that's a little husky. Marcus grins at me and stands up, towering over me. His six-foot-three frame is just as intimidating and beautiful as it was the first time we were together. He nods and steps in to strap my arm to me now that my top half is dressed. As he comes around to tie the sling back on, my breath hitches.

"Easy, Bee. I don't know where your mind has gone, but now," he says, coming before me, kissing my nose, "ain't the time. Give yourself a few days at least, aye?" He looks at me intently, and I'm grateful for his care, appreciating his intimacy but frustrated I can't act on these feelings.

"Sex with you is great, better when Adrian is with us. But…" He pauses and I wonder what he's going to add that will be a kicker. "You're not in a state to go there quite yet. We know, we get it. And we'll find the git that did that to you, trust me."

He kisses me on the mouth and it's gentle, undemanding, intimate.

"Not everything is about sex. We'll just bank that up for the next time we're together and you're able, okay?" His expressive, charming, deep amber eyes, so like his brother's, search mine. I nod and just enjoy the next kiss he gives me.

An hour after I wake up, we're in the office. Marcus put the brunch order in on our way past Flo's, and as we arrive, we both comment on the new glass in the doors and how much better it looks already. Marcus grins then holds the door open for me. We call hello to Bianca and she tells Marcus and I that we're needed in room two. We nod, wondering what wonderful delights await us.

Alasdair is there with Adrian, going over the dashcam footage from two days ago. I wince in reflection as I watch the car tip over. Like any car crash, you want to look away, but you just can't. I watch it again as Alasdair replays certain parts and as he does so, I get desensitised to it. Now, it's like watching a customer's security footage—just a part of the job.

"Bekah is running the plates through DVLA, but I'll bet you a bottle of Single Malt, it's been nicked or cloned." Alasdair's pretty certain on that and with English licence plates, I can see why he'd guess at that. Adrian shows me the still of the guy behind the wheel and asks Marcus if he knows who it might be. He shakes his head, as do I. It's not a face I recognise.

We exhaust the dashcam footage and Marcus takes us through the new camera setups. He pulls up the new outside ones and my heart skips a beat as I see Annie walking past.

"I'll be back!" I say, grabbing my phone and calling my best friend.

"What's going on?" I call out as she answers. "Wait up!"
"Where are ye?" she asks as I make my way down the stairs.
"Coming out of the renovated offices, hauld up, aye?"

"Okay, see you in two," she says and hangs up. I know she'll go mental when she sees me like this, especially since I didn't tell her sooner.

"What the bleedin' hell!" Annie scolds as she marches towards me as soon as she sees me. "How the heck did ye do it again?!" She helps me button my jacket and we walk down Princes Street together. We don't go into Flo's; Annie tells me she's on a cleaning products mission for one of the safehouses she's at today.

"Aye...we got followed, and I took the fight to them. Remind me next time, not to do something so daft?" I lament in a chuckle, trying to lighten the mood. "Tossing a ninety onto its side isn't something I wanna repeat," I tell her. She goes wide-eyed for a moment and then shakes her head.

"Never seen one of those on their side! How are ye coping?" she asks me as she takes a basket from the doorway and I walk around with her so we can talk.

"Doing okay. The guys are helping," I discreetly tell her. She nods and leans into me.

"They've seen it all afore," she winks at me, and I can't help but laugh. She pulls out a list from her pocket and gets what she needs. Annie has to be in a very particular mood to window shop; today isn't one of those days.

"Aye," I reply, grinning. Then I realise I need some personal items, and I get them here; I can at least spare the boys from fetching these for me.

"But I wanted to tell ye, and I just happened to see you walk past as we were being shown the camera updates on the building,"

"There's CCTV on it?" she asks. I nod as she pays for her goods. As we're leaving the shop, she motions for me to join her under the shopping area's canopy.

"Afore we go back and they see us chatting… You *are* okay, aye?"

I nod. "I'd rather not have this," I nod to the strapped arm and hurt shoulder, "but it cannae be helped. Someone is gunning for us, or maybe just Aid. I wanna find out who; I have this need to protect them. If it were someone you cared for, ye'd do the same, aye?"

She pats me on the good arm and smiles warmly. "If ye need some help," she offers. I nod, praying I don't but understanding I might and the offer is there.

~Twenty-Nine~
Marcus

I watch on camera as Blythe leaves our offices and heads out to meet a woman, who, upon receiving a call, stops and turns back towards the building. Blythe practically ran to catch up with her, and they hug, the other woman does Blythe's coat up for her, and then they walk down Princes Street. I can sense my brother behind me.

"That's Annie," he tells me, and I turn to his voice.

"The one that was pregnant?"

He nods. "Aye, her bestie. Dinnae fash," he grins at me and I breathe out the breath I was holding.

"When did ye meet her?" I ask, I was gone for a whole day and beyond Blythe getting hurt, I was told nothing significant had happened. Being introduced to your girlfriend's best friend as one of her lovers in my mind is significant.

"When ye were in Hamilton. We went for food at Flo's, Annie was getting stuff for her daughter, and bumped into us," he grins, "And afore ye ask, no, she'll not work for us. I already asked." He winks. I grin; our minds are on the same thought path.

"What kind of job is she doing?" I ask and Adrian comes over to quietly tell me, his voice low and discreet. As he explains, my mind boggles that someone would even do that, or that it's even necessary. I immediately think of all the ways we can secretly help and I go to jot some ideas down in my notebook. Only, it's not where it ought to be.

"Aid, where's my notebook?" I ask and think back to when I had it last, up in the lab; then I brought it down to our offices, I'm sure. I know I didn't take it to Hamilton or take it to the flat. I began searching for it with Adrian's help. Bekah joins in when she realises we're looking for something, and I explain what it is we're searching for.

"That was in the room upstairs, I'm sure," Bekah says. "I'll go check." And she bounces off as quickly as she can. Five minutes later, she comes back down but shrugs, shaking her head. I head up and try to find it, but it's not here, not even in the secret cabinet we have behind fire-retardant walls.

I'm scratching my head when Blythe comes in. Blythe somehow looks different after her chat with Annie, more fired up, but calmer somehow. Focused.

"Where the hell..?" I ponder, trying to recall things.

"What are you looking for?" she asks me, touching me on my arm, grounding me and sending sparks through me at the same time. I take a deep breath.

"My ideas notebook. It's got a mixture of a wood and leather cover." I stop as she grins and points. I can't see what she's pointing at though, and I tell her so.

She laughs, calls me a typical man, then walks across to one of the workbenches. Wedged between a steel toolbox, a microwelding station, and the wall is my notebook. No way did I leave it there. I blink.

"Someone has moved that," I tell them. Adrian doesn't ask if I am sure. Blythe looks between us, as if working out if I'm mad or not, then she nods.

"Okay, let's find out who and why," she says. We head back to our office and pull up the cameras from before I left for Hamilton. We watch that room camera until we see Bianca come in for the pile of paperwork, along with Alasdair. As they gather the paperwork, I see Alasdair tuck it in where we found it.

"Was that what you've been tearing the place up to find?" he asks, appearing behind us and looking concerned. "I moved it there when we were clearing the paperwork out. I've seen you scribble things into it before; I didn't want it ending up dismantled in the conference room, so I put it there. You always seem to want it when you're up there and you were working at that station last..."

I nod, relieved. "Yeah, just not where I was sure I left it," I tell him and he laughs.

"Can tell you never served," he tells me with a grin. "Ye always put things back where they should go, that way, they're never lost," he quips as he leaves the room, calling to Bianca that we've found it. Blythe and Adrian smother their chuckles.

"Listen," Blythe says, taking in a deep breath. "I get you're on edge, we all are. But, dinnae start getting all paranoid, please?" She reaches out to me and rubs my arm, the same way I rubbed hers only this morning.

"I'll try. I'm a bit lost without this," I explain to her. Adrian gets it; he's lived with me writing my electronic ideas in this book for decades. I've got the pages from years back stored very far away from here. I rebind this tome whenever I need to.

Blythe smiles at me. "Well, you're not lost anymore! Wanna get that idea down afore ye forget it?" she encourages, handing me a pencil. I nod and remember my conversation with Adrian about Annie. Oh yes, that was the idea!

Two hours later, sitting in the communal work area, I finish drawing out the plans for the device that came to me thanks to Adrian telling me about Annie's work.

"What is it?" asks Blythe, looking at the drawing and the pages of notes that hold my brainstorming session. She looks totally bewildered.

"Credit card-sized transmitter and locator beacon. I just need to write the software for it." I grimace. It's the worst part of electronics sometimes, especially with the ideas I have for this device.

Keith coughs and grins. "What do you want it to do?" I go through some ideas I've had and as I list them, Keith adds to them. "Should be able to tinker with that tomorrow, software-wise, if you can do the hardware?" he offers.

I grin at him, pleased I recruited him and his wife. It's late afternoon and I don't fancy starting either aspect right now.

"Where do you build them?" he asks. I look up, and Keith gapes at me. "No backup site?" he lowers his tone to ask, and I shake my head. "You need to get that sorted, and I've got an idea." He motions for me to go around to his desk. The three of us do and we hear his idea of a place in Merchiston that's industrial, small units that already have security on site.

"To hide it, you could do with it being rented by a cover company, just so it's not obvious," he suggests. "We did that at Cal's sites." I nod. I'm aware that Callum McLeod has a few backup electronics sites, especially since I borrowed one.

"We need to write this up." I look at Adrian, who looks at Blythe, who looks at me.

"As if I can with one hand," she tells me with a grin on her face, which makes Keith, Bekah, and everyone chortle too. "Oh sure…laugh at the invalid," Blythe moans, laying on the sympathy rather thick. I grin.

"Our backer should be able to help on that," I state. Keith nods.

"He made Cal's stuff happen quickly too." He grins and gathers his stuff together. "Shall we catch up tomorrow?" he asks. I nod, and everyone collectively agrees. Then we secure everything, Adrian enforcing the clear desk policy. Once that's done and we're happy with the state the offices are in, we head home.

We walk down Princes Street, one of us on either side of Blythe. We talk about uniforms, specifically, what we want it to look like now we're getting more staff. We discuss polo shirts, combat trousers, colours and then, as soon as we're in our building, the discussion turns to food and what exactly Adrian or I are going to be cooking.

Blythe shrugs as best she can with one arm and we help her take off her coat and shoes. I hold my arms out, inviting her to cuddle into me and she does. Gently I embrace her, breathing in the same scent I've had in my nose all day since I helped her shower this morning.

"How are you doing? How's the pain?" I ask her as we break apart. Adrian invites her for a hug while I take off my jacket and remove my shoes. I might not have served, but I understand my brother's need for tidiness. At work, in my workspace, I prefer it if things aren't touched. My chaotic organisation is key to my thinking and creativity.

"Are you calmer now?" she asks me as Adrian lets her go. I nod.

"Yeah, I can't stand people moving my things, especially my notebook." I pat the book with affection.

"This idea in Merchiston," Blythe begins and we nod. "Why haven't you done it before now?" she asks as she puts on her slippers.

"We've not needed to, being honest," I answer as we walk through to the kitchen. I wait as Adrian pulls out a few ideas from the cupboard. One is homemade Chinese, the other is butter chicken. The packet of chicken and rice is off to the side, so it'll be something with rice and chicken.

Blythe looks through the various sauces we bought the other day.

"You decide, I like everything on offer." She grins at us and we chuckle, aware that she's not just talking about the food on offer. I roll my eyes, close them, and lean out to grab one of the sauce packets. Sticky Teriyaki is the one I've picked, and Adrian nods.

"Could you put the others away?" he asks me and I nod as he sets the kettle boiling and grabs the wok from the side. We show off a little as Blythe sits at the kitchen island and watches us make dinner. We could set the table, but we're more comfortable here, collectively together.

"Tell us about your life," Adrian suggests as he cooks. I offer Blythe a glass of wine, but she shakes her head.

"Painkillers means I can't," she tells me. I nod in understanding, and Adrian says he won't either. I see the look in his eyes; he's doing it to support Blythe because she can't. I put the wine away and organise soft drinks for us all. Neither opts for the fizzy stuff, though I love it.

"It'll rot yer teeth," Blythe teases, and I check the sugar levels. There are none and I counter it back to her. "And the salt level?" she enquires, to which I blink.

"Salt, in these?" I ask. She nods and I read the ingredients. Well, hell, there is a little salt in this one.

"Water's better for ye." She winks and laughs as I pull a sulky face. We spend dinner teasing each other gently, but Blythe tells us about her Italian father meeting her Scottish mother, spending summers at her grandparents' place and playing pool with her brother when it rained like cats and dogs.

"That's why you're so good," I admire. She nods and shrugs as best she can.

"And what did you butt heads with my wee brother about?" She nudges Adrian as she asks. He huffs.

"Come on, tell her," I encourage him.

He sighs and begins to clear away the dirty plates. I know how he's going to tell her. He'll do chores and talk, the same way he always has when he needs to open up emotionally.

"It was about someone on base, I can't even remember who," he begins, but I scoff.

"Rosie 'Duckie' Mallard," I remind him. I recall exactly why and grin as he smirks at me. "Honestly, bro," I comment, glancing at Blythe.

"Yeah, Rosie 'Duckie' Mallard. She was with us for a wee bit, there aren't a lot of women in the 47th, but she made the cut. She was paired with your brother for a flight and messed up, due to nerves she was being assessed, along with yer brother. She liked him romantically, so she told me afterwards. What she did wrong was nothing life-threatening or dangerous. The idea was that two would fly a C130 out, the other pair would bring it back. One of four. Theirs was the first one out, and I was assessing along with another instructor."

Blythe nods, listening. She's watching him as he talks, either distracted by what he's doing or by him physically.

"Only, he got snippy at her, nerves I assume, but I spoke up that he shouldn't speak to a colleague that way. Even if she had seriously messed up, there are ways to talk to someone. I just objected to how he spoke to her in an assessment flight and I put it in my notes. He tried to get me to withdraw it and I refused. We've never seen eye to eye since."

Blythe's eyes are wide. "Sounds like By, when he was younger. When was this?" she asks.

Adrian pauses and works it back. "A few years before you came down that one time. Grievance…" He pauses as Blythe reacts to the nickname by pursing her lips together, her eyes light up and she tries not to laugh. Clearly, she had the same one up in Lossiemouth, and he chuckles. "You had the same name, huh?" he confirms as he rinses out the wok. I grab a tea towel and begin drying.

"Yep. Anyway, please go on," she encourages and looks at him whilst he composes himself and remembers where he was in his tale.

Adrian grins a broad smile that makes his eyes dance. "Anyway, yeah, Grievance and I avoided each other after that. I had a few more years of experience than he did. If we were paired together, and we mostly weren't, we kept it cordial. Or, tried to," Adrian says with mirth. "Not that we came to blows or anything, but… Hell, does he know you're injured? Do your parents?"

After spending a few hours getting background stories, I hadn't even begun to wonder if she's told her folks.

She shakes her head. "They're in Italy now, nothing they can do for me that you two aren't already doing." She grins. That smirk reaches her eyes, her nostrils flare, but I daren't ask if her family would get naked with her in the shower too.

~Thirty~
Blythe

The rest of the week is absorbed by Marcus or Adrian talking with clients from enquiry forms, or Bekah and Keith doing what they do. I don't understand firewalls, but making Marcus' little gadget work seems to have absorbed Keith's usual, nervous energy.

Friday afternoon arrives, and Marcus and Keith are in the lab upstairs. Adrian is in the office; the door is closed as he's working on the backup lab business case. I know he wants to give it to Tony over the weekend. That leaves Alasdair, Bekah, Bianca, and I doing whatever it is we need to. Bekah confirmed that the licence plates were cloned; the real owner in Burton on Trent was mortified when he helped the police with their enquiries. I've run out of things I can do one-handed when Bianca tells me that Eric is here to see me.

I roll my eyes, knowing that he's going to start doing some light movements with my arm, and he'll make sure the guys know I'm supposed to be doing them. Not that I'd skimp on it; not doing physio work when you've been told only serves to detriment oneself, and I need out of this damn sling.

I greet Eric, and we head to the smaller conference rooms. Carefully, he unbinds me and starts moving my arm and shoulder, slowly this way and that. I wince at some of the movements, but I expect the pain.

"Well, you've done this before. How does it feel?" He sits on one of the chairs and waits for me to answer. I move my arm without the aid of the other for the first time in weeks and lay it on my lap.

"Where I'd expect it to be. Hurts when I move it, but I know it'll lessen off. As much as I want out of that sling," I look at the faded piece of triangle fabric like it's something from Alien or Halloween that's about to eat me, "I still feel I need it. I can't turn or rotate it in certain ways, say, to wash my hair or condition it." Eric nods as he looks at me.

"How have you managed it then?" he asks me, with no hint of sarcasm or knowledge of my living situation on his face.

"The boys have helped," I offer. He blinks.

"You're staying with them, of course, I forgot. That's nice of them." He smiles, gets up, and talks as he gathers most of his equipment together. "Here's what I need you to do, and this is unique for you because you've had so many dislocations. I want you to take the sling off for about half an hour each day and gently go through the rotations as we've just done. I know your pain threshold is high, but don't push it." He gives me a look that reminds me of my grandparents, and I smile.

"Yes, Doc." I grin at him, and he raises his eyebrows at me. "Thanks."

I look at the sling and decide it needs a wash. Or replaced.

"Oh," Eric says as he closes his bag. "Let's get this style of sling onto you." He hands me a high sling and a shoulder support strap. "You might find either of these to be more comfortable at night, but I'll let you try them both. We'll decrease their use from next week." I nod and tell him I want to try the shoulder support. Something that makes my arm or me look normal has to be worth a try before the other.

Eric is the perfect professional; he slides the sling onto me and helps me get dressed. It's like wearing a gun holster, only the strap is over my shoulder, holding it in, rather than tucking a gun into my side to conceal it. Those days are long gone.

I grin at him, take the old sling and think about binning it. Something stops me and I'm not sure what. I fold it up and tuck it into my back jean pocket. He shakes my left hand and we head out. As Eric is leaving, I hear Bekah cry out in jubilation, and Bianca and I look up to the mezzanine floor, wondering what the heck just happened.

Eric leaves and we lock the office door, then Bianca and I join the others in finding out what's made Bekah's afternoon. It's even made Marcus, Keith and Adrian leave their respective hidey holes. Both the guys give me a look when they realise my arm isn't in the usual high sling.

"Eric was here, tell you later," I whisper to them and get a nod in return. Whatever it is Bekah has discovered needs to be addressed first.

We crowd around her and when Marcus and I see her screen, we understand why she's so jubilant. For over a week, she's been hunting for this guy. Now, we have a social media profile of him. The guy I played car chicken with has a name.

Adrian squeezes her shoulder. "Well done," he praises her and she beams up at him. It's not David Lloyd, but apparently, Andrew Lloyd. A cousin.

"Now, here's what's interesting. His social profile is an old one; it's not active anymore."

"So how did you find him?" I ask, intrigued.

Bekah grins. "Backups and archives. Everything someone does digitally leaves a footprint. Even if they delete it, it leaves behind a marker. I just know how to find the markers."

"Not interesting enough," Adrian pipes up and Bekah grins.

"What Blythe asked me, no. But, this is: he was generally discharged from the Army five years ago, six years into his contract." She keeps Adrian's focus as she says what she's found. He looks at me, but I have no words.

"Can you find out what for?" I ask, understanding that he didn't do his job and was asked to leave the military. Not a common occurrence. She shakes her head.

"What little I can find is redacted and I am not busting into GCHQ or the MOD for anyone," she emphatically states.

"We wouldn't ask you to. Pity we don't know anyone," Adrian begins and then he's holding my gaze. "What? You have got a really funny look on your face, Bee," he says, and Marcus reaches up to touch my hand. I glance at him and smile.

"I might have a way," I muse. "I need to make a call and scrounge for a favour," I share. Taking my phone out of my pocket, I send Annie a text. Social media and Annie don't get on, mainly due to her work style and what she does, so it's plain text, unencrypted. However, on this occasion, she indulges me and sends me back the information I ask for on an encrypted message. Then, I send a message to him on the encrypted software.

B: Long time to speak. Sherlock gave me your number. Need some info on someone who was in the Army but was generally discharged. File redacted, need the skinny. Can you help?

It's as we're walking home with Andrew Lloyd's picture in the company group chat, that I get a response from him.

Unknown: Bloody hell! Long time no speak. Having a swift half in Auld Hundred. Alone.

I stop and look at the brothers, showing them the text reply. They nod.

"We'll be around," they tell me and we split up as I meander down the paths and make my way to meet him, as instructed.

When I enter the pub, I order a small cola and find the guy in question, sitting in a quiet corner. It's still early enough to be drinking and not be too crowded. I choose the table next to him and pull up Lloyd's details on my phone. Discreetly, I show it to him.

"Details?" he asks, and I tell him what we know—rank, unit and number included.

"I'll see what I can do. No promises," he tells me.

I wink. "None expected, appreciate all you can do." I grin. He nods towards my shoulder as he sips his pint.

"How'd ye dae that?" he asks. I grin and tap the screen, hinting at Andrew Lloyd, before putting it away in my pocket.

"He tried to drive us off the road," I share as I finish my drink. "He won, this time." Munroe growls, hence his nickname. I nod to him, take my empty glass back to the bar and leave without looking back at Wolf.

Friday night we decide is steak and movie night. Adrian pulls out the steaks from the fridge and lets them warm up to room temperature. Marcus gets the fries on and I'm left to watch them bustle about. I realise that I'm going to struggle to cut up my food and laugh as I realise it, making the guys look at me weirdly.

I wave my one good hand at them. "Invalid here," I tell them, and they laugh and being swines, they wave back with their left hand, making me laugh.

"Please tell me you have peppercorn sauce?" I beg. They look through cupboards but shake their heads. I roll my eyes and pop my shoes and jacket back on, then I go on the hunt for some and make it back just as the steaks are going into the very hot pan.

I get the sauce warmed up on the hob and as Adrian cooks the steaks, Marcus dishes up the fries, then we sit down to eat. We chat and wind each other up; the guys help me by cutting up the steak for me. We talk about what Eric made me do, the sling changes and my need to be out of it at last.

They pick a movie and I nestle between them both on the sofa. I don't mind comedies, but Will Ferrell makes my skin crawl. I am sure I spend more time with my eyes closed or laughing at the boys laughing at the antics on the screen than I do actually watching the movie. By the time the torture is over and they've berated me for not enjoying their taste in movies, it's dark. Marcus closes the blinds and we head to bed, and for the first time since I hurt my shoulder, I feel I can join them.

    Both kiss me goodnight, sensually, then they snuggle down with me in the middle. I'm not sure if I'm frustrated with just the kissing or if I'm relieved, dressed as I am in a soft bra and knickers. I don't get much time to think about it though as my eyes close and I'm out like a light.

~Thirty-One~
Adrian

I awake the following morning and gently get out of bed to put the coffee on. Blythe is on her side, facing me, but her back is against Marcus, who is cuddling her gently; both are still asleep. I cover them both back over and snap a shot of them on my phone, then I quietly head to the coffee machine and sort it out for the morning.

As the machine gurgles and spews out enticing scents of Italian ground coffee, I stretch, making my back pop and crack. A light flashes from somewhere across the rooftops and I look; there's no reason for a flash to be seen, like a reflection from a window or something. I head back to my room and pull on a top and some leggings, then I check the area out on the map app, out of sight of the window. There's nothing hinting that there's more than flats that way across town. I start to think of what can cause a flash like that and decide it could be any number of things, but my gut tells me something just isn't right.

I reach across and pull the blind half down, then I pour coffee and stand against the counter, contemplating. I need to get this proposal finished and present it to Tony. As I'm thinking, I hear a noise behind me and I turn to see Blythe walking towards me, her eyes half-closed and her hair messed up.

"Morning," I tell her and she yawns halfway through saying good morning back to me. I chuckle and kiss her on the forehead. "Bathroom is that way," I point and she nods but sticks her tongue out at me in a cheeky way. Her eyes dance in a warning and I rise to her challenge. "Be careful," I say, leaning into her, smelling her warm bed scent and sorting out her hair a little. "I might want to kiss that pretty tongue right outta your little fucking mouth," I tease. She stops and looks at me, then sticks it out again after she pours herself a coffee.

I chuckle, pull her to me with her good arm and kiss her. She melts into me and I can feel the blood heading to my cock, reacting to her being in my arms, smelling and looking as fantastic as she does.

"Morning," she breathes at me as we break apart.

"Dinnae stop on my account," Marcus chimes in from the doorway.

"Oh, we won't," Blythe teases and turns to beckon him.

"Coffee first, then privacy," I demand of them. Something about that flash of light doesn't sit right with me, and I can't put my finger on it. The sound of Blythe putting her coffee mug down on the counter brings me out of my head and into the moment before me. I watch as she sashays across to Marcus, then kisses him. He pulls her to him and his hand goes to her arse to pinch it, then he slaps it.

They break apart and I hand my brother his coffee and clear our used mugs into the sink. Then I beckon Blythe to me. She comes to me with a seductive smile on her face, her bottom lip slightly pulled in by her teeth. I widen my legs and as she steps into me, I wrap a hand around her neck into her hair and pull her to me. As soon as our lips touch, she moans and I demand access to her mouth with my tongue. She grants it, and I devour her taste, her smell. Marcus' feet touch mine and he's behind her, his hands reaching up and across to fondle her breasts as he kisses her good shoulder.

I pull back and he stops too. "Bedroom," I demand and they nod. Marcus takes her by the hand and leads her to the bedroom. I follow, closing the door behind me.

They're kissing and I step to them both, then slowly remove her knickers as Marcus devours her mouth. The sight of her being bare, half-naked and smelling delicious, makes my blood run south. I stand and pin her into him, intending on removing the bra, but it's one of those soft ones.

"Here," she tells me as she understands what I'm trying to do. I help her out of it, good arm first, then she turns to me and begins to devour my mouth, making me breathless. Marcus is kissing her back and running his hands down her sides, over her hips and slaps her arse. The more he does that, the harder she's attacking my mouth.

"She likes that," I growl at him and he grins, slapping her arse harder. She pulls away as she gasps, but the grin she gives Marcus is lustfully playful.

"You first," I indicate to my brother and he nods. Then he leans in and orders her to lie on the bed. She does diagonally and he suits up as I kiss her mouth. Moments later, she's gasping as his fingers dive into her. I stop kissing her to lean over her bad shoulder and suck on a breast as he devours her. Her good hand claws my back as we drive her wild and then, she's convulsing, her legs shaking as she comes, though she's trying to crush Marcus' head at the same time. He holds her open and I can hear him licking and sucking, then he stands, lines himself up and impales himself deep into her.

He slowly fucks her as he holds onto her hips and I change position to her good shoulder and aim my cock at her mouth. She grabs it and swallows it greedily, though it doesn't stay in her mouth for long as Marcus' thrusts jolt her around. She swallows and licks as best she can as Marcus fucks her deeply. Seeing her react, enjoying us both, sends a fire through me that I don't want to quench.

"Oh God, oh God!" she breathes out and then, she's arching

against him, against me as he makes her come on him. The sight of her doing so nearly makes me fill her belly. I glance at him, and he nods, indicating we're good to swap, but not before I've checked in with her.

I kiss her and whisper, "My turn?" into her ear. She nods and I grin, the excitement coursing through me mounts up a notch. I suit up as Marcus discards his condom, and as soon as his cock is in her mouth, I bury myself into her. Oh my fucking God, she feels so damn good! She arches up at my invasion, but her scream is held at bay by an occupied mouth. I lift her hips slightly and shove a pillow under her arse.

"Careful of the shoulder," he cautions.

"I will be," I tell him, and I make my thrusts deep and slow, enjoying the feel of her walls contracting around me, trying to hold me still as I dive deeply into her again and again.

"Come on her," I tell my brother as I feel another climax building up in her. He pulls out of her mouth and starts jerking off so he'll come all over her face. She moans loudly, breathes out yes after yes, and I increase my pace. I watch her face break out into bliss as she comes, the "O" she makes, and she's clamping down on me hard as Marcus covers her face, and I thicken deep within her, filling up the condom.

We help her wipe her face, and she sighs contentedly as we snuggle back into her.

"We didn't hurt your shoulder?" I ask as we're kissing her body. She reaches out and touches my face with her bad arm, but she doesn't wince as she does so.

She shakes her head and sighs with a smile on her face. "No, neither of you did. God, the sex is amazing," she breathes; her eyes are heavy. I reach out a little and kiss her.

"You two snooze, I need to work on that proposal," I tell them. Marcus nods and Blythe hmms in a sleepy response. I grin, nod to my brother and leave our bed. I shower, dress in fresh clothes and get my laundry on while they snuggle. Then I get the proposal up on the laptop, pour fresh coffee and I focus on this proposal of investment we're asking Tony to make.

A few hours later, I hear Blythe and Marcus in the shower and Blythe yelp at something, but it doesn't sound like a painful yelp. I grin as I send Tony the file and then I call him.

"Give me an hour and I'll have read it. Feel free to pop around then." Tony's voice is calm, collected, but I also hear the boredom.

"Sure, see you then. We need to eat," I tell him.

"Sounds good. I'm in Hamilton," he confirms.

"Good to know you're not just upstairs. Catch ye soon!" I say and hang up just as Marcus and Blythe emerge. Blythe heads for her room with a towel wrapped around her and her shoulder strap visible. She emerges a few moments later wearing a fresh top and some soft jeans that highlight her figure and her hair is now brushed. Unless you knew, you'd not know she was wearing a shoulder support. She throws me a huge smile, and I close the laptop down.

"Tony says he needs an hour, then we can head over to Hamilton once we've eaten?" I suggest. Marcus grins and heads to the fridge.

"Bacon, eggs and muffins?" he asks. My stomach growls at the mention of food, as does Blythe's and we chuckle. I tidy the laptop away as Marcus gets on with the breakfast. Blythe's phone pings and a second later, she's talking in Italian to someone. I catch Marcus' eye as he glances across to Blythe, then he focuses on cooking breakfast.

Blythe's shoulders slump and she hangs her head as she sits on a chair and talks with whoever has called her. Just as it's ready, Blythe says goodbye (I recognise the word ciao) and joins us for breakfast.

"Parents," she tells us as soon as she's got another coffee in her hands. "I told them I had a new place to live and about my shoulder," she winces, "they weren't happy I hadn't told them about it before now."

I nod and glance at Marcus. "Any reason why you haven't?" I ask.

Blythe nods. "One, they'd worry and two, I'm not in a hospital, so in my head, it's not urgent that they know. Not that my father agrees with that," she shares.

"I've forgotten who your emergency contact is," I tell her as we eat. She seems able to cut up her food this time, so I don't offer to do it for her.

"Annie, or Byron," she states. "I don't need Mama or Papa flying over here and making a fuss. Plus," she takes a drink of water that Marcus poured, "I've not told them I'm involved with you both, though I told them it was your place I was living at."

We both blink and glance at each other, which she sees. "I'm not ashamed of us or what we have, but hitting my parents with you two as well as the shoulder? That would bring them out here in a heartbeat." She places some food in her mouth and chews. "And I'm not ready for their protective streak right now," she tells us. We nod, but it doesn't sit right with me.

"When do you plan to tell them?" I ask as gently as I can.

Blythe sighs and purses her lips. "Give me a couple of weeks, Papa said he'd call again in a few days." Her phone pings and she grins. "Mama," she tells us and types back a reply quickly. "I've just told her that you're more than just my work colleagues, that I'm okay and I'm being looked after better than if I were at Annie's." The phone pings again and Blythe laughs. "She's asking which one of you is my boyfriend; guess now is as good a time as any!" She bites her lower lip and sends back one small phrase, which I can just make out. *Both of them.*

The meeting at Tony's goes well and Blythe acts more relaxed around him as we go through the proposal. Morag times her interruptions with coffee and biscuits perfectly, a fact I tease Tony about.

"They're gonna make you fat," I grin at him. He stands up, his much slender build to ours doesn't even show a podge around that stomach of his.

"Huh uh…" he grins, but it's just a facial grin. We wrap up the meeting and I whisper to Marcus that I want a private word with Tony.

"What's up?" I ask him when Marc and Bee aren't around. He shrugs and his mannerisms are the same as when he started getting divorced. "Millie?" I ask, thinking of his ex-wife.

He scowls at me at mentioning her. "Ach hell, no. But," he sighs, "women in general. Or the lack of them," he pauses. "No, it's not a lack of them. It's a lack of *decent* women who won't take the piss." I pat him on the shoulder.

"There are decent women out there," I tell him, but he gives me a rather sceptical look. I hope I'm around when he finds her. We catch up with the others in the kitchen; Morag is making something great smelling for dinner and suddenly, we're invited to stay. Marcus grins at me and Blythe asks Morag something and then the two of them are chatting away like old friends.

"He's lonely," Morag hisses at me when Tony's out of earshot. He and Marcus are showing Blythe around this huge place. I nod.

"Aye, did the latest one try and wring him for money?" I ask, guessing at what's happened. With Tony, it seems to happen quite a lot. Morag nods and glances where Tony, Blythe and Marcus went.

"Disgusting attitude," Morag spits. I nod, understanding.

"He'll find someone," I tell her. Morag grins and nods.

"Hope so! I'm glad you're all here," she tells me with a smile. "It'll perk him up."

Hours later, after dinner, we started making plans to head home.

"I need to walk this off." Blythe grins and Marcus offers to walk back with her. They thank Morag and Tony, then leave. I talk with Tony about an aspect of the proposal before I drive home. The other two come through the door nearly an hour later, then we chill out the rest of the day and enjoy a quiet Sunday. I point Blythe to a bag that Tony sent me home with. Half a dozen hardback books. If there ever was a kid in a candy store, it was Blythe with books.

~Thirty-Two~
Blythe

I send Tony and Morag a thank you for the books, making a note of where I'd like a bookcase to sit and where my books are going to go. It makes me happy that I get to sit and read in a small, temporary book-nook in one of the chairs.

Monday morning arrives and we walk into work after breakfast. Around ten am, I got a phone call from my credit card company asking me about transactions I tried to make over the weekend and this morning. When I tell them that I haven't purchased anything, or even tried to, since I've returned from Bosnia, save some medication, I get transferred to their serious fraud division. I'm dealing with that when Alasdair's phone goes off and he sends a message around the office, telling everyone he's dealing with credit card fraud. Bianca confirms the same and then we have Adrian and Marcus walking around, offering support, coffee, and squeezing shoulders.

Several hours later, we're all trying to chill out after three of us have had our cards stopped thanks to the skimming when Bianca comes through to the main office and she looks ashen. She hands the folder to Adrian who pulls it out and swears.

"What the fuck?" he growls and motions for me to come over. I do and can see why he's said that when I see surveillance photos of Adrian in the kitchen in just his tight sports pants making coffee, likely taken on Saturday morning.

"That's what the flash was: lens flare!" he growls. "Knew something was off about it."

"What?!" I ask, then he explains what happened as he was making the first pot of coffee.

"Cheeky kimon," Adrian spits. I purse and clench my lips at his use of the dirty slang word.

Then the walk home Marcus and I took through The Meadows when we left Tony's on Sunday. No photos are of us at Tony's place though, which I'm relieved about. Then there are photos of us walking in this morning, three-abreast but not holding hands. The threat made up from newspaper cuttings is real, making me go cold in anger. I glare at Adrian. This is beyond hatred now.

"Police," I state. It's time to get this registered as a crime and harassment. "And I'll bet the credit card fraud is a part of it," I tell him. He nods and places a call to the police while I call Action Fraud.

Marcus sends Bianca out for something and hands her cash, to which she nods and heads off, Alasdair accompanying her.

Bekah is chewing on something and starts tapping something into her computer. Then she asks me for my phone profile details, which I give her. If she can find Andrew Lloyd, she can likely find out where our cards were cloned.

Marcus curses a few minutes later and projects what he's found onto the blank wall. Andrew Lloyd dropped off the surveillance photographs.

"I want his bloody head on a pole," Adrian growls.

He's not the only one.

~Thirty-Three~
Marcus

Finding out it was Andrew Lloyd who dropped off the surveillance photographs of Adrian making coffee in our kitchen, following Blythe and me home yesterday, our walk into work this morning, as three of us are dealing with credit card fraud just short of ten grand collectively, makes me see red. Usually, it's Adrian who goes off like a volcano. I'm just glad we shut ourselves into a bedroom to have fun and not indulge in each other in full view of his camera.

"Police are on their way. They're sending someone out, a DCI Munroe?" Adrian states and Blythe cackles. I mean, throws her head back and cackles, then she howls. Then she has to wipe her eyes and she's still laughing as she heads down to the reception area. I look around as she heads out, but everyone seems as baffled as I am as to why she's reacted like that. *What does she know that we don't?* Bianca and Alasdair are back with the new RFID wallets I asked her to go and buy. Adrian and I carry them, I never thought to ensure that our staff do too.

DCI Munroe walks in with another plainclothes officer just as people are putting what cards still work into their new wallets or purses and I'm tempted to get a card reader just to ensure that they can't be cloned, testing our cards regularly.

He introduces himself to us and we head to a different conference room where Blythe walks him through everything. She seems to know him and I wonder why when Bekah taps me on the shoulder and beckons me over as I extricate myself from the meeting.

She's pulled up a basic social media profile from years ago and matched it to Munroe. It seems he was in the Army, as an MP. The connection is made; they must've crossed paths in their previous working life. I wonder if that's who she asked about Lloyd's background. I make a note to find out later. Bekah also has the social profile of the other person; whilst a police officer now, he has a background in banking and finance, with the surname of Barton.

I nod at her. "Good find, but best ye clear that away," I instruct and she nods. Two taps of the mouse later, the screens are gone. I doubt he'll mind that we looked him up. Munroe and his colleague are in with just Blythe and Adrian, mostly because they feel the attacks are aimed at them. *If that's the case, why skim Bianca and Alasdair's cards?*

Two hours later, Bianca and Alasdair are called in to chat with Munroe and Barton. Blythe calls the credit card company back and updates them with a crime reference Munroe has provided. She is speaking with them and sighs a huge relief then starts to write things down on a notepad.

"Yeah, we've just been told to do that. I'll do it now, and yes, I now have an RFID cardholder," she says, picking up the currently empty accessory that's been left for her. "That's great, though sending it to my workplace will ensure I actually get it." She gives the office details over. "That's great, thank you!" she states and hangs up. "Right, personal admin…fuck," she curses. "The bank still has me registered at Annie's address."

"What do you need?" Bekah asks and Blythe goes through the paperwork she's not yet changed over to our address. "Let's do this," she states, and they make a list, then go through changing it all over.

By the time they've done it all, Bianca and Alasdair are done being interviewed and Munroe attracts Blythe's attention.

"Grievance?" he calls and she snaps her head up, then nods. She motions for me to follow, and I do.

Munroe and Barton take a seat and Adrian has dragged another chair in, making the conference room cosy. I notice that the anti-listening device is on, something I assume Adrian had done when the officers turned up.

"Off the record, Wolf, what did you find out?" Blythe asks as soon as I nod.

"Barton, you weren't here," Munroe says. Barton just nods.

"If it ties into this, I'm all ears and we were struck by inspiration," he grins. I like him and I see Blythe and Adrian's shoulders relax.

"Okay, Lloyd was asked to leave as he let another soldier get hurt down on the Brecon, broken leg. Didn't stay with them, did eventually get help, but hours later. Add in that his colleague got hyperthermia." Blythe and Adrian both wince and shake their heads.

"And they didn't go for a dishonourable?" Blythe winces.

Munroe growls. "He claimed he got lost getting help, but that's not what we're trained to do, or how to fetch help."

"Like fuck we are. Shit, even *we* did a stint on the Brecon and you boys were not fucking gentle," Blythe spits out that fact as if it's a well-known one. Not for me and I can see Barton is confused. Blythe glances over at me, then smiles as she touches my knee discreetly beneath the table.

"Former RAF MP, we had to do orienteering and tracking in different conditions. We did some of it on the Brecon," Blythe nods to Wolf, "some of it up here in the Cairngorms or Trossachs. The Trossachs can be worse than the Gorms though… Ben Nevis…" Blythe shivers.

Barton nods as I smile in understanding. "Anyway," Munroe continues. "There was a court-martial, as you'd expect, but his conduct just wasn't becoming. They asked him to leave."

"That doesn't explain why his file is redacted?" Blythe asks, digging.

"It's down to that, because of who this colleague was. Lloyd's family have influence and there was a donation to the Army Vets Association," Munroe explains further. "But they didn't want his civilian life to be screwed over by his Military conduct. The amount," he writes down a figure that makes me whistle, "was made large enough to make the redaction and plain discharge worthwhile." Munroe looks like he's just stepped in some dog mess or something.

"Money talks," Blythe says, her eyes an icy blue and her lips thin. Munroe nods, leaving the rest of the rhyme unsaid. My mind and tongue finish the phrase off. "Bullshit walks."

"Aye, it does," he growls. Now I get his nickname.

Munroe tells us as he's leaving the small office that Lloyd was also known to be vindictive. We nod, but it's just another piece of the puzzle and still one we can't see the whole thing of.

Everyone mills around at the end of the day in the main office and Bianca enquires about the office renovations. Everyone else joins in and it's another hour before anyone thinks about leaving; we are all reluctant to do so.

"Don't take your usual route home. Go in pairs. We don't think he's after you guys; he's after us," Adrian remarks.

"Gotcha, ya wee bastard," Bekah announces and rolls her chair back. "I worked out how he's done it, and I have him on the building camera's doing it too."

Adrian's grin looks evil. "Good. Send that over to Munroe?" he asks and Bekah nods.

"Already on its way, and he removed the device when he dropped the file off," she tells everyone.

"So it was just because we didn't have our cards in RFID wallets?" Bianca asks, looking at Alasdair and holding his hand.

"Aye. The card company has said you're not liable, haven't they?" Blythe confirms. Bianca and Alasdair nod.

"Yeah, we've not been hit for as much on our cards as Blythe did," he says, nodding to me.

I wince. "Seven grand on a car that didn't go through," she begins to explain. "It was declined because I'd not bought anything since I got back weeks ago and hadn't told them I was going to be maxing my card out in one transaction, so they stopped it. They called the dealership, asking to speak to the person trying to buy the car, but he walked out as soon as the salesperson asked him to speak with the bank." She finishes off the drink that will have gone cold, but Blythe will drink anything coffee, especially if it's Italian coffee. "When they were told *he* was no longer there, they stopped it, knowing my file says I'm female."

I sigh at Blythe's words; this has taken up much more time today than it ought to, and I can't help feeling it's a distraction for something else.

"Bianca, Alasdair, Duncan, you guys head home. Bekah, I need your skills for another half an hour, please. I've had an idea." And suddenly the enthusiasm hits us all.

"Sod it, pizza night here, since we don't wanna leave and big brains over there," Adrian looks at me, but I can tell he's teasing, that look on his face is too familiar, "has thought of something. Let's put the hours in. Bianca, do your stuff." She claps, then she takes everyone's order and calls it through, ensuring we have enough to eat and drink for the next few hours.

As the pizza arrives, Bekah and I are going through the building footage again, watching what Lloyd does in detail. Blythe is standing behind Bekah, then she signals to Adrian and marches off, saying something about "not on her bloody watch." *I wonder what the hell she saw that we didn't.*

~Thirty-Four~
Blythe

Watching Lloyd loiter around the building entranceway as he does gets me suspicious. As Marcus watches it almost on a loop, I spot a shadow that no one else seems to have seen and I have to investigate. Grabbing a high powered torch from the kit room, I signal for Adrian and Duncan to come with me. I could call for Marcus, but him being where he is will probably be more useful.

I bounce down to the entranceway door where the overnight entry panel is located. That's where Lloyd taped the skimming device, underneath the protruding panel.

"Can you check the inside of that?" I ask Duncan. He takes a screwdriver from one of his combat pockets and we hold the torches as he unscrews the front panel.

I'm no expert, but as the insides fall out of the digital access panel, it looks like there are a few extra cables and things inside. Maybe I should have asked Marcus to come with us.

"Fuck me," Duncan whispers and I bite my tongue, giving a knowing look towards Adrian.

"Can you undo it?" I ask. Duncan's mouth is muttering to himself and his screwdriver is tracing wires back as Adrian takes a step back sending hand signals to the cameras. Then, he steps back in closer and holds the other torch up high.

Marcus and Keith join us a few moments later, a slice of pizza vanishing into Keith's mouth as they arrive. Duncan steps aside when Marcus lays a hand on his shoulder. Marcus whistles and asks Duncan for the screwdriver. Thirty seconds later, whatever

Lloyd put into the panel is carefully removed and placed into a metal tray from the electronics office.

"How the fuck did you see that?" Marcus asks me as he screws the panel back together. Then he takes something out of his pocket, dips a screw into it, and fastens in the last screw. I shrug.

"He was just leaning against it too long and I thought I saw someone else behind him," I commented quietly. My mind is churning through ideas, thoughts, trying like crazy to solve the puzzle, to work out the bigger picture. *What was the point of this endeavour?*

"Good job you had a hunch," Adrian says, smacking his brother on the shoulder.

Marcus nods and looks at what Keith is holding. "Let's head in and use hard keys," I state. Everyone nods and we head back up, bolting the door behind us.

We sit back down in the main office area; the aroma of pizza fills the air and there is still plenty of it around. The electronics are still in the metal tray, but at the edge of the desks. I grab a slice as my stomach demands food with a loud gurgle that has the girls in stitches. We all cast looks at the offending article as we go about our tasks as if it'll sprout legs and walk away, or something equally daft.

"Good spot," Adrian tells me as he squeezes my good shoulder. I just nod, but something is still bothering me and it's to do with...

"Oh fuck!" I cry out and grab another slice of pizza as I head up to the conference room with all the paperwork in it. As I stuff pizza into my mouth with my bad hand, my left skims across various piles. Bekah and Bianca follow me, then I recall where I saw this warning.

I pick up a pile of papers, leaving the wool trail there, then I sift through the papers. Finding the one I need, I motion for Bianca to go through it and ask Bekah to find it digitally.

Five minutes later, I show the guys the threat in the email.

"Digitally kippered, on all fronts," Marcus reads aloud. Then there's a shout from downstairs and when we get there, whatever was attached to the front door has just melted in a flash of acid and smoke, but not enough to set off the sprinklers.

We stand looking at the mess for what feels like hours, but I'm sure it's only minutes.

"So that's what that little vial had in it," Marcus mutters as he pokes it with a metal rod that he's secured from somewhere. "You little shitter." He looks at his brother grimly. "We didn't check the car park entry box," he states and then Adrian, Alasdair, and Duncan are off to do just that, each grabbing a slice of pizza as they go. They return twenty minutes later, stating the car park unit is intact and working as it should.

We do eventually call it a night after Marcus calls Wolf about the electronic incendiary in the control panel. Wolf says he'll meet us at the car park entrance to take it in as evidence. We hand it over in the tray it disintegrated in, and Wolf sets his lips thin, but his wide eyes betray his astonishment as he looks at the physical evidence. We've also sent him the video surveillance via a secure cloud.

"What the fuck has this guy got against you?" he asks in his customary growl.

"If we get a chance, we'll ask him," I state. He sighs, rubs his face and calls for another officer to witness the evidence coming in, then we leave.

It's dark when we get to the flat and the first thing we do is draw the blinds so that we can't be seen. I sigh, wishing I had the resources I had out in Bosnia. I'd love to shoot the damn camera out of his hand; a long-range or a sharpshooter rifle would do the job nicely. I've got a lot of nervous, angry, frustrated energy coursing around me and I can't sit still. My shoulder might be better, but it's still too soon to go doing any training, physical or with firearms. I can't even entertain the idea of reading a book and I sure as hell can't go visit Annie. No way am I bringing this to her door; as comfortable as she would be in dealing with this shit, she doesn't need the hassle with the bairn.

I head into my room but don't close the door, ignoring the guys. I could scream, shout, fight. Back in my RAF days, I'd be dragging Annie down to the gym and letting rip with our usual martial arts session. Sex isn't appealing to me right now either, not after the photographs and I look around at the boxes I still have to unpack. Organising them takes my focus and I get lost in deciding what's staying, going, getting another wash, or going away now.

Marcus checks in on me and I give him a nod.

"I'd ask if you're okay, but we know you're not," he gently tells me. I can see Adrian hovering close behind him.

"I know. I can't go to the gym; I can't go out and walk in case he does something else. I can't do a lot of things." I let the anger flow and start throwing things onto the pile of stuff for washing, then I collapse another box with vigour.

"I can't use a rifle, my shoulder simply won't hold it and I can't go join Annie anywhere right now, lest he's watching with that damn camera, or worse, because of the bairn."

Marcus lets me just rant, knowing that it's not aimed at him.

"So, I'm going to sort these out," I throw another pair of jeans that need a quick wash onto the pile and there's enough there now for a load. "Because if I get near either of the Lloyd guys, I might shove them both out of a helo with no parachute, or my good fist down their throats." I grab the pile of laundry and take it to the machine, which Adrian has kindly opened up for me.

Marcus stalks past me and the look on both their faces as they salute me makes me laugh so hard, I drop the laundry. Their antics have cut through my foggy anger, giving it an outlet.

"Fuck," I scream as I double over in laughter. I can't breathe as my body convulses in releasing the frustration and mirth. When I can eventually see, the guys are also wiping their eyes from their laughter. "You pair..." I exclaim as I try to stand up. Adrian helps me to my feet with my good arm, his eyes still dancing.

"Appreciated that, did you, ma'am?" he asks. Technically, he out-ranked me; those days are behind us though.

"Bloody perfect," I tell him and take a huge breath to calm myself. Marcus begins picking up the laundry I dropped and together, we load it and then we watch a movie, Top Gun winning the vote.

The phone ringing the following morning disorients me, until I realise it's Adrian's mobile and not mine. I groan and lie back in bed. Marcus snuggles close to me as we listen to Adrian's side of the conversation.

"Hang on, let me get the other two," he says, then he stands up and opens the door, calling for us and we grin. Whoever is on the other end knows we're here.

"They're here, Tony, say that again?" He presses a button.

"Good morning!" he chirps through the loudspeaker. If he says 'Angels,' I'm so outta here. "I've had an invitation to a Business

Networking event in two weeks here in Edinburgh. I am already booked to be in London and I don't want to miss that. So, I've put down your names. Will Blythe be going with you?"

The guys look at me and I nod. "I'd love to! What's the dress code?" I see their heads drop and I laugh. "Wouldn't be a black-tie penguin event, would it?" I suggest.

"Why would you ask that in such a way?" asks Tony, bewildered.

"You can't see the guys' faces," I retort, trying to keep my humour from showing but failing.

Tony laughs. "Yeah, they don't like these types of events. With you there though, I think you'll be turning heads and attracting more attention than Aid and Marc normally do," he tells me.

"I'd need to go shopping for a suitable dress," I state. "And not being funny, Primark isn't exactly the place to get it!"

"There's a ladies shop in Polwarth Gardens I can highly recommend. I'll have Morag book you an appointment." I baulk at Tony's advice, knowing that while I could afford it, the credit card fraud yesterday has scuppered me.

"Tony, we had our cards skimmed yesterday. We're unable to," Adrian begins.

"I'll pick up the tab," he interjects quickly. "I assume your tuxes still fit?" he asks. I can hear the clicking of a keyboard on Tony's side.

"They should. We'll check later today," Adrian confirms. I lick my lips and the guys stifle a moan.

"Okay, I'll leave you three alone. Speak with you later!" Tony says, then he hangs up.

"Looks like we're going out to a party," Adrian states as he puts his phone back on his bedside table.

Morag contacts me, giving me a day and time to be at this boutique and confirming where it is. It's a short drive from the office and while I could walk, trying on dresses such as these and turning up sweaty is rather rude in my view.

Wolf updates us to say that the Lloyd guys have gone to ground, which we expected. Nothing has been attacked or infiltrated since. I can't help but wonder what they're up to, where they are and why all this is even happening.

My appointment at the boutique is the following day, but the guys try on their tuxedos and check they still fit that afternoon. I must be drooling when I look at them; Marcus hands me a napkin and tells me I've some dribble on my chin. He laughs when I stick my tongue out at him, the swine.

"So they still fit, aye?" Adrian asks as he moves about in his.

"Hell. Yes," I sigh in reply. God, the guys look great!

The following morning, I shower without assistance for the first time since my shoulder was dislocated. While it hurt and took me longer than usual, it was so nice just to wash myself. It was also less fun, but since the photography incident, we've not indulged in each other collectively, all of us still nervous about doing so.

We have breakfast, then I take a cab to the boutique. Morag has said she'll meet me there and the guys head into work after kissing me thoroughly in a corner of the flat with no windows.

Morag is waiting outside and smiles when I alight from the cab. We head inside and we're greeted by Iona, the owner. She bustles about, putting away the tools she's using and picking up a tape measure to drape around her neck.

"Morning, Morag! Is this the young lady Tony called me about?" she asks as she greets Morag with a double cheek kiss.

"Hi," I say, offering my left hand. She looks at me with a slight frown. "Dislocated right shoulder, still healing, so," I explain, and she nods, then shakes my left hand. She takes a step back, bites the inside of her cheek and tilts her head.

"Okay," she says a few moments later. I look at Morag who just winks at me with a smile. "Fabulous black hair, sporty… Are you ex-military by chance? How you carry yourself," she explains and I nod. She grins and draws in a breath. "I think I have just the right dress, but it'll need some adjustments to fit perfectly. No matter, that's what I do!" She marches off but motions for us to follow. Wide-eyed with a grin on my face, I follow along.

Twenty minutes later, I'm standing on a rotating podium wearing a red velvet, wrap-around dress with cold-shoulder sleeves. Iona has it pinned in at my waist, across the back and wherever else she thinks it needs tucking in to fit me.

"There, how's that?" she asks, taking a step back. I blink in the surrounding mirrors, not quite believing what I'm seeing. Beyond stitching it, Iona has it fitting me perfectly. The length has also been adjusted so it's not touching the floor, but just an inch above the ground, even in bare feet.

"That'll lift up when you're in heels, so you'll have a few inches of clearance. In this climate, you dinnae want it touching the floor." She smiles at me as she pins another piece of fabric in to do what she wants it to.

The dress has some volume and weight to it, but it's not too heavy. I move around, looking at the mirror and then I focus on how it moves. You could conceal anything under this dress and it would be invisible; it makes me love the dress even more. I grin at Iona.

"Unbelievable," I tell her. She nods with a satisfied grin on her face, then she wanders off somewhere, but comes back with some amazing black shoes with red underside heels in a matching shade. As much as I was drooling when the guys put on their tuxedos, I'm sure seeing me in this will make them tent.

Morag comes up behind me, "You look amazing in that dress. Pity the lads have nabbed ye," she quietly tells me. "Tony's gonna have to borrow you for events like this for himself." She nudges my good side and grins. Which reminds me, I really need him to meet Annie!

Trying the dress on with the heels makes the dress pop.

"Ye got my shoe size right!" I exclaim as I try the heels on.

"Ach, good, I took a guess at it. Now, give me five days or so." Iona smiles at me as she carefully peels the dress off me so I don't get scratched by any pins. Then she turns to Morag. "I'll email him the invoice when I'm done, shoes included." Both the women smile at each other, hug and then I'm left to get dressed back into my work combats and polo shirt. As much as I love doing what I do, I'm looking forward to dressing up for a corporate event.

"Come on, let's go grab a coffee afore we have to go do the boring stuff called life," Morag strongly suggests to me. I get the feeling I am not going to be allowed to say no, so I just nod, not quite sure how to take Morag's bossiness this morning.

We walk down to Flo's and Morag lets slip why she wanted a quiet word. Tony's throwing himself into work more than usual, whoever his last "hookup" was, has left him not looking at women at all.

"Are you not interested in him?" I ask. Morag's been there for years, from what the guys have told me.

"In that way? Ach no… He helped me when I was down on my luck and needed a roof over my head. We all knew each other from school days; he was just getting divorced and was all over the shop. We kinda helped each other out. Dinnae get me wrong, some days he needs looking after, but this…" She shakes her head. "He should nae be alone."

My mind again brings Annie into focus and I know she'll chew me out for blindsiding her, but one day, I am going to get her to meet him. Somehow.

"He can borrow me for those stuffy corporate events any time he likes," I offer and Morag grins.

"Aye…so how come yer with the McGowans?" she asks.

"I asked," I tell her, recalling the moment I told them both to fuck me. Though it wasn't meant that way, it opened the door. She goes wide-eyed at me, and I laugh.

"Just like that?" she asks and I nod.

"Just like that!" I confirm.

The older woman laughs, then tells me, "well done."

~Thirty-Five~
Adrian

Blythe comes back from the boutique but won't share what kind of dress she's been fitted for, only that it's gorgeous and will fit perfectly when the time arrives. And that Morag had a wee chat with her afterwards.

While she was busy, we dug up more about who would be going, Tony having provided the guest list. There are a lot of other businesses on the guest list for that night, another one in our sector that's just starting out and looking for backers, a few I.T. companies and software houses to name a few. Marcus prints off the high-fliers, the money influencers and we get to work remembering as much detail about each as we can.

Tony's at the opera in London, an opening night event and we learn he's going with his sister, which is why he's not going to be here in Edinburgh. I'll give him a few days, then go and check on him.

"Morag's worried about him," Blythe tells us as we do our research.

"Oh aye?" I ask. She has been worried about him a few times through the years, though it was with justification once or twice before.

"Aye. Seems he's throwing himself into work and exercise," she shares.

"I can think of worse ways to get over someone yer interested in," Marcus volunteers. Blythe looks up at him curiously.

"He was doing exactly that when he couldn't reach you for months," I reveal and Marcus throws me the bird. I chuckle, but Blythe looks like she's pitying him.

"Don't start," Marcus growls, but there's a sparkle in his eyes.

"Ach, ye didn't," she tells us. "Really wish I'd gotten yer message," she tells him.

He shrugs and grins at her, then he turns back to the papers in his hand and focuses on what we need to do.

We get our brains boggled by the high flying socialites this event is pulling in. It takes us two days to get our heads straight about who is who, the high rollers, the amount of cash that the people walking around can summon. I really wish Tony was with us, or even that it was just him going to this event. I find them tedious and boring, but they are necessary. I also do not want to be at the opera; that's beyond my endurance levels. Blythe gets a call on Friday morning, and she yips in joy.

"Perfect, yes, Monday is… Oh, okay, Tuesday then! Yeah, I don't blame you." She laughs and then says goodbye to her caller.

"The dress is ready, final fitting and check are on Tuesday." She beams at us, then she bounces out of the office, and we can hear the squeals from the other two Bees. I look at my brother, and he grins.

"I'm looking forward to seeing her in this dress," he confesses. All we know is that she'll be wearing heels.

Marcus and I get bogged down with quotes, one of which is from one of the high rollers at the event we're going to on Saturday at the Harvey Nichols store. Everything else is quiet, we've interviews to arrange for camera operators going forward and Blythe has volunteered to conduct those with Alasdair or Duncan. When we're not doing quotes, Marcus and Keith have fun.

Well, they're laughing a lot while messing with computers and electronics, so I assume they're having fun. Blythe goes for the fitting, taking the girls with her. Alasdair and Keith seem to be in on some kind of joke and they let slip they know that the dress is red.

Keith and Marcus crack on with the tracker and get the app semi-working; at least, we can beta test it, find ranges, do basic tests.

"Well, why don't I go test it?" Blythe asks the day after her fitting. The dress is now at home in a black dress bag, waiting to be worn at Harvey Nichols on Friday night. The invite specified canapes and drinks, and there are going to be around a hundred to a hundred and fifty people at this investors' business event. Being so close to the city centre, we could walk to the building, though we'll drive the short distance down as Blythe is in heels. A friend of Alasdair's is doing the gate security for the delivery car park, and he's letting us park there.

"Great idea," Marcus grins, rubbing his hands together. Keith grins just as enthusiastically and they hand over the test model to Blythe and Bianca.

"Coming, Bekah?" asks Blythe. Bekah looks up and shakes her head.

"Sorry, no...busy with this, have fun breaking his code," she teases her husband while issuing a challenge to Blythe.

"Oh, I intend to!" she replies cheerfully, then the girls are gone and we gather around Keith and Marcus, leaving Bekah to her task.

We can tell when Blythe turns the tracker on and can see them walking down Princes Street towards Harvey Nichols. Then they take a turn and walk down Lothian Road, as if they're going to the Sheraton Grand Hotel. They're in the old quarter and we lose them for a few moments until we pick up their signal as they come past the Double Tree and back up towards Johnston Terrace on the far side of Edinburgh Castle.

I try to stay focused on reading the CV's and quoting for a personal protection detail for a businessman who doesn't want to go to America on his own.

They take about an hour to walk through the old town, sticking close to the old stone buildings. We lose the signal again near the Dungeons and the Royal Mile. When we get the signal back, they're halfway back up Princes Street, heading towards us.

"Need to negotiate these old buildings," Marcus comments as Keith taps away on his keyboard.

"Yeah, I'll add in some GPS boosting via the mobile masts and Wi-Fi points," he says, writing down what he wants, then his fingers begin to dance. We hear Blythe and Bianca return with a tray full of coffee from Flo's and I grin.

"Nice test run," Marcus thanks her as she hands out the coffees.

"How did it go?" she asks and Marcus runs through what they could and couldn't see as Bekah calls Blythe over.

They talk quietly and Blythe nods to Bekah before squeezing her shoulder and taking a printout from the printer. She is reading it as she heads out of the office but returns half an hour later without it.

We pack up work on time, Bekah hugging into Keith and they leave wrapped around each other, carefully watched by Blythe. Bianca nods to Blythe as Alasdair escorts her home, followed by Duncan at their heels. When it's just us alone in the office, she fetches an anti-listening device, turns it on and guides us to what we've now called the "notice" room.

"We've had another one, or rather, I have."

~Thirty-Six~
Marcus

Keith gives Bekah the biggest kiss to her temple, rubbing her back and holding her close. I get a sinking feeling in my stomach as he reassures his wife.

I nod to them and Adrian calls out a hearty goodnight to them. Blythe is watching them go and smiles at Bianca and Alasdair as they head out with Duncan. When it's just us alone in the office, she fetches an anti-listening device, turns it on and motions for us to follow her to what we now call the "notice" room.

"We've had another one, or rather, I have."

We look at her and she hands us the papers from the printer. It's addressed directly to her, but the text of the email says one word. Meta.

The next five pages are exactly that: email server metadata.

"They're clever," I state, reading through. This kind of information shouldn't be manipulated, not like this. It's like it's been phished through dozens of specific servers before it reached Blythe and it was addressed to her directly. It reminds me of a cypher, something I know Bekah is good at cracking. Only a little of the text is highlighted.

"It's not complete, some of the words are buried in goodness knows what. Bekah is going to run an algorithm on it; I think that's what she said? Anyway, it might take a little while before we can read the whole message," she tells us.

"So we didn't upset her?" I ask. This device won't work without Keith's input and he won't work here without her. I knew something had happened, that sinking feeling in my gut is rarely wrong.

Blythe shakes her head. "Goodness no, my sensitive one." She smiles at me warmly; she knows I show my worry more than Adrian. "She didn't want to worry everyone at the same time and she didn't want to say anything out loud, hence…" She nods towards the anti-listening device I built. I get it. Bekah is thinking the office might be bugged; I need to tell her it's swept daily. "Plus, the message isn't all there… She's been watching our emails, and this one flagged up blue."

We nod, though I can tell Adrian is fuming. He gets up and paces the office, agitation and anger pour off him in waves. Blythe grins.

"About time I got added to the gym list, aye?" she states, turning off the device and heading to the door. "You can vent yer frustrations on the punch bag or weights," she commands as she holds out her hand for him to take. He nods and we lock up, glad to be out of the office for the night and the weekend.

Hours later, we're home, sweaty and we each dive for our own shower units, shutting the blinds to every window as we go. We grabbed an Indian takeaway as we headed home, and I put it in the oven to keep warm as we shower, change, and begin to chill out. We all seem to settle on either pyjamas or sweats and a t-shirt, and before we speak, I sweep the flat for bugs. We don't know Bekah that well, not yet, but if she's concerned about something, I'm quite sure there's a valid reason for it. It's also something I've not done regularly here at home, something I vow to change until this situation is resolved.

I sweep near the windows, especially the kitchen one that Adrian was photographed in his underwear at, but nothing comes up and I can't see anything small flashing around the frame or the glass.

I'm not going to do a Peter Parker and go out to check the walls. These old buildings have beautifully thick Georgian walls. Even a bug placed on a wall outside wouldn't be able to penetrate through; windows are the weaker point.

When I'm sure we're safe, I turn on a device anyway and we all visibly relax.

"What do you think he wants?" I ask. Certain words were easy to decipher and the message so far seems to be an apology.

"Not sure...won't be sure until Bekah's programme does what it needs to do."

"Why email it to you though?" Adrian asks and Blythe shrugs.

"I escorted David down to Brize. I gave him a choice to go quietly or be handcuffed to me; I suggested the quiet route to him. He complied, then we hooked up," she nods to me with a grin on her mouth and fire in her eyes, "but I never saw him once he was taken off the helo and escorted to the fruits' office." The nicknames the RAF have for their commanders are funny. Adrian had to explain that term to me once I got on site. Fruits refer to all the colourful badges Wing Commanders might have earned before taking over the command of a base; they look like a tutti-frutti.

"I didn't either, though I knew he was back, the jungle drums were beating loudly that night, even before I got off base. I really needed a drink." I wink at her. I needed something else that night; we both did.

"And a game of pool," she teases me.

I nod and break a poppadom in half, before indulging in the vegetables and mint sauce that go with it.

"Aye, there was that," I add. "I expected a sultry Italian accent to come out of your mouth when we spoke; my heart skipped a beat when I heard yer voice. Made me miss home," I tease.

Then she replies to me in fluid, rapid Italian with not a hint of a Scottish accent.

"I've nae idea what ye just said," I tell her and she laughs.

"I told you that my heart skipped more than a beat," she says. The light goes from her eyes, her lips thin out and she looks at both of us so intensely, it's scary. Her eyes change hue, a thing I knew they did, but her cool blue eyes go stormy grey as I look at them.

"I dinnae know what's kicked all this off, if it's David, Andrew Lloyd or the damn Duke of Edinburgh…" She's trying to make light of this, but we're all feeling the pressure, the frustration. The way it affected Bekah tonight, affects me more than I'd like to admit to anyone else. Blythe held it together, but now, I can tell she's channelling her anger. "You two have given me something I didn't think I'd ever find. A nirvana, for the want of a better word." She looks deep into my eyes, holding me in place, then she turns the intense gaze to Adrian. "Whatever or whoever is stupid enough to do this, they think they know you, or me. They're so fucking wrong, it'll be their undoing. I. Will. Bury. Them."

Adrian reaches out to her and she lets him pull her in for a kiss that makes our dinner look cold. She comes across to me and I devour her mouth, feeling my cock twitch as she makes her way between us both, then back to the chair she was sitting on.

"Now, let's eat before we have to reheat it," she commands and takes a huge bite of her Rogan Josh.

We end our evening on the couch, huddled together, indulging in one of Blythe's favourite films: Blade Runner.

We awake the following morning together in bed, me spooning Blythe as normal with Adrian facing her. The smile she gives us both makes me feel content, at peace. Home.

"I have a question. Please don't think badly of me," she whines a little, which is so endearing and I snuggle up closer; my cock goes erect at her begging voice and proximity to us.

"Go on," I encourage her. She turns to me and grins.

"Why the Harvey Nichols building?" she asks faintly. I assume she means for the weekend event.

"Have you been up to their fourth floor?" Adrian asks and she turns to him, but she shakes her head.

"Can't say I have, no," she replies quietly. "It's just…not the kind of place I'd have thought of to host a millionaires' business contact meeting."

"There's a glass-walled wrap-around-balcony at the back that overlooks the Castle. The whole backside opens up with bi-folding doors. They do corporate events regularly, and we met our first seed client there, thanks to Tony."

I can't see her facial reaction to Adrian's words, but his chuckle tells me she is somewhat surprised.

"We've struck a few deals at events there, it's rather popular. It'll no doubt be the usual affair, a string quartet, soft music, drinks, canapes," I offer.

"Stop trying to make it sound boring," she tells us. Both Adrian and I chuckle.

"When you've been to a few, they do get a little stifling and boring," Adrian retorts then leans in and kisses her. I follow and kiss her back, run a hand down her sides and she shivers and mews at my touch.

"You'll see, trust me. The fourth floor is spectacular. Just, don't leave your shoes behind, okay, Cinders?" I tease before I thoroughly devour her mouth.

"What are you in the mood for, babe? We're certainly in the mood for you," Adrian huskily tells her and he devours her mouth before she can respond. He lets her breathe a few moments later and she sighs happily.

"Both," she whispers.

"Together?" I ask, making sure we understand and I nudge into her arse. Her bad arm comes over and touches my cheek.

"Yes," she breathes and I can only grin.

"Then your arse is mine, woman," Adrian growls, before pulling her into a kiss that has her gasping as she comes up for air. We shift so that I'm under her. Adrian tosses me a condom and Blythe grabs it.

"You're clean?" she asks, and I nod. We get checked every six months. She turns and looks at Adrian, who nods and leans in.

"I'm wearing one going into your arse," he says and licks her face.

She laughs and wipes the lick off, but she tosses the condom for me aside.

"I'm more than clean," she simply tells us and leans forward to capture my mouth before we can ask what she means. Her small hands are on my chest, her cold fingers are setting fire to my nerves, my whole being. Her nipples are standing to attention as much as mine are. I reach up and tweak her, making her moan and yelp. I hear a smack and she jumps.

"Gorgeous arse, Bee," Adrian huffs in her ear and she grins, then she wiggles it at him, making him smack the other side.

She leans in to kiss me again and I can feel Adrian at her back, between both of us, then she's kissing me down my torso to my pulsing cock. Seconds later, she's taking me into her hot little mouth, her black hair cascading over my stomach, and I groan in pleasure.

"Fuck, Bee," Adrian moans as she sucks me off, leaving a wet trail all over my bobbing dick. She grins mischievously, then she's licking my balls, and I arch up off the bed as she sends sensations through me that I didn't know I was capable of feeling. When I manage to open my eyes, she's lowering herself onto me inch by delicious inch.

She tosses her hair back as she starts to ride me and I grab her hips, helping her stay seated. I dig into her flesh, loving how warm and soft it feels. Her clit is rubbing against my pubic bone as she slowly rises and falls, her groans of pleasure spurring me on. Adrian grabs her hair and pulls her into a kiss as he comes to kneel behind her, making her stop. Then she breaks away and looks at me before she leans down, cascading her black velvet hair around us, capturing my mouth as she leans on my chest. If my heart could explode, it would.

I can feel the bed moving, and Blythe cries out as Adrian slides into her arse, slowly at first. Her face is buried into the crook of my neck and I turn to kiss her cheek, mumbling to her how bloody perfect she is. I grab her arse as I feel Adrian grab her hips and slowly, alternately, we begin to slide in and out of her; I'm not sure who is causing her to scream, groan and moan between us. Hearing her like this, enjoying us both, makes me want to come inside her now. I try kissing her, pulling her hair back to do so, but she's so busy feeling us both, she can't.

Her cries, gasps and screams fill the room making me harder than granite. I capture her mouth briefly before she lifts it to scream again. I dive deeper into her and she tries to tell us something, anything, but she can't form a single word. All I can feel is my dick thickening, filling and enjoying every inch of her velvety warmth, her contracting on me with each thrust from one of us. My brother and this woman above me have me on fire.

Her eyes are closed as her screams and cries get more frequent as we make love with her, then she screams out her orgasm, grabbing the sheets or anything behind me. Her convulsions set me off and I empty myself inside of her, holding her arse cheeks, feeling elation and contentment as I do. Moments later, Adrian grunts out his release as he comes inside her ass. His arms drop to the side of me, supporting himself and he leans forward to kiss her back as our senses return to us.

"Unbelievable," she breathes at me as she collapses on top of me. I brush her hair aside and find her mouth, kissing her deeply.

"Yes, you fucking are," I tell her. She drops her head to my shoulder and Adrian slowly recedes from her and us, and I can hear him taking the condom off. I turn us so she lands on her good shoulder and Adrian tucks himself in behind her as he returns to the bed, stroking her sides, wrapping us up in the quilt to keep warm.

Blythe lets out a contented, deep sigh and she brings her arm up to cup my face as she kisses me. Then she turns to my brother, being careful of her bad shoulder, and kisses him with just as much vigour.

"So you wanted to go bareback? We've not discussed having kids," I remind her.

The look on her face tells us something isn't right.

"You've something important to share, woman?" Adrian growls deeply into her ear. I watch as she shivers and squirms, but she's pinned between the both of us. She sighs and focuses on my abs, tracing them lightly with her fingers, making my skin bumpy. I can see her mouth moving, but nothing is coming out. Then, slowly, she tells us.

"My body fat content is quite low, it always has been, in case you two hadn't noticed." We didn't consider Blythe to be leaner than normal. "Also, I only have one functioning ovary. Well, I was born with only one, not two. I'm that irregular, I've been told I will never conceive. Until now, Annie's about the only one who knows, outside of my immediate family."

"Why didn't you tell us before now?" I ask gently. She's still not looking me in the eyes. She goes to answer, then stops and sighs. Adrian's face tells me this is news to him as well as me!

"Kids never came into the equation, not with you two. I've sat with Annie and cried about it already, years ago now. Just after we finished MP Training, I found out."

"How did ye?" Adrian asks from behind her, his voice low but gentle.

"I'd gone home to Italy and took Annie to meet the family. We were firm friends by the end of that training and we were off to do officers, but we had some leave to use up. I went for my usual check-up, but I asked them for a full workup. There was a guy I liked in MP Training who was also going to do the officer's course and I got to thinking about a lot of things, contraception being the main one. While I had the chance, I asked. Having a large family is an Italian, as well as a Scots thing, aye? I got told a week later, after scans and everything, that I had one ovary, and everything I just shared with you." She shrugs, but the tears are forming.

"You gave up on that idea?" I ask. Adrian is stroking her bad shoulder ever so gently, he's making her aware he's there. I take one of her hands and hold it. She nods in reply.

"It's why I'm so fond of Annie's wee one, Elinor Rose," she says, and the dam bursts.

An hour later, I'm brewing the coffee and bringing it to us in bed. Blythe shared with us that she had thought of adopting on her own when she came out of the RAF, then with the stuff that went down with Annie, her grandparents dying and her parents moving permanently back to Italy, she just threw herself into being a second mum for Elle.

"We're nearly fifty, Bee," I hear Adrian tell her as I come back in with three coffee mugs. "We never thought we'd get to be dads, or have what we have. If you want kids, we can go down the adoption route. It depends on what you want."

"And what you two want," she tells us.

"We thought we'd get the whole nine yards, sure," I say as I place a mug down next to my brother and hand Blythe hers. "Men have it easier on that front than women, for sure, but as Aid said earlier," I look right at her, "there are plenty of other ways."

"So, who gets to be the dad?" she asks and I stop dead halfway into bed. "Legally, it has to be one of you," she sips her coffee, "and do you want the whole marriage thing?" She looks between both of us.

I flounder in my response and she chuckles.

"Things we need to work out. I'm…" She stalls, then takes a huge breath in and pulls her shoulders back, before letting it out. "I'm sorry I didn't tell you both before, or maybe at a different time," she offers.

"Better than not at all," Adrian gently replies as he holds an arm out for her to cuddle into against the headboard. She does and I join them, glad to be back under the covers.

We talk for a little while, but there's one point I feel the need to get across to her.

"Bee," I begin, and Adrian and Blythe stop talking. "Whatever it is we all want, we can get. Most importantly of all, it's you." I turn so I can face her and run a hand to her jaw, feeling her face with my thumb. "You're who we want," I tell her. I pull her to me and kiss her, then Adrian pulls her to him and does the same.

"Hell yeah," he tells us. Hell. Yeah. Indeed.

~Thirty-Seven~
Blythe

I should have told the guys I couldn't have kids earlier, but the timing always seemed terrible. I also don't want to have to use condoms now that we're together. I do feel better now I've no more elephants or bombs to set off for the guys, and they're still talking with me, holding me, involving me.

I stretch and decide what I'm doing today. I walked nearly ten kilometres on the treadmill yesterday whilst Adrian bashed the hell out of a punchbag, aided by someone at the gym who was just as big and as fit looking as he is. Marcus worked on some weights, but I feel the need for something natural today.

Marcus gets a call just as we've showered and dressed. I help Adrian strip the bed and put on fresh sheets as the first half goes through the machine.

"Okay, I'll load it up and we can test it. How's Bekah?" Adrian and I mouth the word "Keith" to each other and we grin. As Marcus finishes his call, we finish remaking the bed.

"How is she?" I ask. She was quite freaked out yesterday; this is beyond her usual remit.

"She's feeling better. Still no further on all the emails, though she's decoded a little more. Keith was saying she got caught up in her head yesterday, imagining what might happen and she got carried away."

"Fear is a powerful tool," I volunteer, understanding where she was coming from. "And this 'campaign' is designed to get into your head. I'm either too pigheaded or too used to this kind of stuff to let it bother me. Besides," I say as I head to the coffee machine and pour myself the last cup from the first batch, "how it's being done it's a coward's way."

I drink the last of the warm coffee from the pot as I begin to make a fresh one.

"The latest email," Marcus begins and checks the device is still working. He plugs it into a USB cable we have that fits, charging it up. "Suggests this is an apology and maybe a heads up to something? Keith's not sure, the words are coming frustratingly slowly."

I nod and set the pot going, now I've rinsed it all out, put in fresh water and coffee.

"If it's not one of the Lloyd brothers sending them, then I want to find out who. And how are we getting there on…what night?" I ask. I don't know why it's not held on a Friday night, but it's not. I'm sure it's this Thursday.

"Friday," Adrian confirms, looking at his phone. I look over his shoulder and he has the invite up on email from Tony. I nod.

"I thought it was Thursday?" I check with him. Then he laughs.

"The invite is wrong, hang on, I'll call and check." I'm glad it's not my head that's messed up. I leave Adrian to call Tony and confirm while I start some breakfast. I find a waffle maker, and I pull it out as I can't decide on what to make for breakfast.

Then I discover bread, bacon and some eggs… Bacon and egg sandwiches will be perfect. I grab a frying pan and start on the bacon. Marcus joins me and I ask him to put the waffle maker back, but he pauses as I point to it.

"Dear God, is that thing still with us?" he whispers, touching it gently.

"Yeah, I couldn't bear to throw it out," Adrian responds, coming to join us. "It was Mum's," he tells me. "She was one for collecting things, gadgets she never used, mainly. But this, she'd make us waffles on our birthday. Think this was her fourth machine."

"What happened?" I ask. They know my parents are in Italy having taken over my grandparents' place, but I don't know a thing about theirs.

"Dementia for Mum, Dad died soon after."

"Oh no! Why?" I ask, going over to them as soon as I've flipped the bacon, holding them as best I can.

"Broken heart. He couldn't live without Mum, even though we said we'd bring him here to be with us. Six weeks is all it took."

"Fuck," I say. There's nothing I can do but hold each in a hug and just be there for them.

"I'll clean it and put it away," Adrian tells me.

"Clean it, yes. But," I pause. "Leave it out. I'll make some mix and we can have them for breakfast tomorrow."

As Adrian cleans the waffle maker, Marcus fries the eggs for me and together, we plate the breakfast sandwiches up and enjoy each other's company, as sombre as that moment has now become.

Tony gets back to us; the event is on the right day, the Friday, not the Thursday as per the date. He promises to forward the latest invite when it lands with him, which doesn't take long. Marcus has booted up his laptop and is updating the software to the transmitter, thanks to Keith working on the code at his end, probably last night. Looks like it's time for another test.

Ten minutes later the tracker has been updated, and he calls Keith.

"Looks good! Okay, yeah, I'll get Bee to test it again." He nods and makes agreeing noises. "Yeah, anything more we want to add to it can wait until Monday." Then he ends the conversation and grins.

"I'm not wanting to walk down to Harvey Nichols in those heels, or carry spare shoes with me," I tell them both when they're together and free shortly after.

"We'll use the BMW."

"Oh, good!" I retort. "No chauffeur driven limousine?" I tease; the boys laugh.

"No, we drive ourselves. The trick is to do what the fruits used to do. Have a drink in your hand, but don't drink it." Adrian winks. He clearly didn't have the same WC as I did.

I take the tracker when Marcus hands it to me, putting on a jacket and some light shoes.

"How do we play this?" I ask.

"Turn it on, walk. Chill out as if we weren't around. I'll be at your six somewhere," Adrian confirms. "And Marc will watch us both from here. Transmitter for you, Google Location for me."

"So, I just go and chill out?" I ask. This seems too easy. Marcus nods. "Yep. Go to Flo's, the library, the Castle. I need you to walk through the Old Town, over the river, loop around and back down for about an hour, I think."

I hold up the small business card holder sized device he's made. "How long is the battery life?" I ask.

"Hoping for four hours, which we need to test, but not right now. For now, I need to check its accuracy and its ability to transmit," he tells me with a smile.

"Aye, okay, I can do that. See you boys in a few hours," I tell them. I grin and call Annie as I leave, wondering if she's in town. It's a good hour walk to hers, but she's not through the Old Town as Marcus needs today.

She says she's not busy, nor in town, but she can hop on a bus and meet me. Ten minutes later, I'm at the bus stop waiting for her and we hug as soon as she's alighted.

"What's going on?" she asks in our customary Non Blondes' style.

"Not much! Testing something for the company, so let's walk and talk a bit, aye?" We head off towards the Castle and I bring her up to date. "Resting my arm, off to a corporate big-wig ball at the weekend, telling the guys about being unable to have kids, missing my girl and you!" I tell her, honestly.

"Oh, look at you! How are you going to manage an event like that with yer shoulder?" she asks and we head through the Old Town. I show her the shoulder strap I still have on and she nods.

"The boys are being mindful of yer injury?" she questions, and I nod.

"Aye, they like kissing it better." I wink at her, and she howls in laughter at me.

"How'd they take your news?" she asks tentatively. I explain how I told them, and she swears at me.

"Could ye not have found a better time? Or method?" she scolds me. "I get they needed telling, but your delivery, hen." She gives me that 'you fucked up' look.

"I know. It's just…really bad. But, we talked afterwards."

"They still talked with ye?" she scoffs at me. "You better keep them!"

I turn and nudge her with my good arm, which makes her laugh and then I join in.

"I'm glad they've fallen in love with your kind of crazy!" she tells me as we finish laughing. Love. There's a word I never thought I'd hear out of her mouth about either of us. As we walk, we talk about her love life or the latest "date."

"Honestly, proper bloody bus driver! Wanted to meet the bairn and everything on the first date, but I didn't give him my number." She winks.

"What if ye meet him again?" I ask.

Annie rolls her eyes. "I picked Livingston because that's where he was. I fed him a line, saying I was from a village just outside Broxburn." I shake my head.

"You'd have had to tell him if it got serious," I tell her, but she shakes her head.

"Tried that afore, with Jim. Look where that got me," she laments.

"Ye ken that not all rich folk are like him, don't ye?" I'm going to be in a room full of millionaires and likely a few billionaires next weekend. I doubt any of them will be as obnoxious as Jim.

We walk around Princes Street Gardens, taking in the mound of the Castle high above us. We walk through more of the Old Town, working our way out to Greyfriars Kirkyard and up towards the Royal Mile as we talk.

"Aye, there are bound to be a few, but once bitten," she tells me.

"I can find ye a nice rich guy, if ye'll let me." I test the waters with her, wondering if she'll let me set her up with Tony. She shakes her head.

"Who dae ye know that's got more money than Mr Bloody Scrooge," she hisses the name out at me, then laughs. "Seriously, naw, dinnae go there." I let the subject drop, only because I don't have the brain capacity right now to make sure Annie and Tony meet, but I vow to find a way.

We take a break in Flo's, ordering a coffee and cake each.

"Can you get any more coffee in yer system?" I ask Annie as she enjoys every bite of the moist coffee walnut cake she picked.

"Aye, if I can get it intravenously, I probably will," she grins at me, "Been hard going at work these last few weeks, as if something is in the air or has been put in the water."

I nod, knowing what she does, but here isn't the place to talk about it openly.

"That busy?" I ask, and she nods. We could be talking about any work situation.

"Are you still as busy?" she asks and I understand her meaning.

"Aye, we are. Not found a solution quite yet," I tell her. "Though, the extra support has been beneficial," I state. She smiles and grabs my good hand.

"Glad to hear it. Now, why has he been following us around for the past hour?" She sits back and glares at me, motioning to Adrian. I laugh and pull the transmitter out of my pocket.

"We're testing this and I needed to walk around for a while. Figured we could catch up whilst I did it. He's been on our six because of the credit card skim." Annie widens her eyes at me and leans in.

"Right, story. Tell. With more cake and coffee," she commands, and she orders another two slices and two very large coffees. I grin. I send a text to Aid and Marcus, telling them I'll be later than I thought, I'm catching up with Annie and I get a thumbs up as a reply from them.

Briefly, as quietly as I can, I bring Annie up to date. She hums in places, telling me she's listening, absorbing. As I'm telling her, understanding falls into place in my head and I can see a pattern forming that's not just based on Adrian. I now want to confirm something with Bekah, so I send her a message.

"Ach, ye still use that awful chatting app?" Annie asks me, crossly. I nod and send the question off, hoping for a quick reply.

"You know I love it," I tell her. She rolls her eyes at me.

"Ye ken I dinnae," she growls with a grin on her face. She won't even have any social media profiles, let alone this chat service.

"Live and let live," I tell her, to which Annie sticks her tongue out at me and grins right after. I laugh too; it's been good today to catch up and talk with my best friend.

"Come over on Wednesday, have tea with us," she invites me. I nod.

"Aye, it'll be good to see her. Can't believe she's seven already," I sigh; I missed being there for her birthday, but her presents were sorted before I left.

I receive a call from Bekah as I'm walking back.

"Hey, boss! Best to explain this verbally, I think! What yer asking for," she begins, and I don't have the chance to ask her not to call me boss, "isn't possible, unless yer in the movies. The warnings are coming in via email and each physical device has two ways to be identified. Following me so far?"

"Aye, just about," I reply as I avoid bumping into a few pedestrians.

"Well, that's how I can tell which device is sending the emails. I can't tell where that device was at the time; it's simply not recorded in the hidden email data. And emails aren't like server attacks, they're passive."

"So much for the good guys knowing what the bad guys are doing! Why can't we have things like in the movies?!"

Bekah laughs. "We're catching up! The movies are setting the pace, but it's taking some time to make them reality! Anyway, see you on Monday, aye?"

"Ye will!" I promise.

I spend Wednesday afternoon and evening in the company of my god-daughter and best friend while breaking in the black and red heels. I walked to hers from the office, the need again to stretch my legs driving me forward. Annie stood and made my favourite prawn ravioli, which she cooked to perfection, including a fresh carbonara sauce. I know she hated cooking this when Grandma taught her; it warms my heart that she's bothered to cook my favourite now.

I indulge in my god-daughter's humour, read three books with her and watch her new favourite movie as she curls up in my lap. Annie grins at me and chills out with a soft drink as we sing along to the movie in question.

When bedtime comes, Elle is clear about one thing.

"I miss you lots, Aunty Bee," she tells me. I kiss her on the forehead.

"I know, but I have two boyfriends and a nice big flat to live in, a job to do that's very different from yer mum's. I can go away to work at a moment's notice."

Elle sighs. "I'd like it if we saw more of you," she tells me. I don't need to turn around to know that my best friend heard and is trying not to laugh at her daughter's directness. She gets that from her mother!

"I'll try to be around more, okay?" I tell her, then I give her another kiss on the forehead and tell her it's time to go to sleep. She snuggles down with her favourite toys, I tuck the quilt around her, then turn the lights off. I close the door and head down to find Annie in the kitchen, trying not to laugh.

"Sorry for her directness, but she's no wrong!" Annie tells me.

"Aye, I know. The stint in Bosnia, then the things here…"

Annie nods. "Aye, I just want ye to be careful." She comes over to me to hug me firmly. "But enjoy this, okay? They care, at least I believe they do." She goes over to some paperwork by the back door and hands me a small pile of envelopes. "I've thrown out the fliers, or the ones I could tell were fliers. That lot has been gathering up here since you got back from Bosnia. I forgot to give them to you when you collected the boxes." She smiles.

When I was out in Bosnia, she had my permission to open my mail and check it for the important stuff.

"The last one came in a few days ago; there's a credit card in it," she tells me. I sigh.

"They were meant to send it to work," I moan. Annie shrugs.

"It's here, came this morning, or maybe yesterday?" she questions herself.

Her power of recall is good. "You don't remember?" I ask, checking. She grins.

"Aye, I do, yesterday. But I knew you were coming tonight, so…" She shrugs, but I know she'd have given it to me if I wasn't going to be here tonight, somehow. Opening the envelope, I check the details on my new card, and because of the skim, it has to be activated. Annie makes us both a hot drink and I take the heels off whilst I call them, enjoying the freedom my feet now have. As I'm putting on the flats I'm going to be wearing to walk home, Annie kindly puts the shoes into their box, wrapping them up carefully, and smiles at me when she's done, grinning back as I confirm some details with the card company. Once the card is activated, I put it in the new cardholder and sip the herbal tea.

"I take it yer walking back?" she confirms, and I nod, wiggling my feet in front of her.

"Can't do anything else, walking's all I get to do these days and will be until the shoulder heals up." She nods and smiles, touching me on my good arm.

"Bet that's messing with yer head," she tells me.

"Like ye wouldn't believe," I affirm. "Oh, let me show you what I'm wearing this weekend," I tell her, excitedly.

I show her photos of the final fitting that Bianca took and her jaw drops. "Bloody hell, you'll knock them dead," she tells me. Then she helps me get my jacket on so I can make my way home with the heels in a bag over my good shoulder.

When I get back, I mix up some waffle batter from a recipe I found online and place it in the fridge to sit overnight, keeping my promise to the boys. Then I shower, change, and head to bed.

Marcus and I are up early the following morning; Adrian turned over and went back to sleep, which is quite uncharacteristic of him.

I mix the batter as the now clean waffle machine comes up to temperature and carefully pour in enough mixture to make two waffles each for Marcus and me. Marcus sets up the fruit and toppings selection as I watch the waffle maker do its thing.

"So the test last night was helpful?" I ask him as the machine hisses a little.

"Yep! Annie didn't ask?" he questions.

"I didn't tell her." I grin.

Marcus tsks me and I shrug. "I turned it off when I got there. Besides, you two know her address, it was on the CV she drafted for me." He blinks at me. "I was doing retail security and hated it. She saw your advert, drafted everything out for me to just double-check and send when I got back from that shift if I wanted to apply. I did and, well..."

"Here you are," he finishes my sentence with a grin.

"Yep, here I am." I grin as I check the machine. The light hasn't changed to green so they're not ready yet. "I'm glad she saw it." He nods and reaches over, touching my left hand.

"So are we." He smiles. "Does she know about the device?" he asks as the light changes colour and the machine clicks. I nod, being careful to open the machine and pry the waffles out.

"She's seen it, briefly, she's not yet worked out that it's for her to use and for us to track her down if she's hurt. I'll explain it all when we're ready to hand it over. She thinks it's just something for work."

I plate up two waffles each and make up another half batch for us, leaving the rest of the mix for Adrian. We hear Adrian's shower start and grin, setting up our waffles as we want them. For me, it's fruit and golden syrup; Marcus drowns his in maple syrup.

As we're serving up the last two for us, Adrian joins us, looking refreshed.

"Your waffles will be a few minutes," I explain as Marcus gets him some coffee.

"Great, thanks!" He downs about half the mug before he comes up for air. I swear the man has asbestos insides; that coffee was hot! "So, how was the first distance test?" he asks. Marcus and I laugh, then we repeat the conversation.

Later that day, we're in the office. Marcus is keen to do a battery length test on the transmitter while Adrian gets involved with providing quotes. I'm doing interviews today with Alasdair for some new camera operators we need for certain sites, which leaves Duncan free to kill four hours and drive somewhere. He heads off with the device, watched by Marcus while Alasdair and I get on with setting up the interviewing space.

Bianca may be in reception, but she's good at observing. She'll feed into our thoughts with body language and everything else. We place a 'speaker' on the coffee table, playing something classical, but any private chit-chat won't be so private.

The first candidate arrives and within moments, Alasdair and I are indicating that this person isn't right. Their CV doesn't match who we have in front of us and my skin crawls as I try to work out if I can work with them and if they'll do as they're told or even supposed to. When I feel a negative reply to all three points, I know my answer and fifteen minutes later, we're parting ways.

The next candidate is on time and reminds me of Bekah. Unassuming, hidden in plain sight, and they know their stuff. Their CV isn't as strong as the first person's, but they're a much better candidate and they have camera operation experience with the City Council. Alasdair flags the pre-agreed hand signal under the table; he says yes. I like Alyshia and I concur with him.

The third and final candidate is running late but does call ahead to tell us. They work for another private firm for security and the next shift person didn't turn up on time; or at all. We thank him for letting us know and I tell him to get here when he can.

"I know who this is," Alasdair comments as he reads through the CV.

"You do?" I check. Maybe Alasdair shouldn't interview him.

"Yeah, I can't be by your side… Is the boss finished?" he ventures.

I shrug as best I can. "Let me check." I find him in the kitchen, pouring himself a coffee.

"Are you all done? We've got a conflict of interest I need your help with," I explain and he raises his eyebrows, then wags them at me. I am glad I don't have a coffee in my hand; I'd have spilled it when I tried not to laugh like a hyena at his antics.

"Not us, you eejit," I slap his arm. "Al knows the next candidate," I explain as I grin at him.

"I can jump in. What's it been like so far?" he asks and I bring him up to speed.

"Okay, I trust your judgement. You are good at reading people," he grins. I smile, embarrassed because I know someone who is a heck of a lot better.

Adrian smiles at me as he hands me a coffee he's poured for me as he tops up his own. He motions for us to head down to the reception area and just as we sit on the sofa and chairs, our candidate comes in, hassled and flustered.

Alasdair introduces us, then vanishes for a few moments before he comes back with a coffee for his friend and a nod to Adrian and me. Then, he's gone, probably up to the main office to listen in. Adrian leans forward and casually turns the device off. I glance at the device and him, scolding him with a glare. He shrugs slightly and his lip curls up. Yeah, he doesn't care that Alasdair won't be able to listen in to his friend's interview.

"Take yer time. Thanks for telling us you were going to be late," I begin. I hand signal to Adrian we should chat here and I get the confirmation signal in response. The guy is hassled enough.

"I work at the Harvey Nichols building and the next guy on shift…he just didn't turn up. I couldn't leave the place without any security, but the boss has come in. Thanks so much for seeing me, and I'm sorry I'm in uniform still, I had no chance to change," he begins and Adrian waves his comment off.

"Shows dedication to the job if you're still willing to do that while interviewing for somewhere else. So, why do you want to leave?" The floodgates open, and he walks us through the standards he wants to work to, the reliability and working community he wants. Work is work, but the need to feel safe, secure, appreciated and not taken for granted are his driving factors. I like the guy, and I signal to Aid that it's a yes from me.

He answers with the same signal but tells me to wait. Then he grills the guy for another twenty minutes about camera protocol, the laws of CCTV and everything we expect someone of his position to know. He doesn't get flustered or frustrated at Adrian's questions or change of tact.

"How long is your notice period, Greg?" I ask and he grins.

"My contract is zero hours, but I've done forty-five this week alone. I'm working tomorrow too," he shares and we grin. "But I'd like to give them a week at least." Adrian nods as he writes it down.

"You're letting our car into the rear of Harvey," Adrian says to him, and Greg nods.

"I am. Alasdair asked for a favour." He glances at me, but I have no idea why.

"Sorry, am I missing something?" I ask, looking between the two of them. I knew we were driving the short distance.

"So ye dinnae have to walk far in those heels," Adrian enlightens me and I chuckle, feeling warm and cared for; they've arranged a spot right at the venue. These guys!

Greg, Adrian and I negotiate a salary after we ask Bianca to check on Alasdair for us. She nods and heads off and we quickly narrow down the salary and go through terms and conditions, hours of work and other details. Some of the work we're picking up now is live feed, but most of it is camera review. We've worked out what we need in staff, and Greg and Alyshia will be two of those. I mention to Adrian two won't be enough.

"We can go through more applications next week. The advert is going out again tomorrow in the newspaper and on the recruitment websites," Adrian tells me as we pack up for the day. I nod.

I try to call Alyshia, but she's not answering, so I leave a message, asking her to return my call, then I send the "thank you, but you weren't successful" email to the first candidate. Alyshia calls when we're home and just as dinner is being served. She accepts the offer and terms, and I tell her I'll get the paperwork sorted for her tomorrow morning and that I'll have it all emailed to her. Then I ask Bianca via our chat service if she will draft it all up and send it for me. She says she will and I leave it in her capable hands.

I sigh as I finally sit down, relief sweeping through me. While today hasn't been physically taxing, my mind is shot, my head hurts and my shoulder is whinging, though I'm not sure why.

"Need some painkillers?" Marcus asks as I sit.

I nod. "Yes please, the black box ones? I don't need anything stronger than that right now."

I tuck into the homemade fish and chips Marcus has cooked. Beautifully battered fish in a golden crumb with homemade wedge chips.

"You've outdone yourself," I praise him, and he grins in response. "This is better than the chip-shop and just as indulgent."

"Very glad you like it," he tells me. I hear the guys talking as I eat, and it takes me until halfway through dinner to remember to take the painkillers Marcus handed me what feels like ages ago. As I finish eating, the pain starts to ease, and I can finally join in with what the guys are talking about.

"Suits are back from the cleaners; Morag fetched them for us."

"You two had Morag fetch your suits?" I ask, incredulously.

"One, she offered as she had to fetch Tony's too. We're all wearing the Marcella wing collars this weekend at some point," Adrian says as he stacks the plates and rinses them before putting them in the dishwasher. "Two, we were caught up in work and we didn't want to ask anyone else."

I grin. "She spoils the three of you." And I get struck by an idea. "I think Annie would be good for Tony. We need a way to get the two of them together," I suggest, and they stop, then look at me, each other, and grin.

"When he's out of the funk because of the latest tagger on, that might be a good idea. He's a dad three times over, but his kids are at Uni, youngest starts in a few weeks," Marcus volunteers. "He should be able to handle her wee one," he says with a grin.

"See how he handles her first, she's fiercely protective of Elle," I say. "Last one wanted to meet the bairn on the first date. Annie wasnae having that." I grin.

"No, I can imagine she wouldn't entertain that," Marcus chuckles.

"So what's your dress like?" Adrian asks, not too subtly. I throw my head back and let my mirth show.

"I'll show you tomorrow, when I wear it," I tease. I stand and bring some items from the island over to the sink to be rinsed. "Until then, you have to wait." I wink at him. Then I walk over to the shoes and put them on again, teasing them for an hour as I walk around the flat, swaying my hips. I'm enjoying their physical reactions as their obvious bulges show. As I tidy the last of my things away into the dresser in my room, I can't help but feel that I'm home. Finally, this isn't just a place to rest my head. It's a place for my body and soul to recharge.

~Thirty-Eight~
Marcus

Blythe is teasing us about what her dress looks like, thanks to her wearing those god-damn hot heels around the flat. I groaned last night when she wore them; I noticed Adrian was watching her, not being all that discreet about it. She's keeping the dress a secret and she made the girls swear to do the same. We know it's red; that's all Keith and Alasdair have shared with us because that's all they've been told.

Friday morning sees us tidying the flat then heading in to send out contracts via email to new staff and quotes to potential customers, or a refusal because we're not just an alarm company.

Bekah calls us over mid-morning, the printout in her hand. The hidden cypher in the emails has now been cracked and not just the one in the email to Blythe.

We go through all the emails, from the very beginning and build the picture up. Every single one begins with an apology.

"There are cyphers in cyphers, hence why my programme took a while. It started then went through and found another, decoded that and found another."

"Listen to this," Blythe says. "This is the last one which was sent to me." Blythe coughs and changes her voice.

"You did well facing him off the other day; he hates being challenged. Remember that about him: he's not as weak as D, but hates head-on confrontations. I can't stop them; they're planning something for a few weeks' time. I only hope my warnings help."

"So who is warning us?" asks Bianca, but there we all draw a blank.

"Every single one of the warnings ends with the letter L, Lima," Bekah confirms. "So they either work with the Lloyd brothers..." She starts typing on the computer and gets her search programme to look for connections between the Lloyd cousins that begins with L. "This might take a while." She grins at me.

Adrian's chair rotates side to side, rocking slightly and he's drumming his fingers over the arm of the chair.

"Marc, can we get access to the Harvey camera feed?" he asks me and I shrug.

"We installed it, but it's against ethics and protocols, not to mention a total breach in their trust to do so. However, if they've not changed the password, yes, we can get in. But I did tell them to change the admin passwords when I left them to run things on their own. Why?"

"This warning to Blythe, if I recall, came before we agreed to go to the Harvey Nichols evening. But it's a well-known event that we've been to before. I'm just expecting trouble," he states. I nod in agreement.

"We need to be as prepared as we can be, so if something kicks off, we can deal with it," Alasdair suggests. "We go with earpieces in our pockets. As for the password, they won't know we're watching too." He grins.

"You can't compromise Greg," Blythe counters vehemently.

Alasdair shakes his head. "I won't need to; I know Greg's boss, so I'll just offer additional services, given what is happening on-site tonight," he reasons. Adrian nods.

"Do it, if he says no, then don't force it," Adrian tells him as he looks at Alasdair, who nods in acknowledgement and heads off to make a call. "As for the ears, yes. Bee, you're maybe better off with the battery charged ones tonight. Does anyone fancy some overtime tonight?" he asks. Keith, Bekah, Duncan, and Bianca nod.

"I'd rather be here watching than be at home wondering; that's not good for me," Bekah states.

"There's information about us you'll maybe need if you have to call the police," Blythe states as she looks at Bianca. "Can you give Bekah our details? Ranks, numbers, etc." she asks, and Bianca nods, settling into a workstation and beginning to produce the information she's been asked to.

As Bianca hands Bekah our information, Alasdair states he has access to the Harvey Nichols security cameras.

"I told him there might be trouble tonight and offered some additional support, given who is on the guest list. He told me yes. He sounded stressed."

Blythe grins and offers up another solution. "Al, get access to the City ones too. One pair on the Harvey Nichols place, the other pair on the City ones."

"City ones are a bit harder to gain access to," he states.

"I ken it's gonna be tricky, but the more eyes we have on things," she strongly suggests. The Lloyd brothers are planning something for tonight and I'm not sure what.

We always have the earpieces charged up, but we take a set out and test it, picking a smaller design as the usual big bulky ones are too conspicuous. She does however pick a left earpiece, where she usually favours a right one.

"Easier to reach this side than the other," she explains and we nod. We get the earpiece set up with the correct internal ear channel and check the frequency we're meant to be on. The test runs smoothly, much to my relief and judging by the exhales of the others, they're relieved too. Alasdair confirms he's gotten into the City CCTV systems with Keith's help.

"They won't know," Keith promises me and I give him a nod. We've banks of monitors across all the tables, and half an hour from the earpiece test, they're configured how Alasdair and Keith want them. There's not a spare monitor in the office.

"I hope nothing happens though." Bekah smiles at us.

"So do we. I suggest you all go home, get something to eat, and be back for around eighteen-thirty?" Everyone nods in agreement, and we lock up and head off. Alasdair and Duncan have keys and the codes to let everyone back in.

We do the same, though we don't eat anything heavy. I cook some omelettes with cheese, Italian meats and mushrooms. I make Blythe's first as it's bound to take her longer to get ready than us, mostly because of her shoulder. Then I whip up Adrian's and mine, casting sly glances at Blythe as she makes small sounds of enjoyment. The small moans of pleasure that escape her lips stir my cock, making concentrating on the cooking very difficult.

"I'll see you when I'm dressed. I take it you can do the ties?" she asks and we nod.

"Tony had us taught by the tailor the first time. It's not a lesson we've forgotten," Adrian reminisces with mirth.

She grins, clears her dinner things away and stacks the dishwasher. Then she vanishes and we hear her door lock and the shower start. Darn, we can't sneak in for a peek at the dress!

An hour later, we're in the wing collar Marcella dress shirts and trousers, but not the full suit. Blythe comes out to grab a drink of water and her makeup is on, but she's in her dressing gown; the dress isn't on her yet.

"Could you tighten the strap for me?" she asks, and the dressing gown slips down on that shoulder. I create a little distance between us, hiding the fact I've gone hard again, seeing her nearly naked, the anticipation building within me. Adrian lets out a small groan as he turns to see me helping her. Fuck, we've got an hour before we need to leave; having our way with Blythe beforehand isn't on the agenda.

"Down, boys, you'll be tenting those suit trousers all night, I promise ye," she teases us. "Later, when we're home," she drawls out seductively, then she bites her lower lip. I notice the word she uses. Home. This isn't just a place to rest our heads, a factor I told her about down in Carterton that first time.

"That's a promise," I tell her, and she grins at me, cups my face, and kisses me lightly. I growl as her scent surrounds me, and I can't help but inhale slightly as I help her with the shoulder brace, gently tightening the strap before dropping a kiss on the shoulder.

Then she kisses Adrian before she vanishes back into her room, taking a glass with her and locking the door behind her again.

Half an hour later, she emerges wearing a coat over her clothes. Her makeup is red-carpet standard.

"Wow!" I declare, even though I can't see the dress.

"No peeking!" she tells us with a grin, "I'll show you at Harvey Nichols," she confirms. She grabs her shoes and sits down to put them on. I can't help but watch as her feet slide into them. The coat parts at the bottom, revealing red velvet. Then she stands and she's nearer five-foot-eleven rather than her usual five-eight.

"Bows, boys," she tells us, and we grin.

"In the car, before we get out," Adrian stiffly replies.

"Make sure you do," she tells us. "I want pictures of you both in those suits." She winks at us.

"We want a picture of you in that dress too," I remind her, speaking for the both of us.

"Oh absolutely! Shall we go?" she asks and leads the way out of the flat.

~Thirty-Nine~
Blythe

Marcus drives us the very short distance to the Harvey Nichols building. There are a few cars and catering vans in the small rear car park, which is usually where the delivery lorries arrive. We have the earpieces in by the time Marcus is applying the hand-brake past the security barrier. He parks near the gatehouse, then he reaches for the box of false toys to show off to some potential clients once they've put on their bow-ties. We've packed a few live samples and left them in a metal box in the back passenger footwell.

Adrian helps me out of the car. I'm excited by this event, the first one I've ever been to. My RAF years never saw me do things like this. As we arrive up on the fourth floor via the elevator, we're guided to the cloakroom and it's time to reveal the dress to them. Marcus helps me remove the coat, his feather-light touch on my shoulder sends shivers through me. As Marcus hands the coat to the younger concierge, I do a slow twirl, enjoying the lustful looks from them both. I've had a little longer to get used to the men in their tuxedos, but my breath still hitches as I take them in.

"Fuck, Bee, you're gorgeous!" Adrian mutters. The young concierge is unable to take his eyes off me until Adrian steps directly into his line of sight. I can only grin as the poor lad quickly returns to his job.

There's a photographer set up under some LED trees decorating an archway in the foyer, and I motion to it. The guys grin and we pose for a photo. I'm not sure whose hands are the most possessive. Theirs on me or mine on them, maybe that's not important. I smile, the flash goes off and we head in to mingle.

The fourth floor is decorated like a hidden woodland glade, a much bigger version than the photo booth hinted at. There are a few tables at the edges, but the floor is clear and servers mingle, offering canapes and drinks to the guests. There are more warm white LED trees scattered about, softening the mood, and just as Adrian promised, there's a string quartet in the corner, playing classical music.

They escort me to the balcony, and I understand now why this is a sought after venue. Level with us is Edinburgh Castle, lit up against the slowly darkening night sky. We're looking almost parallel to it, not up at it. It looks so very different from this angle and I take a moment in the calmness of the men standing beside me to appreciate the historic landmark.

"Beautiful, isn't it?" someone states and we turn.

"Fraser," Adrian greets him. "Allow us to introduce you to Blythe Grievson, one of our newest and best assets," he boasts. I beam at the praise and Fraser takes my hand, shakes it gently, then kisses the knuckles.

"I'm charmed." He smiles at me.

"As am I." I look at Adrian. I know who Fraser Michelson is, but not what he is to Adrian or Marcus. Fraser's hands are warm, slippery, and his lips linger a little too long on my knuckles for my liking, but I bite my tongue and play nice; for now.

We switch around who is listening to the reports from the office for the first half an hour, keeping abreast of what our team is reporting. I catch his glance once or twice, but Marcus shakes his head quietly. Nothing is happening yet. Then he removes his earpiece as Adrian takes over and we carry on mingling.

"Who is Fraser?" I ask when we get a quiet moment or two. The prop drink in my hand has been swapped out for water, thank goodness.

"He was very keen to back us before he learned Tony already had. Laid it on thick, wee bit smarmy, but a decent enough backer." I nod. Smarmy is one word for Mr Fraser Michelson, but not my chosen one.

I get introduced to a lot of people, and my mind gets foggy with who is who, despite the preparation before. An hour or so in, the drink I'm holding is switched out again for water. Pretty soon, I'm wishing I hadn't sipped so much; now I have to go visit the ladies. I tell the guys where I'm going and they nod in acknowledgement.

When I come back, Adrian is talking with someone and I can't see Marcus.

"Where's Marc?" I ask, finding my earpiece and placing it in my ear. I'm glad we ate earlier; my stomach is in knots with the nervous energy of anticipation and agitation.

"He was just here," he says and we look around. We can't see him. I glare at Adrian and tap the earpiece.

"Can't see M. Can you confirm location?" I ask as I find a quiet corner out on the balcony. Alasdair and Duncan are used to how we talk, they served too, but in different arms and units.

"We have eyes on the place, we can see you on the balcony. Checking the other cameras…" Duncan's voice trails off. "Bee, M just fired up the transmitter." I turn to find Adrian right next to me, listening via his own earpiece.

"Need eyes on him," Adrian growls quietly. I wait for his cue; even though Marc is my lover, he is Adrian's brother, so whatever his decision is, I'll back him if it's not going to break the law or get Marc hurt.

"We've got him. Ground floor. There's a gun pointing at him."

I swear. "D, call it in. Give them the details. Tell them guns are involved, that this is possible terrorism," I state, using the adrenaline that's now pumping through me as I was trained to. "It'll bring down all hell and trust me, that's not a bad thing." I nod to Adrian and we start making our way down to the rear car park and Marcus.

Adrian is slightly ahead of me and reaches the gatehouse first. I catch up just as Greg tells him that he saw what was going down and called the police too. These shoes are killing my ability to run, but I can stride well enough in them.

"ETA?" I ask into the headset. Calling a gun incident in progress will have the Edinburgh armed unit out here in minutes.

"Three," is the reply. I begin counting in my head, starting at one hundred and eighty, backwards.

"What can you see?" I ask as I pull out the spare car keys. Taking my shoes off, I tuck them under Greg's desk, then I crouch, keeping my body low as I sneak my way to the car and the back passenger door. Thank goodness the weather is playing nice and it's dry. Adrian stays in the gatehouse, but I can hear him on the earpiece. He's being very quiet. In Bosnia, we'd often split up, playing to our strengths and skills. I trust him to get to Marcus, but I have to distract whomever this is, and my gut is telling me it's Lloyd.

"Marcus is at the far side of the car park, behind a white catering van. Not sure who else is there, can't get a clear visual."

"How do you know it's Marc?" I whisper fiercely, knowing my voice will be picked up easily by the earpiece.

"Tracker," Duncan's voice comes back to me. I quietly grab the metal box, closing the door behind me very gently, then I head back towards the gatehouse. We've about two minutes before the armed units turn up.

"Confirm visual on armed units when they arrive," I tell Duncan. I pause, open the box and take out a smoke bomb. "Get him outta there," I tell Adrian, who nods back, then I push the old metal munitions box towards the gatehouse and stride towards the corner Marcus is in.

~Forty~
Adrian

I watch as Blythe shoves the metal box towards the gatehouse, then heads towards the white catering van, standing fucking tall. She told me to get him outta there, then I caught her meaning and nodded once. She means Marcus. Greg looks at me with dread on his face, but I get the plan.

I know her strengths, how she'll most likely play this out.

"She'll distract them; she's bloody hard to not see, aye?" I tell Greg. He doesn't know us; he's in the deep end. "You know what to tell the police?" I ask as I grab the box, then the other device Marcus rigged up and place the box with others under Greg's table.

"Yeah, we've got the cameras on them." He points to the rack of displays. Guests are piling out the front of the building; the evacuation is well underway.

"Don't let anyone take that," I tell him and he nods, then he puts it in a locker, out of sight along with her shoes.

"Get as many lights on them as possible, blind them to anything but what's in front of them." Greg nods and presses a few buttons, bringing more light into the service yard. I smack him on the arm and crouch low, then head out of the gatehouse to follow Blythe's path.

My heart is in my mouth, this is worse than what we ever faced in Bosnia, all because of what I feel for her. We've another minute before armed police turn up and two, maybe three more minutes for them to be deployed.

Keeping low, I head past the barrier and sneak towards the catering van, hoping that the caterers have been silly and left the keys in the ignition. In my earpiece, I can hear Blythe breathing, counting quietly as I watch her stride with confidence, barefooted, towards whoever has Marcus at gunpoint and I pray. In Bosnia, she was formidable, but she often had a gun of her own to use or she was higher up with a sniper rifle. Not so in this country. I have prayed a few times in my life, but never as hard as I am right now. We'd better fucking come out of this alive. All of us.

I watch as she stops and my heart leaps into my throat. Hands held out, feet steady and set. I assume she's tucked the smoke bomb somewhere, and I wait.

"Armed units coming upon location. Thirty seconds," Alasdair's voice is low in my ear. Blythe's not moved, and I realise she must still be counting down their arrival. With about ten seconds to go, she calls out Lloyd's name and steps into his view.

As she does, I check the driver's area of the van that's blocking the camera view, but the keys aren't in the ignition. I leave the door open, then check underneath. On the other side of the van, I see black trousers sitting on the floor, the back of a tux jacket leaning against the van, his left hand behind his back. Marcus.

I slide low to get under the van, then I slowly, quietly, creep towards my brother. Blythe's bare feet on the tarmac make me feel cold and I shiver, both due to the situation we're in, but mostly because of my fear of what might happen to her. In my head, the armed units are here, and the distant, repeated flash of blue reflects off something, confirming it.

~Forty-One~
Marcus

A gun pointing at me is something I never want to have happen to me again. How my brother and Blythe did this for a living, I'll never know. I've already said a quick prayer of thanks to whatever God I'll meet, thanking him for the time I got with Blythe and I pray she'll stay with Adrian if they make it out of here. I have already accepted that I probably won't.

"Lloyd!" Blythe's voice cuts through my thoughts and she's there, in *that* red dress, like an angel sent from hell. Her blue eyes are lighter; either that or the floodlights are playing tricks on them. There's smoke or steam from somewhere behind her, adding to the vision that hell spat her out just to help me.

"You fucking beauty," I mutter under my breath.

"You, again!" David Lloyd turns the gun towards her as he screeches.

"Oh!" she coos. "A thirty-eight special, nice!" She tilts her head at him. "Revolvers like that are illegal in this country though."

"I don't care about that!" he spits. "You're a fucking pain in the arse! A nice little accident is all we needed," he begins.

"Needed it for what? Come on, man, make some sense, will ye?" I can see her hands twitching, but I realise it's not a twitch. It's a pattern and while David's attention is on Blythe, I push my earpiece back in. "I want to know what all this was for!"

"Armed units are on site. They're asking for your frequency," Alasdair's voice quietly seeks permission.

"Granted," Adrian's low, gruff voice replies before I can say a thing. Great, we'll have them in our ears in a few seconds. There's a crackle, then we do.

"Tac Advisor Jimmy McVay. We're deploying the unit now. Are any of you armed?" he asks.

"Negative. Lady in red is former RAF MP Blythe Grievson," Adrian explains. His voice is too near to just be on the earpiece. I release my held breath, knowing he's around me somewhere. "She has a smoke bomb on her to use if you need it. That's all she's armed with."

"Understood. Where are you?" I hear McVay ask. I pull the earpiece out slightly, so I can focus on what Lloyd is telling Blythe.

"You were never meant to get involved! Why did you get involved?" he screams at Blythe. The gun is in his right hand and he squeezes his eyes with his left. "You were nice to me! Why did you have to interfere?"

"Get involved in what? What are you trying to achieve? Let me help you," she offers.

"You can't! He fucked it up!" David begins to wave the gun around. "It's all fucked up!"

"What did he do that he shouldn't have?" she asks him. Then I hear her voice in just the earpiece although I can't see her mouth moving. "He's no right in the head."

"Understood," McVay's voice comes back. "We'll have units in place in two, keep buying me the time, Grievson,"

"I'm in place to extract my brother," Adrian's voice whispers into the headset. Then he says one word and I understand how. "Shed."

We would often hide under the shed, having dug out underneath it one summer due to the heat. I'm leaning against a catering van; I can only guess that he's underneath it. I feel three taps against my left hand and know it's him. I wiggle my fingers at him, keeping an eye on Lloyd, but acknowledging my brother.

"Where is Andrew, David? Tell me what he did that he shouldn't have?" Blythe asks and she's still moving her fingers so very slightly. "Tell me where he is." Then he looks across at me.

"Andrew? He's in the van! Said I had to do this, but I can't..." David looks directly at me. I stay perfectly still, aware I'll give Adrian's position away if I move.

"You can't, what?" Blythe asks. David loses his focus on me and turns to her.

"I can't have him; he never wanted me," he points to me without looking at me, "but he won't get to decide after tonight!" he screams.

I feel the catering van door open, the vehicle rocks slightly and Andrew Lloyd comes down the stairs. He displays no emotion and the fact he is also holding a gun like his cousin makes my blood run cold.

"Fuck, hurry up!" I mutter, hoping that the earpiece catches my words. Please God, let the armed unit be in place already.

"Oh, you got her into the open," Andrew coos, pleased. He turns towards Blythe after casting a glance at me. I can't tell where Adrian is right now, but Andrew is pointing the gun at her too.

"You might as well tell her," Andrew declares. "Not that she'll live to do much about it."

I hear Blythe chuckle into the headset. "ETA?" she breathes.

"Sixty," McVay answers back.

"Hurry the fuck up," she instructs.

"You were always nice to me," David says to me, his eyes soft. "Your brother always seemed to attract your attention away from me with the women he'd bring back to your flat." Then he turns to Blythe in a way that chills me. He's not a puppy; he's a deranged, rabid dog. "Then you turned up after I mistook the Commander's son's teasing for advances," David explains. "I wanted him to come and join us, his tech with ours would rock this industry. I need his help to get the damn things to work right!" He clutches his left eye again, screaming as if in pain while the gun wavers in mid-air.

"Andy said he'd persuade him, and set his focus on us..."

All this for...what?! *He has got to be fucking joking. What the fuck is wrong with these two?!* That job offer was a joke and I've never known David to mess with electronics. We've never spoken about it, it's never even been hinted at, and there was nothing suggested in the "offer." Moving four hundred miles for a job that meant I'd be working for free was never an offer. Working with my brother was the only dream I've ever entertained. Until Blythe.

"I was never into other men," I state, clarifying a point he made. David turns to me and he looks like I've just injured his puppy. "Never have been. My brother..."

"Should be dead!" Andrew cuts me off. "We missed him in Bosnia, though our guy..."

Blythe cackles demonically. "That was your sniper?" I have no idea what they're talking about, but I hear Adrian in the earpiece.

"Oh shit," he mutters. "Blythe killed him." I can't help but feel proud, hearing that she killed someone who aimed a gun at Adrian, long before they were anything more than employee and boss. I realise quickly these feelings of mine are probably rather sick too.

Blythe continues, "Your man, the one who took a crack shot at Aid *and* our client one dark night?" She waits. But I'm not sure what for. "The one I killed, if you're wondering what happened to him." She pauses again, then she growls the remainder of her sentence out. "Through his left eye," Blythe declares slowly, punctuating exactly how she did it. Both Lloyds freeze and turn to her.

"You?!" they declare and Blythe's fingers stop moving.

"Smoke," Adrian declares in the earpiece and Blythe puts her hands behind her back. Given her shoulder, I know that what she's doing now has to hurt.

"No smoke. Ten," McVay instructs and Blythe lifts her chin.

"You've less than that man!" Adrian growls.

"Aye, me! What? Ye think I'm just a pretty wee face?" She pulls the smoke bomb ball out from behind her, pulls a pin, and then she throws it at the Lloyd brothers with her left hand. I go wide-eyed as they watch my smoke bomb roll towards them like it's a tennis ball. Nothing has happened. It's misfiring.

"Go, go, go!" I hear in my ear. Suddenly, there's a swarm of armed police surrounding the Lloyd brothers, and I duck under the catering truck to join Adrian. I almost want to turn around to see what is happening from here, but Adrian commands me to move my fucking arse. The patchy tarmac is dirty, dry and scratchy as we crawl out, then we scramble to our feet, making our way quickly to the front of the vehicle. The police have surrounded the Lloyd cousins, their huge guns drawn.

They're read their rights and handcuffed as an already long list of charges is rattled off to them. Then Andrew makes a dash for Blythe as he's hauled to his feet, even though he's cuffed. He tackles her into the wall and she brings her left elbow down onto his neck, making him crumple. A knee to his face catches him on the way down, her red dress flying around as she pulls off several close-quarter martial art moves. Several officers take aim at Lloyd, letting Blythe do her thing.

"Tango down," I hear an officer say as Andrew glares at Blythe from his crouching point, then charges into her as he roars. How can he still be moving? Then a blood-curdling scream pierces the air, one I've never heard before and never want to again. It matches the smoke bomb as it finally goes off, obscuring our view for far too long.

When the smoke clears, Blythe is leaning against the wall, tears streaming from her eyes, but Lloyd is out cold, slumped between two huge armed officers as they drag him off, literally. I notice her shoulder is out of place again and I swear as I point it out to Adrian.

~Forty-Two~
Blythe

I cry as the paramedic resets my shoulder for the seventh time, but at least he listened to how I needed it done. I resign myself to needing the operation now; I can't keep avoiding the damn thing anymore. The paramedic unit has gas and air, thank the Gods and I take a few deep breaths of it before and after the shoulder is reset. The dress...I dare not look to see what state this beautiful dress is now in. McVay comes and introduces himself to me and he brings my men to me. With my good arm, I hug one after the other, glad we're at least alive. I cry as both gently hug me, the pain from my shoulder, the adrenaline drop and seeing them alive, dirty but unhurt in general is a huge relief. When I take a moment to try and compose myself, McVay says he'll get a statement another time, but soon. He tells me that he'll speak to Munroe, who he now knows has a long list of background information that they need to discuss.

"You're alive!" I touch Marcus' face and try to kiss him, but the gas and air are making me light-headed and unstable on my feet. The paramedics try to force me to lay on the gurney, but I don't want to! Marcus joins me in the ambulance and tells me I need to go to hospital and to lay down. My mouth is awfully dry, my head hurts and my shoulder is taking all my attention. I watch as he hands the keys to Adrian who nods at me, tweaks my toes and leaves the ambulance so we can get underway.

By the time I'm in an A&E unit being assessed several hours later, I finally get a drink of water. Then I'm told I'm allowed home. McGowan's private health care will take care of the operation. I blink. What private health care? I wasn't aware we had that. I thought I'd be waiting months to have it done on the NHS, not that I minded, but at least I won't have to wait that long.

A nurse comes in with Marcus tailing behind her. She motions to me and he steps up to the bed I'm sitting on as she vanishes.

"Wanna go home?" he asks me in a careful whisper, and I nod.

"Yes, please," I breathe. I've been trying to process all that's happened over the last nine months or so. Our trip to Bosnia was to train the businessman's own team. Learning that the sniper attacks weren't probably just aimed at the client, but at Adrian too, makes me cold to the core in sheer anger. *Were they attacks even aimed at the client at all?*

As we're in the BMW heading home, I struggle to fathom out why David Lloyd would do this, or why his cousin would get involved. I pull myself out of the mind funk I've sunk into and listen to the brothers.

"Their assets will be frozen, accounts, business, the whole lot," Adrian explains.

"Why?" I breathe the question. "I never worked out why?!" I tell them, then I sit back and close my eyes. *I want to know why.*

"We don't know either, not yet, not for sure. I'm going to let Edinburgh's finest work that one out; Munroe will have fun passing that file along," Marcus tells me.

I sigh, frustrated because I hate not knowing the answers to things.

"Bee, darling, put your earpiece back in would you?" Aid asks me as we drive near Annie's estate as we head home. I do and then I hear Bekah and Bianca's voices in my ear, asking questions.

"Is she okay?" Bianca asks. Her voice is high, tight.

"I'm fine," I sigh and Bianca yips in delight. "I'm alive, but I hurt a lot. I want to sleep, but I need answers," I reply.

"I can provide you with one," Bekah's cheery voice chimes in. I glance at the car clock; it's four am. "I know who the L is. She's Andrew's ex-girlfriend. She's helping the police with their enquiries, or will be when they go find her. They have her details now. And I've one disturbing fact; those black market guns had live rounds in them."

I shiver, knowing that at the range I was at, just about eight feet, any of those bullets would have wrecked parts of me that would never be recoverable. I might have walked around military bases with a Bond style PPK as a part of my uniform and training, but being actually shot was something I'd thankfully avoided. Shot at? Yes. Avoiding other physical injuries? Not so much, the shoulder being testament to that.

"Go get some sleep, you guys. Thanks for having our backs." We say good night, then I remove and turn off the ear-piece. I close my eyes for a second, then we're home.

The men help me up to the flat, practically carrying me. I'm exhausted, full of painkillers and I can just about keep my eyes open. I'm sure they're just as tired as me, but still, they lend me their strength and care. Nothing but their love for me makes sense right now. I don't know who helps me undress, gives me the big painkillers, or who puts the pillow behind my shoulder. I drift off to sleep in a darkened room, floating on a warm fluffy cloud that I know I can't fall from.

I awake to the muffled sounds of people talking. I try to work out who they belong to as I wake up a little more. Until I hear one that is awfully familiar, but I can't call out, my throat is too dry. I get up and head to the bathroom, trying to do what I need to, my feet are just about working. I hear my door open and Marcus pops his head in.

"Oh, hello, you! You've got a guest…" he tells me. "Do you need some help?" he offers, and I nod. "Here," he tells me, as he pours me a glass of water. "Eric said those drugs last night with the gas and air might make you really dehydrated. How are you feeling?" he asks.

I can only groan, I can't formulate the words in my head, let alone get them out of my dry mouth. Two glasses later and I still feel like I'm in a desert.

"Feeling better?" Marcus asks, and I nod a little. "Blythe, talk to me."

"Dry throat," I croak and pour myself another glass, but then my bladder becomes painfully full, making me use the toilet again. Marcus vanishes then comes back with my dressing gown, or rather, a dressing gown that is neutral in colour and is far too big for me. It smells of Adrian. Marcus helps me into it then guides me out to the living room. Adrian isn't around, but my brother is.

"Gently!" I squeak before sitting down gingerly in a chair. I can just make out my younger brother's tight features, thin lips, and pale blue eyes. The same blue I display when I'm annoyed.

"Marcus has brought me up to speed about what happened. How are you feeling?" he asks as he moves to the seat nearest to me.

"Sore throat," I croak. Byron looks at Marcus with a frown.

"She was on the gas and air before she took the doozy of a pain killer. We were told it would knock her around for forty-eight, but they'd lessen the pain."

"What exactly did they give her?" Byron asks as he watches me.

"I'll go fetch them, I forget their name," Marcus offers. "Don't let her wander off," he instructs my brother, who nods. Marc comes back with the big horse tablets that I took one of before I went to bed. I have no idea what time it is now, but I've not slept enough.

Byron looks at the drugs, then me. He puts them down and there's a sadness in his eyes. "Back to bed, sis, come on," he instructs and I have no issue with that. He leads me back into bed, sets me up and then leaves. I don't hear the door close.

~Forty-Three~
Marcus

Seeing Byron Grievson standing at the building door was a shock, but I let him in. Adrian went into the office for an hour or two; his agitation levels were just as high as they were last night and I'm not sure what has caused it. Whilst Blythe was being assessed by medical staff at the Royal Infirmary, we were giving statements to Tac Officer McVay and DCI Munroe in an empty doctor's office.

Lloyd had separated me from Adrian by dressing as a waiter, cliché I know, but it worked. The gun in his hand into my back was all he needed. Learning on the way home that it was live ammunition still scares me.

Byron wanted all the details when he arrived. He saw the incident on the news. When he recognised his sister in the photos that had been taken in the reception area, that the press had somehow gotten pretty quickly, he took emergency leave from his base in Waddington, driving straight to us. I'm not sure how he found us, but it wouldn't be hard, I guess, remembering that he is one of Blythe's emergency contacts.

The first thing I did was get his car into the car park beneath. The last thing he'd want would be a parking ticket when visiting his sister. As I come back with coffee, he's on the phone and talking Italian after he's tucked Blythe back into bed. He's flipping her horse-tablet medication around in his fingers and even I know he's swearing. Just like Blythe, he doesn't sound Scottish at all as he talks with his family.

"Thanks, Mama, see you soon!" he tells her. Then he hangs up and rubs his face.

"Bad news?" I ask, sitting on the sofa and pointing to the black coffee he asked for earlier.

"Well, not for me. For Bly and you pair, yeah." He sighs deeply and holds up the small pack of extra-strong drugs Eric told us to use sparingly with supervision for Blythe's pain. "This family of drugs were given to my grandmother for her dementia. They cannot, I repeat, *cannot* be given to Blythe again." I blink at his commanding statement. "Ever."

"Hang on," I tell him and bring up her medical records on screen. That drug, or the basis of that drug, isn't listed as something she's reactive to. I showed him the records that we had no idea about. "But why can't she have them?"

He sighs. "They made Grandma worse. She'd take one and lose three days. No memory, total wipeout of those days. You could give her one on Monday, as an example. When she became aware on Thursday or even Friday sometimes, she'd think it was the day after, or the same day. She'd have no recollection of the days in-between, conversations she had, what she said or did. It may have taken her pain away, but the other side of it…" He shivers. "Please, don't give her these again."

"Bleeding Nora, we had no idea," I breathe. We'd been there with our own mother.

"We didn't, until we had several instances of it almost back to back. She had packets of these scattered around the place, and we think she was taking them, thanks to stashes hidden around her room. We had to burn the ones we found; Italy doesn't take their drugs back once they're issued."

"I'm sorry for your loss," I tell him. "We know what it's like to lose a relative to dementia. Our mother went the same way," I tell him. He nods and there's a soft look in his clear blue eyes.

"So you know," he says quietly, and I grimace.

"Oh hell, yes we do."

I take the medication and put it in the back of the medicine cupboard. Blythe isn't tall enough to reach right to the back and neither am I, unless I take everything out. She won't be able to do that at the moment, so for now, they're safe. I'll take them back another day.

At that moment, Adrian calls and explains the reason for his agitation. The Lloyd cousins interfered with our initial seed site, taking down all of their cameras and security. Thanks to that seed client, we had many other clients as he was also someone we used as a reference, beyond Tony.

"From what I've been shown on video call, they placed some smaller EMPs down there and set the lot off at the same time."

"Fucking dickheads," I curse them, making Byron snort.

"Who else is there?" asks Adrian, picking up on the extra sounds. I turn the camera around and show him Byron. "Bloody hell, Grievance! Never expected… Is Bee okay?" he asks in alarm.

"She's fine, but those meds Eric gave her, she shouldn't have. We've got a case of bad mum days on our hands until this gets through her system," I explain.

I can hear Adrian curse; he understands the bad mum days reference. "Understood," he sighs in acknowledgement. "We need to go down, but it's going to have to be both of us because of what the bastards did."

"I can't stay with her, I have seventy-two off base and then have to have my arse back on site." Bryon grimaces. "I'll be glad when my tenure is up in eighteen months."

"Can we wait a day or two, until this is out of her system?" I ask, but Adrian shakes his head.

"I wish, I promised we'd be down tomorrow. I didn't realise Bee was affected like that," he explains.

"What about Annie?" Byron offers. "She's the only other one Bly will listen to, and trusts."

It might just work.

~Forty-Four~
Adrian

We take turns in driving back from Bristol, leaving at three am, eager to be home to see Blythe. She's not answered our calls or texts since yesterday afternoon, and as the dawn breaks outside of Sheffield, I get more nervous, especially after the garbled, almost drunken message at nearly five am to Marcus. Marcus' mouth is set; he's usually one to fidget on long car journeys. Not this time.

Marcus calls Annie at around seven am, a slightly more sociable hour than oh-five-hundred. She answers on the first ring.

"Hello?" she answers, slight concern in her voice.

"Annie, it's Marcus and Adrian. We can't reach Blythe, is she with you?" he asks.

"She should be, hang on…" We hear Annie climb the stairs and call for Blythe. Then Annie swears. "She's not here. And her kit bag is gone. When the hell…hang on, putting you on the loudspeaker."

We can hear other movements and Annie telling her daughter she's coming down now to get breakfast for her. When we left two days ago, Blythe was staying at Annie's for a few days so that she was somewhere familiar with a friend.

"Camera on the door shows she left just after four am. I recognise the taxi firm; let me call you back." And Annie hangs up. Twenty minutes later, she does exactly that. We're a few miles closer to home, but it might as well be five hundred.

"They dropped her at Edinburgh Airport, she was blethering on about catching a flight to Bologna. Let me see…" There's a pause. "Yes, darling, you can have some juice; I'm trying to find out where yer Aunty Bee has gone." I hear a little voice ask a question, but I can't quite make it out. "No, petals, she's not supposed to be gone yet." A few extra seconds pass. "Elle, it's important I do this so we can find Bee. Can you get yer breakfast like ye usually do, please?" I grin, Annie reminds me so much of Mom. "Good girl," Annie praises as things go quiet.

"Right…There was a zero six-thirty flight to Bologna. It's a three and a half hour flight from Edinburgh. She'll not have landed yet, and they're two hours ahead. I'll call her folks, explain what's happened. Yer gonna have to go chase her down, lads."

"Oh fuck!" I spit out. Maybe one of us should have stayed behind, and I kick myself for it, not appreciating the extent of what Byron was telling us.

It's nearly eight am before we can call the office; Bianca and Alasdair are usually the first ones in.

"McGowan Security, how can I direct your call?" Bianca answers cheerfully.

"Good morning, it's Adrian," I tell her quickly.

"Oh, hey, boss! How are you? Are things okay?" she asks in a slightly concerned voice.

"Bianca, Blythe's headed out to her family's place in Bologna, but she left at half six this morning. Can you book us on a late afternoon or an evening flight?" I ask. Bianca is good at this.

"Of course, I can! What time are you likely to be here to drop that dead kit in?" she asks and I can hear the tapping of the keyboard.

"We're just near Sheffield, so five hours or so? Depends on traffic."

"Okay, there's an eight-thirty flight...sorry, boss, twenty-thirty flight." I grin at Bianca's self-correction, but only because she picked up on it and flustered herself. "But that's one seat...there's a twenty-one-fifteen flight, which is going to make it pretty late arriving as it's a three and a half hour flight."

"Book us on what you can and have the details ready with our paperwork, would ye? We'll have time for a coffee and a quick wash afore we go."

"Sure thing! On it!" she replies, and we hang up.

Four and half hours later, we're parking the car up in the garage spot as usual. Leaving our clothes bags in the car, we take up the faulty kit we had to go and replace. I kick myself again; I should have sent Duncan or Alasdair down with Marc and stayed here. Catastrophic failure of the surveillance kit didn't need us both, but it showed us in a better light to be there together given it was the Lloyd boys who killed it all. I'm in the kitchen, grabbing a coffee, when the buzzer sounds and Bianca's voice rings out over the speakers, "Adrian, Marcus? You've a video call coming in, and he wants to speak with either or both of you. He looks like Blythe."

We head to my office, and I fire up the video chat software. It's only been a few days since I set eyes on Byron Grievson.

"Grievance..." I nod at him. He nods back.

"Have you got a few moments? I...kinda need a favour."

"You want a favour from me?" I ask incredulously. He nods slowly and sips from a mug.

"I'll let you know exactly where to find my sister, smoothing the way with my parents, if you can help me find Duckie." I blink a few times.

"You want to find Duckie?" I ask, hesitantly. I'm still in contact with her, sure, but do I want to send Grievance Junior her way?

"I need to, please?" he requests. He's never asked anything of me before, and his voice is gentle, almost begging.

"Give him the details," Marcus mouths at me. I pull my phone out and dig out Duckie's details, then send them straight to Byron's phone when he gives me his number.

"She's down in Milton Keynes," I tell him. He nods and sighs.

"Thank you," he tells us. A few seconds later, my phone beeps as he sends me details back. An Italian address and a phone number. "When you get out of Bologna Airport, call Luca on that number. He'll take you straight to Papa's. I'll advise him and Mama you're coming, or he might get the shotgun out. Blythe might be older, but she's still his baby girl." He nods and taps something into his phone. "Good luck," he says, then he ends the chat.

"We so fucked up," I growl to Marcus, annoyed with myself. We have to sort this; I thought she understood that with the chat we had with her brother and Annie. "One of us should have stayed." I state, sighing heavily. That sinking feeling is too bloody accurate at times.

"Shoulda, woulda, coulda," Marcus replies. "Let's fix it, aye?"

I give him a single, sharp, determined nod in reply.

Bianca appears at the door and knocks, then she hands us two sets of papers. Flights, business class out of Edinburgh tonight to arrive at nearly midnight Bologna time. Boarding passes are already issued, thanks to Bianca knowing our details better than we do and her checking us in.

"First flight I can get both of you on." We look at each other, and Bianca shakes her head. "Will you two get off your arses and go chase her down already?"

Marcus moves and then hesitates.

"Now!" Bianca instructs, pointing to the door. "You won't get answers here! Shift! Shoo!" She waves us out of the offices, and the others are gathered on the mezzanine balcony. "I want my nice boss back!" she tells us.

"Don't screw it up!" Bekah tells me, which gets an "oi!" from Keith.

"Go! I'll cover for a few days!" Alasdair tells me, his arms around Bianca.

"Good luck!" Duncan and the others chorus.

We nod and head to the car, then Edinburgh airport.

~Forty-Five~
Marcus

As Adrian parks the car in the long stay car park at Edinburgh Airport, I call the Italian number and in sketchy Italian, Google translate and broken English, I manage to get Luca to understand we'll be arriving late to surprise Blythe; that Byron told us he'd take care of us.

We refrain from alcohol; both of us are too keyed up to drink. We want clear heads when we land. As it's a three and a half hour flight, we have a chance to nap a little. The flight is uneventful, and Luca is there with a sign, waiting for us.

"Come, come!" He motions for us to an older car out front. He speaks rapidly to the parking attendant that's threatening to do something to his car and both of us load up, then we tap Luca on the shoulder and tell him we need to go. He nods, still spewing what I think are profanities to the other person.

Luca drives us out of Bologna and down to a small village, Monterenzio. It's too dark to see exactly what we're passing, but the car drives smoothly for a good while, then we're on winding roads, taking corners that throw us against the sides, and sometimes the car judders as we cross over stones. Then Luca is pushing the accelerator to get the car up a tight hill and at a parking spot, he stops.

"Come, come." He motions to us and we get out, grabbing our bags. He rings a bell at a gated entrance and speaks to the man who answers, who is a dead spit for an older Byron. The older man looks us up and down and motions to us to follow him. We thank Luca, tipping him, and we follow the older man inside. He leads us through the house to a courtyard at the back. No one else seems to be around.

"So which of the two of you abandoned my lass?" he asks. We both lower our heads. Meeting her father like this was never the plan.

"Can I explain?" I ask. He nods and sits down in one of the chairs at the small table he's taken us to. Then a maid comes out with three glasses, some cognac and vanishes without a word.

"You talk, I drink. You may drink if I don't kick you out," he states in his accent of a strange, heady mixture of Italian and Scots. We nod and I begin. From Blythe taking down Lloyd after the kidnapping, to him smashing her shoulder and sabotaging our first ever client's systems, the drugs Blythe was on that Byron told us would affect her, to her leaving Annie's at four am as we were coming home to be with her before, during and after her operation, which she'll have to reschedule now.

"Both of you want to do that?" he asks. "You both want my daughter?" He queries, hesitantly.

"Yes, sir," Adrian answers. "We thought we'd explained clearly to her we had work to take care of before her op, that she'd spend a few days with Annie, so we could then have these six weeks of just light work and recovery time with her at home. Either we didn't do a good job of it…"

"Or she was still too drugged to hear and remember." Another voice, a softer Scottish one, joins us. It's not Blythe, but the way Blythe's father wraps his arm around the lady's waist and pulls her close, the older look about her, those blue eyes, I'd say we're meeting her mother for the first time.

"I'm Ava, by the way." She extends her hand to us, and we shake it, giving her our names as she does so. "And this is Lorenzo." She turns and kisses his head.

Ava says something in Italian to Lorenzo and then smiles at us. "I have a twin room for you both, Byron and Annie told me you'd need it."

"Does she ken we're here?" I ask. Lorenzo has stood, so do we and I eye up the cognac; I could do with that to help settle my nerves. Lorenzo shakes his head.

"No, she does not. What you say about her babbling, being not herself, we understand. You may take your drink," he says and smiles at his wife, then says something else in soft Italian to her. She slaps his pec with a giggle and motions for Adrian and me to follow her once Lorenzo has handed us a good measure of cognac. Lorenzo brings up the rear.

"You can see her in the morning. Family rooms are on the other side. You both..." Ava climbs a small set of stairs and swings open a set of double doors. There are two double beds, made up and ready for occupancy. "Can sleep here. The dogs patrol at night to keep the smaller pests away. An electric fence around the property keeps the wolves and larger wildlife at bay. The dogs don't know you, so you might get hurt if you venture outside of this room. We'll retrieve you in the morning." She smiles at us, but there's a look of fierceness and defiance in the older lady's eyes.

"We understand," Adrian confirms. "Thank you." Both her parents nod and leave us. We each claim a bed and sit on it for a few moments, then Adrian checks that the door isn't locked. It's not and I sigh in relief.

The en-suite bathroom is both clean and functional, in character with the villa we find ourselves at. I drink half my cognac in one go.

"I can see where Blythe gets her characteristics from," I offer and Adrian nods then sips his cognac.

"I wonder if they'll tell her tomorrow...or let us talk with her first?" he ventures. We might both be half a century old, but meeting the parents of the woman you're in love with usually takes some planning.

I stop with my cognac halfway to my mouth. "I'm in love with her," I blurt out to my brother, who nods in return with a coy grin on his features.

"Aye, we both are." He pauses. "Weird feeling, I tell ye. We just need to tell her in the morning." We finish our drinks and turn off the lights. The sounds are alien to me; I can hear a wolf howling in the distance. It doesn't get an answer back.

~Forty-Six~
Blythe

I get dressed slowly, reluctant to get out of my comfortable bed. There's a change in atmosphere this morning. I can hear the voices of the workers and they seem chirpier, happier, even the birds' singing seems more joyful and louder. I sigh, realising that things are much clearer today. I can't recall why I'm here, or how I got here, but I know where I am. I look at the city of Bologna so far away in the distant valley, yet so close and my insides churn. I feel I'm in the wrong place, but not, at the same time. I am supposed to be at Annie's, I'm sure.

My mother comes in to help me dress, which distracts me from the thoughts and emotions I am currently trying to digest. She helps me put on the low sling and ensures that I'm comfortable.

"I'm good, Mama," I tell her gently. She smiles at me.

"Yer dad is out on the terrace, breakfast is being served," she softly tells me. "How are you this morning? Does it hurt? How is your head?"

"My shoulder hurts, but I'm okay. What's going on?" I ask as I slide my feet into something easily manageable. "And I feel okay in my head." I look at her. "Mama, how did I get here?" I see tears in my mama's eye, and I know something is wrong.

"Yer papa's on the terrace. Come on, we'll work out all our answers there." I blink at my mother as she marches towards the terrace. I follow, the pitting feeling in my stomach changes, and the kaleidoscope of butterflies emerges, making me unsure about what I'm about to find out.

The terrace is set as it normally is; Papa is at the head of the table, his back to the kitchen. The sun shines, making me feel warm as it touches my skin. There's a warm breeze over the whole veranda and the smell of hibiscus and oranges gently scents the air.

The table is laden with croissants, fette biscottate, coffee, jam, bread, cheese and meats. I kiss my father good morning at his temple and pour myself some coffee, taking the seat next to him as is traditional, being the eldest. There's more food here than the three of us can manage.

"What's going on, Papa?" I ask in fluid Italian. Before he can answer, my mother's voice calls out for him to help her with something. He kisses me on the head before I watch him go into the kitchen, muttering, and I turn my attention back to the food before me. As I reach out for a croissant bun, my eyes are covered. Without thinking, I twist around and lash out with my left hand. No family member would ever dare to do that, not to me. There's an "oomph" sound, the feeling of something hard, masculine, and then my name is called as the darkness surrounding my eyes drops.

"Blythe, it's only us, darling! Shit!" I blink a few times, then I see Marcus crouching down over his brother. I push my chair back and crick my neck. Every knuckle cracks.

"What the... I'm so sorry!!" I screech when I realise what I've done, and to who. My parents rush out and my father helps Adrian to his feet, his right arm is holding his left rib and my mother is telling me off in Italian. I hold up a hand and wait until my father has backed away from the brothers.

"Mama, please, how did I get here!?" I demand.

"You caught a six-thirty flight out of Edinburgh yesterday to get here. You left Annie's at oh-four-hundred," Adrian explains as he winces.

"I did what?!" I ask, and Papa makes me sit down.

Marcus repeats what Adrian said as they sit down at the table in response to my father's gesticulation.

"Have you two been here all night?" I ask. For them to be at the breakfast table, my parents knew. The chirpier staff, the louder birdsong now makes sense. I knew they were here too, somehow.

"Aye, yer parents kindly put us up last night. We got here quite late."

I watch them as I reach for my coffee. My father is still at the head of the table, my mother to his right, me to his left. But, he's placed Adrian directly opposite him and Marcus to his left, facing me.

"You came out to find me?" I ask as I try to keep my excitement under control. *Did they come all this way to find me?*

"Aye, we did, though *here* wasn't quite where we expected to find ye," Adrian retorts. "We were expecting you to be with Annie, where we left ye."

"Bee, do you recall the client in Bristol we had to go and see? The Lloyd cousins trashed his system like he tried to trash ours. Only, they succeeded this time. We took you to Annie's for a few days, but you walked out at oh-four-hundred yesterday."

I look at him. "I don't remember being at Annie's," I tell them. "But I did wonder why I wasn't there when I woke up," I admit.

"You don't remember Byron being at the flat for two days?" they ask and I shake my head. I can't look at them, I'm so embarrassed. I'm not usually an emotional mess! *What the hell is happening?*

"Did we stay in touch, talk, chat? I don't remember anything of what you're telling me."

"We installed a new app on your phone," Marcus tells me. I dig the phone out of the sling and look at it. The screens are different from what I'm used to. Marcus gets up and comes to sit next to me when I do nothing more than simply look at my phone. I can't remember how to use it.

"Unlock it for me?" he asks and there's a wiggly symbol on the bottom of the screen that he makes me press my thumb to. *Oh, that's what I need to do!*

I watch as Marcus scrolls through my apps after I've unlocked it, feeling like a child being shown how to play with their favourite toy.

"Your layout has changed," he mutters. Then he swipes upwards and finds an app I'm sure I've never seen. "This one was on the home screen," he tells me and puts it back on the home screen. Then he pushes the phone to me. "Open it," he tells me and stays where he is. I click it open to find a whole new chatting app that I am not used to. But, I have a profile, my number is there, and there are a few private message channels, one from each of the guys, even one from Annie. A small group section for the three of us, then the company wide one, which I've apparently replied into. In all, there are about fifty unread messages, over twenty are just from the guys.

"When was this installed?" I gently enquire.

Adrian blinks at me. "Do you really not recall?" he asks, and I shake my head. "We set it up for you before we left for Bristol, in Annie's kitchen," he continues. "Call her if you want. Ask."

I take my phone and dial Annie, jumping the call to the loudspeaker as it rings. She answers almost straight away. "Heya, where the hell are ye?" she asks me in a concerned, aggressive tone. "Please tell me yer okay?!"

"Yeah, I am, sorry! Out in Italy," I begin, but she cuts me off.

"Aye, I thought that's where ye were heading, leaving me at four am like that!" She sounds relieved but annoyed with me. "Elle's been worried about ye!" I wince as she confirms what the guys have been saying.

"Would you believe it if I said I don't recall how I got out here?" I tell her and she gasps.

"Whatever the hell they gave you in hospital, can I have some, please? I'd like to forget the last few days myself." I hear her drink something in the background. "What *do* you recall?" she asks me and I can hear her munching on something. "Are yer parents there? Ciao, Ava, Lorenzo! Come state entrambi?" she asks. Languages and Annie make me grin. She knows so many languages conversationally.

My parents reply in Italian, and Annie responds. "So," she says, switching back to English. "What is the last thing ye remember, Bly?"

I cast my mind back, sighing. I drink some coffee. "My arm being reset in the back of an ambulance, being given gas and air," I tell her, sounding pleased with myself.

"And ye dinnae remember anything until this morning? Bly, darlin'...that was four days ago." I gape, frozen in time by Marcus' statement.

"Annie, it's Adrian," he begins and she laughs. His voice makes me look up at him and his brother. I'm unable to remember four days?! *What the hell have I done? And why?*

"Okay, you two were hot on her tail, good!" I sit back and pick at a croissant roll which my mother has put butter and honey onto.

"The last time the four of us were together, tell us about it would ye please?" he asks.

"Aye, sure." Annie's voice rings out true and clear. Her power of recall is impressive. "Bly got hurt that Friday night; ye said you got back about oh-four hundred Saturday. Byron arrived at your door Saturday afternoon, which is when you said you found out about the Lloyd boys scuppering yer seed and reference site. Ye both needed to go down; Byron couldn't stay any longer as he was on emergency leave. You asked me if Bly could stay here until you got back. You told us both that the horse sized drugs Eric gave her, she shouldn't have; Byron recognised it as a drug her grandma took for her dementia that made her condition worse. It wasn't on the list of recognised drugs not to give to Bly, so no one knew. Hell, I didn't even know. It should be on my list too, perhaps? Anyway..."

"I don't remember that at all," I tell them.

"Bee, the pharmacist and Eric told you not to take it unless you were being supervised. I get why now!" Marcus counters.

"Aye, I honestly don't feel like I've got a hole in my memory," I tell them, and my stomach knots up. *If I don't recall the visit to her house....is my short term memory now affected?*

"Bly, yer gonna need to let this run through your system afore you come back home. Which is going to be fun because yer not meant to be flying in that state! I need to go and do the school run!"

"Love you, Aunty Blythe!" I hear Elle shout out down the phone.

"Love you too, munchkin!" I sing back, trying to sound cheerful so she stops worrying.

"Arrivederci, tutti!" Annie calls out and hangs up. My mother purses her lips and my father rolls his eyes. I just smile, knowing I'll correct her Italian later.

I put my croissant roll down, unable to eat anymore, though I've hardly touched it. I'm absorbing the confirmation of a conversation and seemingly days I don't recall. If it had been anyone else, I'd call them a liar to their face. But not Annie. If she said we spoke and could repeat the conversation verbatim, and said I was somewhere, did something, it happened. That's all there is to it.

"Excuse me," I say as I push away from the table. There are too many people here, too many bodies around me, the air is thin and I forget how to breathe. Marcus reaches out to me as I make to go past.

"We're not angry, not with you. We get it."

"That'll explain your state when Luca brought you here yesterday," my mother says. I turn to her and then sit back down.

"What do you mean?" I ask, becoming more overwhelmed and Dad chuckles. He reaches across and rubs my bad arm gently.

"Annie called us, telling us you might be heading this way. We sent Luca out to meet you," Mama tells me. She reaches across for my father's hand. She did that when grandma was really bad. I blink, understanding that I've worried them greatly.

"Do you not remember how you talked and talked, but made no sense? Or that you tried to go horse-riding at three in the afternoon? With your arm as it is?" I shake my head at my father's questions. "You freaked the guards, and us, out. The dogs knew it was you, but they acted weirdly around you. Do you not recall that?" he questions, and I shake my head.

"I did not," I tell him and he pulls up his phone. Using similar cameras as we do for work, Dad pulls up the recording from three pm yesterday afternoon, after I had arrived. I tried to saddle a grey mare, but I kept falling over. The mare isn't having any of it because of the seemingly drunken state I am in, and backs away from me a lot. Then I see a stable hand try to stop me just before my father appears and guides me away. We watch as the stable hand settles the mare back into her stall, then tidies away the tack I had pulled out one handed. My father appears on another set of cameras, guiding me into the villa and back to my bedroom. Five minutes later, my mother is at my door. After a short time, she and my father leave. I blink.

"What the heck?!" I exclaim. *Did I run to Italy for reasons I can no longer remember, because I didn't want to be at Annie's? Or did I deeply want my parents to be there for me when I was in so much blinding pain?*

"Giorgia?" my father calls to me in a stern voice, using my Italian middle name and snapping his fingers. "Blythe Giorgia Grievson Mancini, get your focus on, Sergeant!" he barks, and I blink as his voice sinks into the fog, pulling me up from it, my brain responding to the military rank that I used to hold. Half the breakfast has been cleared away, Mama is rubbing my good arm, there's a blanket around me while Adrian and Marcus are giving me weird looks.

"What is it, Papa?" I ask, frustrated at his finger snapping.

"Bee, honey, you have sat there unaware for about ten minutes," Marcus tells me. "Did you take any tablets this morning?"

"I haven't," I state, but I stop. "Mama, I didn't, did I?" I ask, looking at her pleadingly, being pretty sure I hadn't taken anything. She shakes her head.

"You've not taken anything since I fetched you for breakfast, love," she tells me.

I swear, profusely, in Italian and then English and my parents wince.

"The best thing you can do is let it go through your system, as Annie suggested. I can ask Eric how long this drug usually lasts," Marcus suggests.

"Lorenzo's mama would take her medication twice a week," Mama pipes up.

"Guess you'd better stick around and help my parents keep an eye on me then, huh?" I suggest, offering the guys an olive branch.

"We'd love to," Adrian adds. At least we have that sorted!

A few days later, having suffered only one more, small "blackout" episode, I am sitting on the terrace with them at sunset, enjoying their closeness and warmth. My mother has already demanded details in private about our relationship and I've been honest with her. It's been a relief, I think, to talk to someone in the family about it, to find out that I'm not the first and she doubts I'll be the last to need more than one lover. It involved a bottle of wine on her part, a glass for me and the sun loungers facing towards the moon.

"Honestly, Bee, darling, we're as glad as fuck you're alive and not hurt beyond what we knew." Marcus is on my bad side, sitting close and stroking my leg. "You scared us."

"We had no idea the drugs were doing that and I wish one of us had stayed behind," Adrian adds sullenly.

I take a deep breath, trying to keep the knot deep within from overpowering what I need to say. "Well, I didn't either. So, can I withdraw my resignation?" I look between the brothers, unsure how this is going to go. I hope they tear it up, but I can't be sure I even sent it now.

Earlier, the girls set up a smaller, private chat with just us, and I told them I was going to ask about my resignation letter today. They told me they weren't aware I'd submitted it and they're waiting for me to respond back, telling me that they didn't want me to leave. Annie's been in touch too, sharing her relief that I'm here and safe, getting better. The fact she'll use this software is fabulous!

"Resignation?" Marcus throws me a confused look. "What are you talking about, honey? I don't recall receiving one, did you, Adrian?"

He shakes his head. "Nope, not I. Did you Marcus?" he adds, and I grin and chuckle a bit.

"I didn't? I was so sure I had!" I exhale deeply, letting the regret of having sent it dissipate. *I was so sure I had.* "Thank you."

"Aye, well, we genuinely didn't receive one, even if you think you sent it! Not that we'd accept it from ye in the state yer in." Adrian grins, but then his mouth goes thin and he drops his voice. "And dinnae thank us yet, I have to go back to Edinburgh tomorrow."

I sigh, letting my annoyance manifest. He leans in to me, loud enough for his brother and me to hear, but no one else.

"And I want to fuck ye long and hard afore I go, to keep me warm when I know yer here with Marc for a few more weeks," he tells me, then he reaches over, cupping my head in his hand and guides his lips to mine. He doesn't pull at me; he brings himself to me.

"How do we do this, here?" I ask. The three of us together, under my parents' roof, isn't something I've contemplated.

Marcus leans in. "I take your room, you go with Aid to ours. I'm here for another week at least, and your father has kindly given me the Wi-Fi password, so I can work during the day if I'm needed." I nod. The group chat has been busy, but not overly so.

Marcus kisses me fully. He groans as we break apart and then he stands.

"See you both at breakfast," he tells us. Then he's stalking off and I whimper a little at him going, but Adrian is there beside me.

"We know. We spoke about it last night. He'll get his moments with ye later this week," he tells me and kisses me softly. "Come on," he stands and extends his hand, then he guides me to the room that he is sharing with his brother.

~Forty-Seven~
Adrian

I hold the courtroom doors open for Blythe and Marcus as we head into the gallery for the spectacle that these proceedings have been so far. This is day three and already, Andrew Lloyd has had to be removed from court every day. When Blythe took the stand, he jumped up and down, trying to reach her, calling her all sorts of vile, disgusting, derogatory names. She didn't react, flinch, or respond to his theatrics.

We're hearing from Lucy today, the witness who was emailing us in crypto form, trying to warn us. She is one of Andrew's ex-girlfriends who got dragged into this mess. Because of her emails, we were able to avoid some of the issues he'd planned for us, but not all. Now, she's turned evidence against him. Before the Judge can call the witness, or get an usher to do so, Andrew kicks off again, threatening to find and end her.

He's removed from the courtroom and Lucy pulls her shoulders back and nods in our direction. Then, she sits and answers a barrage of questions from Lloyd's solicitor as well as the City's. We know the guy has a job to do, to try and get both Lloyd men off, but Lucy's evidence—along with our evidence, recordings of conversations, hard and digital copies of emails, and incendiary devices—make it pretty damning.

What's even more damning is the ex-lovers of both of them who come forward as character witnesses. Blythe even called a few anti-character witnesses; they weren't favourable to the Lloyd cousins at all.

At the end of the first week, we're worn out. Alasdair, Duncan and the others have held down the fort as we've wanted to be at the trial, but the reason why any of this happened is the kicker.

Marcus wasn't the first object of their joint affection. He was, however, their last. The mention of the situation in Bosnia came up, but the judge told the jury to dismiss all but the fact the sniper was sent to kill me by the Lloyd cousins, as the evidence of that was on the recordings. Blythe wasn't on trial and what she did in a foreign country whilst working was not relevant here.

We checked in with the Bosnian businessman, who assured us that because the sniper was a wanted criminal in their country and because their gun laws are very different from ours, no charges would be brought against Blythe for her actions whilst in his employment.

The court case picks up again on Monday and so this Friday night, we're chilling out. Or, we're trying to. Blythe seems stuck in her head and nothing Marc or I do seems to shake her out of it.

She had her shoulder operation when we got back from Italy; we actually got her back early so she was here on time for the pre-op meetings and checks. They've reworked half a dozen points in her shoulder, which is still strapped to her and will be for another two weeks. She's in her room and we can hear her talking, but we're not sure to whom. What hurts is it's not us she's talking to.

Then she comes out of her room and sighs. She comes over to us and gently sits between us, leaning into me and holding a hand out for Marcus. There's nothing we can do or say that is going to make anyone feel any better.

"Diminished responsibility," Blythe blurts out, her voice heavy and somewhat sad.

"What is?" Marc asks without looking at her.

"That's what they're aiming for, grounds of diminished responsibility for Andrew, and they'll throw the book at David. They're looking to lock Andrew up in a psych ward for the rest of his days. They requested a psych evaluation today. David will probably get twenty or so. They're claiming Andrew suffers from diminished responsibility thanks to the Army. Now they're trying to prove he's schizophrenic and that the Army caused it."

"Do you think that's how it's going to turn out?" I ask as I shake my head in disbelief. There are a few more weeks of evidence yet, but I doubt we'll be at the rest of the trial. It's had seven court days as it is and I'd hate to be on the jury.

"Yeah, that's what Annie reckons they'll go for. We don't have the death penalty here anymore, but they'll still lock him up. The question is, where and for how long?"

Annie's probably right and it explains who Blythe was chatting to. "It's not long enough, whatever they decide," Marc volunteers.

"No, it never is. We're all dealing with trauma in our lives, we're all dealing with something," she counters. "But the Lloyd boys think they are the 'victims' here; they don't see the consequences of their actions. They've become bloody good gas-lighters, everyone else is to bloody blame."

I sigh. "Conduct unbecoming," I offer.

"Understatement of the year," Blythe says as she picks up the remote to bring up a movie.

We flick through the choices and settle on something we've all seen before; even though it's not Christmas, Hans Gruber falling off Nakatomi Plaza cheers everyone up.

Weeks later, Blythe is being assessed post-operation on her shoulder. Marc and I are waiting in reception as she goes to be assessed, then the doctor calls us in.

"Ms Grievson is healing well," he begins.

"I am still here, ya know!" she yells from behind a curtain and we grin. The trial is over, and the Lloyd cousins were sentenced for more years than we thought they would be. They'll be in their eighties by the time they're allowed out on parole, or dead. The latter suits us more than the former. Both have been incarcerated in different psyche facilities, with a court order that they're not allowed to contact each other through family members, or directly.

"Sorry," the doctor blushes. He does at least wait until Blythe pulls back the medical curtain and we help her with her coat before he carries on with the postoperative results. The weather is turning, it's colder out, but as we're Scots, we'll just put on an extra jacket or layer and get on with life.

"Okay, I want to see you one more time in four weeks. Do those exercises as we've discussed and we can start going back to the shoulder strap once I'm happy you have some mobility back. No driving yet and just the painkillers as we discussed."

"The stitches are dissolving okay?" Blythe checks and the doctor nods.

"Exactly as they should be. You might feel some itchiness as they do. Try not to scratch the top layer, but rub the area with your knuckle," he glances at us, "or get some help," he suggests.

Blythe grins.

"Just, do yourself a favour?" he asks as we get up to leave. "Don't make it eight times, okay?"

Blythe grins at him demonically. "I'll try! Not promising ye anything, Doc," she teases. Then we leave and slowly, we go get our lives back on track.

Epilogue - Blythe

Italy, the court case and my operation seem so long ago in the cold January rain of Glasgow.

We're keeping tabs on Tony as he hired us when he started getting threats for a reason we can't as yet fathom. Duncan and Alasdair are with him at a business meeting he insisted he had to be at in Glasgow, and so far, things seem to be going well. We've tracers on our guys and we're watching them from a rendezvous point on the road out of Glasgow back to Edinburgh. The plan is simple, we'll follow his Lexus limousine as they pass, but not too closely; our guys will be in the front of the vehicle, Tony can sit in the back and do his work or whatever he wants. The boring part is the waiting, but Tony's due to start making his way home with Duncan and Alasdair in the next ten minutes or so. I stretch the kinks out of my neck, my repaired shoulder and my knuckles.

As we wait, the radio plays some long forgotten song and my mind wanders to my now married little brother. He and his new wife spent five days out in Italy, meeting parents and chilling out. After the disastrous end of year Duckie had, I can't blame him for taking her away for a few days. I'm glad I was able to help him make it happen.

We watch the car GPS follow its designated route out of Glasgow for a few miles, then it deviates, stops and turns back. Adrian and I look at each other. I get a sinking feeling in my gut, an instinct I trust, having cultivated it in military training.

"That's not right," I say, starting up the Ninety we're in. This is still my favourite of the fleet of vehicles. I'm as grateful as heck that the garage was able to repair it after I played chicken with Andrew Lloyd months before.

"No, it's not," he says and tries to reach Alasdair and Duncan on the headsets. Neither responds to his calls and I swear, taking action. I shift the car into gear, turn on the lights, and head towards where their GPS says they are as he does what he can to reach our crew. As we're approaching the car's GPS location, I get a signal from Marcus' latest credit card transmitter. The only one we have in the field belongs to my best friend. Bad. Fucking. Timing.

My phone goes a few minutes later and I answer it on speaker.

"It's not me, but you need to find the signal. Code Two." Then the line goes dead. Adrian reacts to the words she told us and we pick up where the transmitter is coming from. The empty pitting feeling I have gets a whole load wider as we find the Lexus with the back door and front passenger doors wide open. Adrian quickly secures it, swearing as he goes, grabbing the keys which were in the ignition. Duncan and Alasdair aren't near the car, but this was the last location of their personal trackers.

"Code Two?" he asks questioningly as I drive onwards to Annie's signal.

"Aye, same as our code for someone's hurt," I tell him. "I taught her it when I gave her that transmitter after the trial." Adrian nods in acknowledgement, his lips thinly set. The location is not too far away and I pray to the Gods for some good luck. Losing our financial backer on our watch just cannot be allowed to happen.

Adrian taps on his phone and then compares it to mine.

"What are you comparing?" I ask, unable to look at both screens and drive.

"Mine is where Tony was, according to his phone's GPS. His signal died about when the car changed route. The transmitter signal is from the same location." I throw him a quick glance at some traffic lights.

"She couldn't have," I breathe out incredulously. "No way." I shake my head in disbelief. As I turn the corner, there's police everywhere, blue lights lighting up a ruined building like it's the Fifth of November or Hogmanay. I park up next to a police transport van and kill the engine, giving us time to think.

"How the hell are we gonna get in there?" Adrian asks, but I spy someone I know.

"Wait here," I say and climb out, grabbing the chance.

"Wainright!" I hiss as I approach an officer with sergeant stripes on his arm. He turns to me and curses.

"Ain't got time for you tonight," he tells me and turns to walk away. The rain is steady, relentless.

"We've someone in there. Do you want all that extra paperwork?" I ask him. If Annie's transmitter is in there, I hope whomever she's found is worth us not finding Tony for, but I've no other leads. Wainright stops and turns back to me, then he motions to a side panel.

"Move that piece three up and be quick!" he hisses. "Afore I get bollocked." Then he turns away, ignoring me. Adrian is already on his way over to that panel, and he signals for me to get to the car. I do, starting her back up, and reversing her up to the panel. I open the back door and grab some blankets out of the storage box, laying them on the cold vehicle floor. The police are thankfully busy around the corner, giving me enough time to set the back of the Ninety up as best I can for an injured someone.

I see the panel move five long minutes later, and Adrian is dragging Tony in his arms.

"Dear God, what the hell?!" I exclaim as I help get Tony into the back of the Ninety, as cramped as that is for his frame.

"No idea. She's stitched him up though," he breathes out and I follow his pointing to Tony's bloodied side, which is bandaged up, though it's been peeled off. "Had to look to see if I could move him," he explains and I nod in understanding.

"Is that him smelling like piss?" I ask, trying not to gag on the stench. Adrian nods and removes the smelly coat from Tony, throwing it back towards the old Woollen Mill.

"Do we have any more blankets?" he asks and I shake my head.

"Lexus has a first aid kit, there'll be thermals in there," I suggest, removing my jacket and putting it on Tony like a blanket. He can pay for it to be cleaned later. Adrian nods and I shut him in the back with an unconscious Tony, the smell of urine and more questions than we can answer.

Hours later, I lift my head as Eric leaves Tony's bedroom, pulling the door closed behind him gently.

"I think you're right, but he'll maybe remember when he wakes up," he points and I nod. "Those stitches are clean and even; your friend did a good job." I smile and push my chest out a little, feeling prideful. "But I agree with your original thought," Eric gives me that look that tells me he doesn't doubt himself, "He was doused with Chloroform."

I nod and let the exhaustion kick in. Eric nods at us both and leaves, telling us he'll be back in about eight hours.

"Any luck reaching her?" Adrian asks quietly when it's just us. It's some silly hour of the morning and we're aware of it. I shake my head in reply.

"She is still in Glasgow and said she'd talk with us tomorrow." I want answers now, but Annie's focus isn't on us. I wonder why she was even there. Adrian looks towards Tony's bedroom; the lines of worry are etched upon his handsome face. Tony's a friend, far more than just a silent backer to us.

I rub my hand up his arm, across his bicep and squeeze. "He's in good hands; Eric has added to the stitches, checked him over and he's breathing normally. Nothing more we can do now, but let him wake up on his own."

Adrian nods then looks at me. "Go get some shut-eye. Tony's not going to wake up for hours. I'll stay here." The tone of his voice suggests he's not wanting to argue, only to be obeyed.

I relent; I'm too tired to argue and there are a whole load of questions to find answers to, but I need sleep so I can. "I'm going to go back to the flat to crash, then I'll work with the guys after I've slept, and I'll speak with Annie when she tells me she's back. Get. Some. Shut. Eye. Too," I instruct him, kissing him softly and then I depart. As I head to the door, I see Adrian enter Tony's room. Someone has hurt the one who believed in the brothers long before they ever did. *Who the hell wants him hurt, why, and how the hell did Annie get involved?*

Read the next instalment; Trodaiche.

Glossary

There are a lot of RAF military terms in here, especially in chats with Blythe and Annie. If you've ever heard military people speaking to one another, you'll understand how these two talk. You can find most of what I've used on this site:
https://en.wikipedia.org/wiki/RAF_slang

Dìonadair (djon-ver) is a Scots Gaelic word and the title of the book. It means Defence and the title was inspired by its counterpart, Trodaiche. It's the first in the duology of the Tango Down Duet.

I have put together a Spotify Music List for this duet, I listened to it a ***lot*** when I was writing these; you can find it here: bit.ly/TDDMusic

This work and any/all others are listed on my website (louisemurchie.com) where you can sign up for my FREE Newsletter. I'm Scottish, I like things that are free - I hope you appreciate them as much as I do too!

Thanks for reading this story/duo and for any reviews you leave. I deeply appreciate it!

MURCHIE

Printed in Poland
by Amazon Fulfillment
Poland Sp. z o.o., Wrocław